THE TEMPTATION DUET

THE FORBIDDEN SERIES

TRACY LORRAINE

A NOTE

The Temptation Duet is written in British English and contains British spelling and grammar. This may appear incorrect to some readers when compared to US English books.

AVOIDING TEMPTATION

"**Y**ou all set?" Eddie asks, glancing at the first slide of my presentation projecting on the wall and to my neatly stacked folders and worksheets.

Tonight is my first class at my new job. I've been an English teacher since I graduated from university eight years ago, although I'm more used to teenagers than adults, but I didn't have the time or money to be fussy when I moved to London. I almost snapped Eddie's hand off when he offered me this position.

He's the only person I know in this city. I knew it was a risk going to him, but he was my only option. Thankfully, he was still at the same address he gave me years ago, and when he unlocked his front door he welcomed me in like it was only yesterday we'd last seen each other.

"Yeah, I think so." I shake my arms at my sides, willing my nerves to disappear before my students arrive. I don't need them figuring out my weakness the moment they walk in the room. The thought of teaching adults terrifies me, even if they've made the decision to better themselves. Put me in an entire hall full of teenagers and I wouldn't bat an eyelid, but adults are a whole other story.

"You're going to be fine. This'll be a walk in the park after the spoilt rich kids you're used to."

"If you say so."

The classroom door opens and both Eddie and I look over. It takes a couple of seconds for someone to enter but, when they do, my chin drops a little. I didn't have any expectations of who my students might be. Eddie explained to me that the classes are usually a total mixed bag of people, but I can say with absolute certainty that I was not expecting someone like him.

His eyes find mine briefly before he looks away to take in the room. With his head down, he walks to the back and takes a seat in the last row. It gives me time to assess him. His eyes are hiding behind thick-rimmed glasses, but it's his outfit that really catches my attention. His white dress shirt is perfectly pressed, stretched across his wide shoulders and rolled up to the elbows exposing muscular forearms covered in tattoos. The black braces that sit over his shoulders make the corner of my mouth twitch up. Although his demeanor right now doesn't show it, I've no doubt that on a normal day this man is full of confidence.

"Told you, all walks of life in this place." Eddie's obvious distaste for the man at the back of the room drips from him, reminding me that although he's here helping me, he's still firmly from my old life. "Probably part of his rehabilitation or something."

Feeling eyes on me, I turn back to look at the guy, who's now staring right at us. His previous hesitant look seems to have vanished as his eyes drop from mine in favour of my body.

My skin tingles with his attention. I can't lie, it's a good feeling after being practically invisible for so long, but this is neither the time nor the place.

After lingering on my leather skirt for a few seconds too long, his eyes find mine once again. The brightness of his blue irises makes my breath catch. Surely they're not real?

A commotion at the door forces us to break our connection as others enter.

"Time to get to work, Miss Smith." Eddie winks before lifting his knuckles to my cheek. "No need to look so worried. I couldn't think of anyone better for the job."

His eyes bore down into mine and my stomach twists. I assumed Eddie would have a girlfriend by now. He's a great guy, but it was immediately obvious that he was still living life as a bachelor after he invited me to his flat when I turned up on his doorstep. He's been an amazing friend, more so than I think he knows, but that's all there's ever going to be between us. I'm just not attracted to him like I think he wants me to be. Although he didn't really fit in my past life, hence why he moved on a few years ago, he still reminds me of everything I hated about it. He still wears the flashy suit with the pretentious pocket square and tie pin. I've had enough of all of that shit for a lifetime. If there's ever going to be another man in my life, I want him to be as different from what I've known previously as possible.

"Thank you. You'd better go before you're late for class."

He nods before mouthing good luck and stepping away from me, and I feel like I can breathe again. He's been the perfect gentleman and friend since I arrived, but I fear he might be expecting too much. I'd hate to hurt him after everything he's done for me.

Just before he walks out of my classroom, he looks back over his shoulder, and my stomach drops at the twinkle in his eye. I'm sure it works on other women—unfortunately for him, I'm not them.

When I look back towards the desks facing me, I see that they're almost all full. Doing a quick head count, I realise we're still missing a couple. "We'll give it another two minutes, and then we'll get started."

I spend most of the first lesson outlining what they can expect from the course, the kind of assignments they're going to have to complete, and which books we're going to be studying. It's weird, because although everyone here is much older than I'm used to, I still see the same stereotypical students. At the front are two women who look overly keen to learn—it makes me wonder why they need to re-do this qualification if they're so enthusiastic. Behind them are a few rows of what I'd class as average students who follow all instructions to a tee, followed by a couple of guys in suits who, although they do what I tell them to, look like they want to be anywhere but here. Then of course, there's *him* at the back. The man who, every time I look up, I find staring right at me.

With only ten minutes left, I set them all a quick task to write a poem like the one they've been analysing that will help me get to know them.

Everyone puts their heads down and gets to work, aside from him. His eyes follow me as I walk to my desk and pick up the stack of folders. A shiver runs down my spine as his attention holds. He's the kind of guy I dreamt of running away with when I was a teenager, if I ever had the chance. I wanted the bad boy to rescue me from my life of china tea cups and pearls. It never happened, and, as was inevitable, I'd ended up becoming one of them. If only I'd had the strength to get out sooner.

I drop a folder on everyone's desk and ask each student if they have any questions or concerns about what we've done so far. I can only imagine their heads must be spinning, especially if they haven't been in education for a while.

Swallowing my trepidation, I step up to his desk and drop a folder.

"How are you doing?" I glance at his still blank page. "Is there anything I can do to help?"

He drops his pen on top of his paper haphazardly, and my fingers twitch to straighten it as he sits back. His eyes crawl up my body until they find mine. The blue is even more striking up close.

"I'm sure there's plenty you could help me with, Miss Smith." His eyes flit around my face, and there's no way he misses the brightening of my cheeks. My temperature begins to increase the longer he stares at me, and I know that I need to walk away—only, my legs don't seem to want to cooperate.

"So, tell me...will you be our teacher every Thursday night?"

"I would think so, yes. Problem?"

"Oh no. That is most definitely not a problem."

"Brilliant. Any concerns about the course or the work...Joe?" I ask, glancing at the name he's written on one of the forms I'd given him.

He shakes his head, and finally my legs allow me to get the hell away from him.

The second I dismiss the class, everyone starts moving, some faster and keener to get away than others.

"How'd it go?" Eddie asks, slipping inside the room when there's a break in students leaving.

"It was good. I'm not sure I'm ever going to be able to thank you enough for this."

"No need. When our new appointment decided against the position after his first day, we were pretty stuck. We should be thanking you for turning up when you did."

A chair scratching across the wooden floor makes both Eddie and I wince. Turning, we both watch as Joe collects up his stuff.

"Great class, Miss Smith. Very...inspirational." He winks, and I want the ground to swallow me up.

"Please, call me Quinn. This isn't school."

"Sure thing, Quinn." The way my name sounds rolling off his

tongue has tingles erupting in my belly. "Already looking forward to next week." With a nod of his head, he drops his books into his bag and heads for the door.

"Looks like you've already got yourself a pet." The way Eddie's lips curl up in disgust as he watches Joe leave ignites a fire in my belly. I thought I'd left all the judgemental arseholes behind. "Lift home?"

I want to say no after that last comment, but the thought of navigating through London on a cold and dark winter night fills me with dread. I'm sure it'll feel like second nature soon, but right now, I don't feel like I belong, let alone know where I'm going. I begrudgingly agree and start to gather up my things.

"Still think you made the right decision?" Eddie asks once we're on the road. His eyes flick over to me every few minutes, and I wish he'd just focus on the road ahead.

"Most definitely. I just can't wait for this place to feel like home."

"It won't take long. You fancy going for a drink?"

"Um...can I call a rain check tonight? I'd really like to be prepared for tomorrow, if that's okay?" I hate saying no after everything he's done for me recently, but I can't help feeling like agreeing would be giving him the wrong idea.

"No, that's fine. I totally get it. I know I've thrown you in at the deep end. I'm not taking no for an answer tomorrow night, though. I'm on the VIP list for one of the best clubs around, and I want to show you what London really has to offer."

"I...uh..." The thought of being thrust into London's thriving nightlife kind of terrifies me. Well, it terrifies the old me. I need to remember that she's long gone. The girl sitting here right now is ready to start experiencing life, start living it to the fullest and taking some risks. Suddenly, a little excitement I remember when I first got here tingles in my belly. "Yes. I'd love to."

"Get out your best dress, Quinn. I'm going to show you how it's really done."

Dress. Shit.

I school my features before thanking him for the ride and jumping from the car.

I make quick work of getting inside my building and up the stairs to the studio flat Eddie helped me find.

The small space is nothing like I'm used to, but, for the first time in my life, it's *my* space. It might be tiny, but it's mine to do with as I wish. Well...as long as the landlord agrees. I've wanted my own life for as long as I can remember, and I'm finally here.

I drop my bags onto the small coffee table that sits in front of my sofa bed and head towards the kitchen for a glass of water. I down it before popping a couple of slices of bread into the grill for dinner. I might have my own life now, but, at least until I get paid, it's not exactly what my dreams were made of.

Once I've stripped out of my jumper and skirt, I pull on an old pair of pyjamas and stare at the number of items I've got hanging in my wardrobe.

I left my previous life with only a handful of essentials. I hated the majority of my clothes; they represented a life I hated. The first thing I did when I arrived here was head to a shop and purchase a couple of items I'd always wanted to own. The knee-high boots and short leather skirt I've just taken off were two of those items. Looks like I'm going to have to hit the shops again if I need something for a night out tomorrow.

I spend the night working on lesson plans and, sometime after midnight, flip my sofa to a bed and curl up under the blanket.

My flat might be cold, and I might not have much in the way of possessions, but I still fall asleep with a smile on my face because this life right now is everything I've ever wanted.

"Whoa this place looks...fancy," I say as I walk beside Eddie towards the club he's spent almost all day telling me about. Suddenly, the little black Primark dress I thought looked pretty hot when I was in the fitting room first thing this morning doesn't seem good enough.

Looking down, I run my palm over the figure-hugging fabric and let out a sigh.

"You look stunning," Eddie whispers, assuming correctly where my thoughts are at. "That look suits you much better than the twinsets I'd become used to."

"Thanks," I mutter, but when I glance up, I see a little fire in his eyes as he drops them down my body. I stand up a little straighter. I don't want him looking at me that way, but if he is, then it must mean I don't stand out like an outsider trying to force my way into a new life.

Eddie walks straight up to the bouncer and gives him his name. Glancing over my shoulder, I take in the long line of people waiting to get in. This place, The Avenue, is clearly popular, and I can't help yearning to be part of that crowd. It might sound crazy because almost anyone would love to be in my position now, being waved through to go to the VIP section, but all I want is a normal life. I want to blend in with the crowd and disappear.

"Come on," Eddie says, grabbing my hand and pulling me towards him when he realises that I'm not following. "What's wrong? You want to join the peasants?"

His words have anger burning in my stomach. Does he really think he's so special? Pulling my hand from his, I follow him up the stairs to the second floor before we walk around the edge of the vast room to another set of stairs that are guarded by security and sectioned off with a red rope. The music is so loud, it vibrates through my bones, but I can't deny that it doesn't make me want to dance.

Eddie speaks to the bouncer as if he's a regular—which he probably is—giving me a chance to look around.

I've always wondered if clubs are like they're portrayed on the TV, and standing here right now I can confidently say yes. Everything about this place is exactly what I was expecting. Its floors are polished black with silver flecks, and all the fittings are chrome with huge glass chandeliers hanging from the high ceilings. The bar is packed, the queue of people at least five deep as they wait a little impatiently for their next drink. But the majority of the room is given over to a dance floor where hundreds of bodies move and gyrate to the beat.

I'm totally lost watching their movement when Eddie slips his arm around my waist and moves me towards the stairs.

"We can dance later if you like. I need a few drinks first to loosen up a little."

A shudder runs down my spine. I'm not sure I want him loosened up. He's free enough with his hands as it is.

Gritting my teeth and fighting my need to step away from his touch, I allow him to guide me up to the bar.

The difference in the clientele up here is stark, and it only increases my desire to go back down and mix with the masses. I look around at the designer suits and fancy dresses, and it's just like being in the middle of my old life where everyone's biggest concern was how they looked and how much money they had.

Eddie leans over when the barman comes over. At no point does he look back to ask what I want, which irritates the hell out of me. I know he's been my confidant over the past few years, but he couldn't possibly know what I want to drink right now.

It's only a few seconds later when I realise why he didn't bother asking, because the barman reappears with a bottle of champagne and two glasses. Eddie hands over his credit card before grabbing his purchase and leading me over to the balcony. He places the glasses down on one of the high tables and pulls over two stools for us to sit on. Glad to have some space, I pull the stool a little closer to the glass balcony that allows us to look down over the dancefloor below.

It's like I blink and there's a glass of champagne shoved under my nose. I guess now wouldn't be the best time to tell him that I don't really like the stuff.

"To new starts, new jobs, and...friendships." His eyes twinkle as he says the final word. "I'm so glad you reached out when you did. I think this is where you're meant to be."

"Eddie, I—" I'm just about to explain to him that there's not going to be anything between us when someone approaches and holds their hand out for him to shake.

The two men start talking like they're old friends—it's not lost on me that at no point does Eddie bother to introduce me. Clearly, I'm not that important.

Ignoring them, I take a sip of champagne and try not to turn my nose up too much. I really shouldn't complain; it's not like I can afford to buy my own drinks in a place like this. I dread to think how much this bottle cost. It seems that Eddie could take himself out of my old stuck-up and pretentious life, but he couldn't remove his inner snob.

Rolling my eyes at my thoughts, I look down over the mass of bodies below. They've all got smiles on their faces as they dance and laugh with friends, and my muscles ache to know how that feels. Eddie is the closest thing I've had to a proper friend since I was a child. The thought makes my stomach drop. I'd kill to have a girlfriend to share everything with, to go shopping with and share my dreams and fears. I had that when I was a kid, but Suzi ended up moving to the States with her parents not long after we finished school, and the distance between us put pay to our friendship.

I let out a sigh as I once again think about what a lonely life I've lived up until this point. The knowledge that I've done something about it at last has a little hope starting to filter into my depressing thoughts.

I'm not all that different to the adults I've started teaching. For whatever reason, they've all decided that now's the time to better themselves. I might not need qualifications like them, but I am in need of other things. I just hope that I'm able to find what's missing in my life in my new home, and I don't end up going back to where I came from with my tail between my legs, just like I'm sure they're all expecting me to do.

Someone's exuberant dancing below catches my eye. I have to do a double-take when a familiar figure comes into focus.

It's the guy who sat at the back of my room yesterday evening. He's dressed similarly, only his white shirt is grey tonight, his braces firmly in place over the top, and his thick-rimmed glasses sit on his face. That's where the similarities end, because where he was a little unsure of himself last night, right now he's full of confidence as he dances with a group of friends.

I can't pull my eyes away as he pulls a petite redhead into his body and wraps his tattooed arms around her waist. Their hips move together in time with the music. They're so in sync they could be making love.

Jealousy hits me like a truck. It's not because I want to be the redhead—I don't think—but because I want that connection with someone. I want my body to connect with someone else's so easily that I don't even need to think about it.

I find myself downing the glass in my hand, needing something to dampen the emotion bubbling up my throat. I continue watching and, before long, he spins the redhead away from him and pulls the equally tattooed man standing to the side of him to dance.

Oh...

He moves as effortlessly with him as he did with the girl, and it only sparks even more questions about my elusive nerdy bad boy student.

The other guy soon gets fed up and, with a laugh, pushes Joe away and pulls a girl into his body before shoving his tongue down her throat. When I eventually drag my voyeuristic eyes away from the couple, I find Joe sandwiched between another guy and a girl. The girl's at his front, Joe's hands roaming over her body as her head rolls back in pleasure, but what really holds my attention is that his lips are attached to the guy's. They kiss like they'll die without it, and I can't pull my eyes away.

Something inside me erupts, lust descending to my core like I've never felt before. I've no idea if it's him, him and the guy, or just the three of them together, but fuck, it's hot.

"Jesus, don't they have any morals? It's embarrassing," Eddie tuts, following my stare.

"They're just letting their hair down and enjoying themselves."

"They might as well just fuck each other while everyone watches." I glance up at him through narrowed eyes before finding Joe again. "What? Don't tell me that you'd rather be down in the middle of that than up here with me?" He hands me a refilled glass as if I should be impressed by the expensive golden liquid I'm supposed to be enjoying.

I don't respond, knowing that he wouldn't like or understand my answer, because, yes, yes I really do want to be down there in the middle of all that. I want to experience everything I've missed out on with my sheltered life. I want to act wild, to do things my parents would be ashamed of but what normal young people do on a weekly basis.

Eddie manages to drag me away from my spot looking down over the fun below in favour of introducing me to some of his friends. I take one look at their designer suits, handbags and botox, and I know that I'm not about to be making friends with any of them.

I try to smile and nod at all the right times, but aside from being in a different location, I may as well be back in my old life. This is the kind of pretentious bullshit I was desperate to get away from.

My imagination sees me through the rest of the night, and, by my fourth glass of champagne, I've almost plucked up the courage to abandon Eddie and his self-obsessed friends in favour of finding my own fun. But just as I've decided to excuse myself to the toilets, his hand lands on the small of my back.

"You ready to get out of here?"

A little disappointment settles in my belly, knowing that I missed my opportunity to escape. But am I ready to get out of here? Yes. I was from the moment he directed me up to the VIP area.

***

EDDIE QUICKLY FINDS the taxi he'd ordered and ushers me inside. He slides across the seat until he's sitting a little too close and, after barking my address at the driver, turns his heated stare on me.

"This place suits you." His fingers capture a lock of my short black hair as his eyes flit around my face. He knew me in my previous life as a blonde. The first thing I did when I left, before I even got to his place, was find a hairdresser. Gone are my long, golden locks in favour of a short, dark bob. I'd always thought I'd suit short hair, and the excitement I felt at being able to experiment almost got the better of me as I sat in that chair, my head spinning with delight.

"T-thank you."

It amazes me that he doesn't mention the other—what I would think is obvious—change, but he seems to have forgotten what colour my eyes were when we first met.

"I missed you when I left. I thought of you often and whether or not I should have come back for you."

"That wasn't for you to decide. I needed to wait until the time was right. You'd already caused me enough drama." I laugh, but it's anything but amused and more clipped and uncomfortable as he edges even closer.

"We could be really good, you and me, *Quinn*." The emphasis he puts on my name makes a shudder run down my spine.

"I'm not sure that's such a good idea."

"Why not? You came to me for help. You must have known I'd want more with this second chance."

Lifting my hand, I place it on his chest in an attempt to make him back off a little.

"You're my friend, Eddie. I appreciate our relationship more than you could know. But that's all it is. You know what I've left behind and must be able to understand that I just need to be me for a little while."

"But—"

"No buts. I came here for me...not for you. I came to you as my friend, as someone who could help me. That's what I need right now. A friend. Can you be that?" I ask, my voice stronger than I thought it would be when I was brave enough to have this conversation with him.

His eyes bounce between mine as if he's waiting for me to tell him I'm joking. But I'm not. I'm deadly serious. Eddie's been a really good friend since the day I met him, but that's all we're ever going to be.

The taxi slows to a stop, and, when I drag my eyes from Eddie, I find we're outside my building.

"Thank you for a nice night. I'll see you at work next week."

"You sure you don't want me to walk you up?"

I look around at the dark and deserted car park, my heart starting to race a little, but I refuse to give him the wrong idea, even if he only does mean well. "No, I'll be fine. See you soon."

Before he can argue, I hop out of the taxi and all but run towards the front door. I know I'm safe here, but it doesn't stop me looking over my shoulder, especially at night.

CHAPTER THREE

Butterflies flutter in my belly as my Thursday night class starts to filter into my classroom. Tonight marks a week at my new job, and although it's very different to my previous teaching position, I'm quite enjoying it. There's something so easy and relaxed about teaching adults who mostly want to be here. It's miles away from the privileged kids I'm used to.

Each student finds their seat and pulls out the folder I gave them last week, ready to get to work, but the desk at the back remains empty. I try not to dwell on the fact that I was kind of looking forward to seeing him again after the show on Friday night, but it's there nonetheless.

It's two minutes after the lesson is meant to begin, and he's still not arrived. Pushing him from my mind, I address the class and get started.

I've just about finished explaining what I'd like them all to do when the door flies open and crashes back against the wall. Everyone in the room turns to see what's going on, but his eyes only find mine. Our contact holds for a few seconds too long before he breaks away in favour of finding his seat.

"Nice of you to join us, Mr. Kingsman." He tips his chin, telling me that he heard, but he still remains mute as he falls down onto his chair. He doesn't bother pulling anything from his bag, causing anger to erupt in my belly. What was I saying about the difference between teaching adults and teenagers? This defiance is something I'm much more used to.

"Don't worry, Miss Smith. I never stand up a good-looking woman." He winks, and my breath catches in my throat.

Fuck.

A gasp echoes around the room.

"Right. Well. In case you hadn't noticed, this is school, and your lack of punctuality won't be tolerated."

"I'm sure I have a few ways to ensure it's overlooked."

"Good for you." Picking up the worksheet he should be making a start on like some of the less nosey members of the class, I walk towards him.

Picking up his bag, I make a show of dropping it to the floor with a thud before pushing his foot from the top of the desk. "This is evening school, Mr. Kingsman, not primary school. I suggest you start acting appropriately. I'll catch you up on what you missed after class seeing as you couldn't get yourself here on time." I give him some very short and sharp instructions before turning and walking away, hoping to find some air to drag into my lungs.

I spend the rest of the class trying to ignore his piercing stare from the back of the room and the fact that whenever he's finished a task I've given him, he puts his feet up on the desk. He's baiting me, I'm aware of that, but I'm falling for it hook, line and sinker.

Everyone else is still reading through the first two chapters of 'Romeo and Juliet', ready to discuss it, but even with my head down, looking at my planner for this week's homework assignment, I can feel his stare.

Unable to resist the urge to find out what it is he wants, I lift my eyes.

A smug smile tugs at the corner of his lips in accomplishment.

Damn him.

Like he knows exactly how to wind me up, he makes a show of screwing up a piece of paper from his pad and making a half-arsed attempt at launching it towards the bin.

I fight my need to look at where it actually lands and put it in the bin where it should be. I'm strong for a few minutes, but eventually my desire for everything to be in the right place gets the better of me. As I'm summing up what the students should have just read, I bend down, pick it up and drop it in the bin. I feel his amusement behind me, and, when I turn around, I'm proved right when I see a wide smile on his face.

Arsehole.

"And make sure you're all on time next week," I call after I've finished going over their assignment. A couple of sniggers fill the room as all but one of the students put their stuff away and leave the room.

Joe, on the other hand, puts his feet back up on the desk and crosses his arms over his chest.

My teeth grind as I stare at him. The fabric of his shirt strains under his muscular arms and across his wide chest. I take in the ink covering his forearms, and my stomach clenches as I wonder how many others his clothes could be hiding.

I came to London with the intention of doing all the things I've craved since I was old enough to appreciate what a sheltered life I'd led. I wanted to be my own boss, wear clothes that I wanted and listen to the music I loved. Nowhere on my list was to be tempted by a bad boy, but shit, if he isn't exactly what I need after the boring, vanilla life I've led. I've no doubt that he'd help me break all the rules I've been forced to live my life by.

His eyebrow lifts as if he's waiting for me to do something, and before I think against it, I stalk towards his desk, place my palms on the smooth surface beside his feet, and stare deep into his eyes. Just like with a teenager, he needs to know I won't cower down to him.

"I'm still waiting for an apology for being late, Mr. Kingsman."

Unfolding his hands, he reaches for a pen that's lying haphazardly on his desk. Lifting it to his mouth, he taps a couple of times and, just like he probably planned, my eyes zero in on his full, soft looking lips.

My mouth waters, and I swallow as I fight to remove the inappropriate images playing out in my head.

When his eyes drop from holding mine captive to my cleavage, I almost stand, horrified that I've put myself on show like that in front of a student. But he's not just a student. He's the kind of guy I've been dreaming about since I discovered them. He's the bad boy I've imagined running away with a million times, and, with the way he's biting down on his lip right now, I'd say his thoughts aren't too opposite to my own. A bolt of excitement races through me about how wrong this is. Anyone could walk through the door any moment and find me giving my student an eyefull.

My temperature spikes, and my breasts swell under his gaze. Thank fuck for padded bras.

Bending down, I bring myself so we're at the same height and force his eyes back to mine.

The bright blue that has been staring back at me for the past two hours is significantly darker, almost black.

Clearing my throat, I start to explain what it was he missed when he decided to turn up almost twenty minutes late. "So, as you've probably now figured out, we're going to be studying 'Romeo and—'"

"Quinn, are you ready?" Eddie calls from the doorway. "Oh, sorry. I didn't realise you were running a late session." His eyes bounce between the two of us, deep lines forming across his forehead.

"I'm not. I'm just catching Joe up on what he missed as he was a little la—"

"Lateness will not be tolerated around here," Eddie barks, his angry stare homing in on Joe. "If it happens again, I will be forced to reevaluate your position on this course."

"Fantastic," Joe mutters under his breath, making me chuckle to myself. Why am I not surprised that this man isn't even a little concerned that someone of authority is giving him a dressing down?

He slips his feet from the desk, collects his stuff and shoves it all into his bag. My fingers twitch to reach out and arrange it inside properly, but that's none of my business, even if the pages of 'Romeo and Juliet' are now getting dog-eared. I shudder at the thought and rise to full height.

"We've got reservations. Are you ready?" Eddie eventually says, turning his heated stare from Joe to me.

"Y-yes. Let me grab my bag."

I quickly swipe a Post-it Note from my desk and scribble my email address down.

"Mr. Kingsman, any questions, just shoot me an email. I'll see you next week."

He shrugs on a leather jacket before throwing his bag across his body, nods in my direction, and takes a step to leave. His eyes stay locked on mine the entire time, ensuring that the tingles he initiated earlier continue to simmer just under the surface. I sense

Eddie looking between us, and eventually I manage to pull my eyes away.

Pulling my own bag over my shoulder, I walk over to Eddie. "Be careful, Quinn. That one's got trouble written all over him."

"Don't worry. I've handled worse."

"I know. I've met them," he says sadly. Unfortunately, he's right, and I know he's not necessarily talking about my past students.

He takes me to a Chinese place not far from my flat. Thankfully, after my little speech in the taxi last week, he seems to have backed off a little.

"So what's that guy's story then?" he asks once we've ordered.

My heart starts to race at just the mention of him. "No idea. You probably know more about him than me, seeing as you'd have processed his application, right?" Eddie is head of department at the college, so I'm assuming part of his job is vetting applicants.

"I guess I did. Sadly, they aren't required to supply a selfie."

Anger twists my stomach that he's once again judging him based on his tattoos and style.

"He might be the brightest student in that class. How he looks has nothing to do with it."

"But what kind of job will he ever get, looking like that?"

"Plenty. Tattoos can be covered, Eddie. Bad attitudes are harder to hide," I mutter to myself, but, by the narrowing of his eyes, I know he heard me.

We have a nice enough night, but at no point can I forget about the judgmental side of him that he's too quick to show. Maybe it's always been there, but because previously we were surrounded by people who were much, much worse, it wasn't so obvious. But now I've removed myself from that life, I want all of it gone, and I'm afraid that Eddie is going to be part of that unless he fixes his attitude.

It's not until I've securely locked myself inside my flat later that night that I pull my phone from my bag.

It's nothing special, just the cheapest smartphone I could find when I first arrived, but it does the job.

No one aside from Eddie has this number, and only one other person knows where I was headed, so I'm a little surprised when I find a notification for an email when the screen lights up.

To: Quinn Smith
From: Tatstwatsandarseholes
Subject: Romeo seeks Juliet

Dear Miss Smith,
I sincerely hope you had a wonderful evening with Mr. Boring,
although I can't imagine he fulfilled all of your desires.
I wanted to thank you for taking the time to go through our current
assignment with me seeing as I was so rudely late to class. I can
assure you that it won't happen again.
I always come on time.
Yours,
Joe Kingsman

I stare down at my phone with my eyes wide and my mouth gaping open. Did one of my students just tell me he comes on demand?

What the hell have I got myself into here? My temperature spikes as I begin to type a reply.

To: Tatstwatsandarseholes

Who in god's name has an email like that?

From: *Quinn Smith*
Subject: *Romeo needs to work harder*

Dear Mr, Kingsman,
I'm glad I could be of assistance. Any problems with the work,
please don't hesitate to ask.
Regards,
Miss Smith
PS. My evening was...boring.

The wine Eddie ordered us is clearly having an effect, because before I've really thought about it I hit send. I regret it instantly. What the hell am I doing, and why am I more excited right now than I've ever been in my life?

The screen lights up.

To: *Quinn Smith*
From: *Tatstwatsandarseholes*
Subject: *Juliet deserves more*

Dear Miss Smith,
I think you need some excitement in your life, and I know just
where you can find it...
Very much looking forward to our next lesson.
Mr. Kingsman

With a smile spreading across my lips, I close down my email app and silence my phone. This has already gone too far. The moment I didn't move when I knew he was checking out my cleavage was a step over the line, but this? This is way beyond the kind of rule breaking and excitement I was looking for.

CHAPTER FOUR

I've never been this nervous to start a class, but when my Thursday night students begin entering the room, my whole body is vibrating with anxiety.

I knew I shouldn't have replied to his inappropriate email last week, but I couldn't help myself. He's just too tempting with the bad boy geek look he's got going on. It calls to the wild side this boring English teacher has kept hidden for most of her life.

I expect him to be late just to push my buttons again, but it seems he took his warning from Eddie seriously, because he's the fourth student to enter.

I follow his movements as he walks towards his normal desk and pulls out his folder, pad of paper and pens. Then he just sits and waits as everyone else gets themselves ready. At no point does he look up, and it annoys the shit out of me that I've been so worried about seeing him all day, and he's totally indifferent.

My nerves give way to shame and embarrassment as I think about how easily I played his game, because clearly that was all this was to him.

I welcome the class and set them up on the first activity, which is to be done in pairs.

Sitting down behind my desk, I watch as they all move closer to their allocated partner and begin their discussions, but before long my eyes find their way back to him and the woman he's working with.

The second I look up, I meet his blue eyes. My breath catches as a smirk spreads across his face before he turns his attention back to her.

Tingles erupt and my thighs clench. It's not the reaction to a student I should be having, but my body doesn't seem to care as I fight to drag my eyes away from where he's leaning into his partner and absorbing every word she's saying.

The next thirty minutes of my life are possibly some of the most frustrating I've ever experienced. No matter how hard I try, I can't stop myself from glancing up at them, and every time I do, I regret it. It's like he knows and intentionally does something to wind me up.

His partner is young, and even I can admit how pretty she is. He makes sure that both she and I know it. He runs the back of his knuckles up her arm, tucking a lock of hair behind her ear when they're both looking down and studying the text I've given them. He laughs animatedly in a way I'm sure isn't all that natural when she says something. And although I'm pretty convinced he's acting for my benefit, it hits the exact spot he was intending.

It's infuriating. *He's* infuriating.

Once they all return to their own seats, Joe goes back to ignoring me. It's much easier to deal with, but the nagging need to make him look up at me gets more and more impossible to ignore.

There's only ten minutes left of the lesson, and I'm walking around, collecting what everyone's been doing so I can mark it, when the sound of a pencil dropping on the floor in front of me catches my attention. I step towards it, my need to have everything just so too much to ignore, and just as I'm about to bend, someone shifts behind me. It's only then that I realise this is a game, and I have a millisecond to decide if I'm going to play on the wild side.

Moving here was all about pushing boundaries.

In a moment of madness, I bend over and pick up the pencil. Excitement fills my veins, knowing that I shouldn't be joining in with his games, but I can't help myself. My stomach clenches at the thought of someone watching me openly flirt, but the risk isn't enough to stop me.

I slowly turn and place the pencil back onto his desk, lining it up perfectly alongside his paper. Risking a look at his face, my breath catches when I find his dark eyes and his teeth digging into his bottom lip.

Every muscle in my body freezes as his eyes drop from mine in favour of taking a leisurely stroll around my body. I'm dressed differently this week, seeing as I haven't been able to get to the laundrette yet, so my old trusty twinset and a-line skirt have sadly made a reappearance.

Desire still fills his eyes, but when he opens his mouth, something else entirely comes out. "Mr. Boring rubbing off on you, teach? Didn't have you down as a cardigan and pearl necklace type."

My shoulders stiffen at the reference to my old life, although I'm equally as glad I've managed to pull off my new persona as I am frustrated that he's noticed the change.

"Don't always judge a book by its cover, Mr. Kingsman."

"I'm beginning to learn that, Miss Smith."

When I eventually pull my eyes from his and glance to the clock on the wall, I notice that we're about to run over.

"Right, well. Looks like we're done for the day. I'll have all these marked for you for next week. Any questions about this week's assignment, feel free to reach out. I'm here to help in any way I can." There's a scoff from behind me, and my cheeks flame.

The sound of people packing up fills my ears, and I take my time in cleaning off the whiteboard I'd scribbled all over during the lesson and restacking some of the text books on the shelves beneath that were a little untidy.

A few 'thank yous' and 'see you next weeks' ring out, and I acknowledge each one with a hesitant glance towards the student.

I don't turn back around until I'm confident everyone has gone, and even then it's only to grab my bag so I can get away from here and all the thoughts he conjures up in my head.

"Shit. Fuck." My hand comes up to cover my racing heart when I find him still sitting at his desk with his feet once again on the fucking top and his chair rocking back. A surefire way to piss off any teacher.

"Did you need help with the assignment, Mr. Kingsman?"

"Um...no, I think I've got it covered." His feet hit the floor and he stands, taking all the air in the room with him as he stalks towards me.

My heart continues to race and my palms start to sweat as he approaches the other side of the desk.

"I was more wondering what I could do for you."

"How's that?" I squeak. Wishing the ground would swallow me up for showing my vulnerability, I reach for my pencil case, ready to stuff it inside my bag, but he stops me. His large, calloused hand lands on mine, and I'm forced to freeze as sparks shoot up my arm. I glance at the door, knowing that Eddie will most probably barge through at any moment to check up on me.

"I'm not totally sure. I was hoping you could help me out with that."

When I turn back to him, he's staring at me with narrowed

eyes as if he's trying to work me out. My lips part to respond, but he beats me to it.

"What I do know is that what you need isn't Mr. Boring, and it also isn't this poncy fucking twinset." He reaches out and pops open the top button of my cardigan like a freaking magic trick. "I also know that you're looking for something, and I'm pretty sure I can help you find it."

"I uh..." I've no idea what to say to any of that other than to be freaked out by how spot-on his assumptions are.

"You don't need to tell me that I'm right. I already have my answer." His smug smirk pisses me off, but it's nowhere near enough for me to make him leave. "So, are you in?"

"In with what exactly?" My eyes find the door again as I try to pull my hand from under his, not wanting to get caught in this position, but he squeezes harder to stop me.

"Giving me a chance to find whatever it is you're looking for."

"I've no idea what—" The door opens. My eyes fly up and my heart pounds against my ribs as Joe rips his hand from mine and steps back.

"You all done for the—Mr. Kingsman, in trouble again?" Eddie looks between the two of us, his eyes calculating.

"Not this time. Just had a couple of important questions for Miss Smith before I left to make a start on my assignment in the coffee shop down the street." He turns back to me and winks.

It's probably the most unsubtle invitation I've ever heard. I expect Eddie to say something but, to my surprise, he side-steps Joe's random statement. "You ready?"

I hesitate for a second, giving Joe a chance to return to his seat and pick up his bag, but he's not yet out of the room when I say, "Actually, I'll find my own way home tonight. I've got a few errands to run. I wouldn't want to hold you up."

"Oh, okay. If you're sure."

I barely hear the words, because I'm too focused on the wide, triumphant smile Joe graces me with before he walks out of my classroom.

What the hell are you doing, Quinn?

I tell myself that I'm just going to get a coffee for the journey home. I want to see if he's really there and what else he has to say. I'd be lying if I said I wasn't interested in hearing it.

I feel him watching me the second I step inside the coffee shop, but I come up empty when I quickly scan the tables as I walk towards the counter.

"Cappuccino, one sugar, chocolate sprinkles," is whispered in my ear, sending goosebumps racing across my skin.

Turning, I find him right behind me with two mugs in hand.

"How'd you know?"

"Good guess."

I follow him to a table in a dark corner at the back of the shop, my entire body shaking with nervous energy, and sit with my hands wrapped around the mug so he doesn't see them trembling.

"So tell me, Miss Smith. What is it you're looking for?"

"I don't—'

"Don't lie to me. I can see it in your eyes every time you look at me. Tell me what you need. I'm sure I can deliver everything you desire."

Need sits heavy in my stomach. I might be wanting to experience new things, but there's no way in hell I'm asking him to cure that little issue.

"I want..." I hesitate, and he leans forward as if I'm about to tell him a secret. "To really live. To do all the things I've never been able to do." A rush of adrenaline hits me at admitting that out loud for the first time in my life.

I expect him to laugh, because it's more than obvious that this guy does exactly what he wants and when he wants, but all he does is rest his arms on the table and ask, "Like what?"

"So many things. I want to wear the clothes I want, I want to dance to the music I want, I want to get drunk and dance all night, get a tattoo, have a one nig—" I stop when his eyes widen in delight. That's not what this is about.

A man clears his throat behind Joe, and I damn near jump out of the chair thinking that we've been caught, but when I look up there's just a man helping his wife into her coat.

"Why haven't you done any of this before?" he asks, ignoring my skittishness, sipping on his own coffee and swallowing his reaction to what I almost admitted.

"I lived a somewhat sheltered life."

"In London?"

I shake my head, already knowing that I've revealed too much. "I've only just moved here."

"So I was right earlier about the twinset, then." His eyes drop to my chest, and I sigh.

"I fucking hate them."

"Right." He tips his mug up to finish off what's left and stands. "Let's go, then."

"Where?" I ask, my eyes wide in shock.

"To experience life."

"Uh..."

"What, you scared?"

"No, I..." His eyebrow lifts in challenge, but there's no way I'm backing down. "Just need to finish my coffee first."

"Oh...wild," he says with a laugh, sitting himself back down.

CHAPTER FIVE

oe waits around the corner as I run back into the college and drop my bags off in the staff room. Thankfully, the department is empty, and I don't run into any colleagues who've only just seen me leave.

I don't allow myself time to think about the reality of what I've just agreed to. Instead, I focus on the excitement of what he might be about to show me.

I find him in a hidden doorway on his phone when I get back outside.

"I thought maybe you were going to bail."

"I don't back down from a challenge, Mr. Kingsman."

"Joe, please. I can't cope with all this surname bollocks."

"Sure thing. Where first?"

"To get rid of that godawful twinset."

"Won't all the shops be shut?"

"You really haven't been here long, huh?" I shake my head in response and fall into step beside him. "This is London. You can get anything whenever you want it."

"I don't have much money," I admit with a wince.

"Okay, we'll steer clear of Bond Street then." He chuckles. "I'm not sure they'll have the kind of thing we're after, anyway."

Side by side, we walk towards the tube station. He looks relaxed as ever while I feel like I could pass out any minute at the rate my heart's pounding in my chest. I might be breaking all the rules, but I'm about to get a taste of the life I've always wanted, I'm sure of it.

"I've never stepped foot inside a Topshop before."

"Where did you come from? Narnia?"

"Might as well have been," I mutter as we descend the escalator.

"We'll need to be quick. They close soon."

We step from the escalator and Joe darts right, as if he knows exactly where he's going.

"Do you trust me?"

"Uh..."

"Go to the fitting rooms, get undressed, and I'll get some options."

"How much do you know about women's clothes?"

"Enough. Now go."

Thankfully, there's no assistant hovering at the fitting rooms, so I rush into the first cubicle and strip out of my twinset.

Standing there in my boring cotton underwear, I start to question my sanity. I'm standing basically naked waiting for one of my students to bring me a new outfit to wear on a crazy night out.

I should be concerned, but everything I've been worrying about seems to vanish when I'm with him. That might freak me out, but it's also such a relief after looking over my shoulder every second since I arrived here.

"Quinn?"

"In here." I poke my head out of the curtain. Joe's eyes drop despite the fact that I've got the curtain draped around me.

"Put these on." He thrusts a couple of hangers at me, and I slink back behind the curtain.

"Uh...where's the rest of the top?" I ask, eyeing the tiny bit of fabric in my hands.

"Probably in the bin, which is exactly where that bloody twinset is going in a few minutes. Now stop complaining and put it on."

Rolling my eyes at him, I pull the skinny black jeans from the hanger and attempt to pull them up my legs. I feel like Sandy as she tried to get those leather trousers on in *Grease*.

Amazingly, they fit like a second skin, and even I can appreciate how good they look. I've never seen my legs like this before. I always thought I was a little short and stumpy, but I'm realising that might have been the a-line skirts.

Next, I remove the scrap of fabric that I'm assuming is meant to be a top from the hanger and pull it on. What little there is of it is covered in silver sequins. It's short enough to expose my midriff, something I can honestly say has never seen the light of day before, and apart from the spaghetti straps across the back, it totally exposes that as well.

"I'm not sure about this," I say to the curtain.

"Show me," he demands.

"Fuck." I stare at myself in the mirror, and it's like there's a different woman looking back at me. Gone is the boring, nondescript woman I'm used to, and in her place is a stylish, young lady who has the city at her feet.

I run my fingers through my bobbed hair in an attempt to give it some volume and blow out a deep breath.

My hand shakes as I lift it to pull the curtain back. The second it's in my hand, I shut my eyes and just go for it.

"Fuuuuuck," Joe groans, and my eyes pop open in horror. Only, the expression on his face doesn't show that of disapproval like I was expecting. It's full of heat, and the sight of it has desire pooling between my legs.

"I feel naked," I admit, covering my bare stomach with my hands.

"Trust me, you're anything but naked right now."

"I've never shown this much skin," I whisper, more to myself than him. I know it's crazy, seeing as I'm wearing a full-length pair of jeans, but still. It's the top that makes me feel so exposed.

Lifting his arm, he signals for me to spin around for him.

Sucking in as much confidence as I can muster, I close my eyes and begin turning.

"Waaaait."

"What?" I look over my shoulder when his warmth hits my bare skin.

"This," he says, snapping my bra strap, "needs to go."

"I don't think so."

"Trust me." Before I even have time to consider if I do or not, the fabric around my ribs loosens and he's pulling the straps down my arms.

"What the hell are you doing?"

"Pushing you out of your comfort zone and making you live."

"Why the hell did I admit that to you?" I mutter, taking over the job of removing my bra. The second I pull it out from under the tiny sequined top, I really feel naked. The fabric tickles against the sensitive skin of my breasts, and the cool air surrounds them. My nipples pucker, but thankfully the sequins cover it. Showing him just how much this is affecting me is the last thing I want.

"Because you know I'm the one to do it. And if it was a one-night-stand you were too scared to admit to wanting, you shouldn't have any problems looking like you do right now." One of his hands brushes up my exposed spine, and his breath tickles across my neck.

I shudder, and there's no way in hell he doesn't notice.

"What the hell?"

He steps back, giving me a little space to breathe, but then he pulls the back of the jeans away from me and tugs at the tag. "Do you have any regard for people's personal space?"

He rolls his eyes and reaches out again, I assume for the tag on the top, but knowing it's currently pressed against my right breast, I turn away from him and pull it off myself.

"You planning on ruining all my fun?"

"You ask that like you're not having the time of your life right now."

The smile that curls at his lips makes my breath catch.

"What size feet are you?"

"Five, why?"

He glances down at the cute ballet shoes I wore to work today and quirks an eyebrow.

"Fine. But I'm keeping them. I only bought them a few days ago."

"Fine. Sort your shit out, and I'll meet you at the entrance."

He takes off with the clothing tags, and I panic. "You're not paying for those." He doesn't bother to turn around and respond. Instead, he lifts his hand over his shoulder and flips me off.

I fume, my fists clenching. Why did the guy who caught my eye have to be so infuriating?

I fold all my old clothes into a shopping bag that's at the bottom of my handbag and slip my feet into my comfortable flats. I dread to think what he's going to find for me.

When I emerge, the shop is deserted. I start to panic that I've been locked in until I take a few more steps and find my partner in crime standing to the side of the doors with a pair of black strappy sandals swinging from his fingers and a woman's leather jacket draped over his arm.

"There's no way I can walk in those."

As if he knows just how competitive I am, he drops his gaze to my feet before he says, "I bet you can. Loser buys dinner."

"Jesus," I mutter, holding my hand out.

He offers his support once I've got the first shoe on my foot and start wobbling about as I attempt the second one. The moment his fingers wrap around mine, sparks fly up my arm. My eyes search his out, and, when I find them, he's staring right back at me.

"I don't want a one-night-stand," I blurt out, probably sounding like a total moron.

"That's good, because I wasn't offering one."

"Really?"

My eyes search his. From the way he was looking at me earlier and the way he touched me, I was convinced that was where he hoped this was heading.

"I'm not the type of man to do that kind of thing." He reaches out and tucks a lock of my hair behind my ear. The move is so soft and gentle, the total opposite to what I'd expect from looking at him.

"I don't believe that for a second. I saw you—" I cut myself off when I realise I'm about to admit to watching him the other night.

"You saw me what? Have you been stalking me, Miss Smith?"

"What? No. It's just...Eddie took me to The Avenue last week and you were...enjoying yourself."

"Ah, I see," he says sadly. Dropping my hand, he turns to leave.

"Wait." Without thinking, I slide my hand back into his when I catch up with him. "You just looked like you were having fun. I was...jealous."

"Jealous? Wasn't Mr. Boring keeping you entertained?"

"He took me to the VIP section. It's not really my kind of thing. I'd have been much happier down with you."

"That's because I'm such a good dancer."

"I saw. Everyone seemed to love you."

"I know how to show them a good time."

"So what are you waiting for? I want a good time."

CHAPTER SIX

Our first stop isn't the craziest of locations. I was kind of hoping he'd dive right in with the wild night he had planned. That said, takeout Chinese sitting in the middle of Leicester Square is pretty awesome.

"Oh my god, this is so good," I moan around a mouthful of sticky chicken. Aside from going out for dinner with Eddie, my diet has been pretty limited since I moved here, so this tastes incredible. "You've got to try some. Here." I hold out my fork for him, and, after a slight hesitation, he opens his mouth. I realise my mistake almost immediately. His full lips wrap around my fork, and I can't take my eyes away from them as he chews and then swipes his tongue across the bottom one to lick up some stray sauce.

"Keep looking at me like that and I'll get the wrong idea about what you want from me tonight."

His words cause desire to fill my veins, but as much as I'm enjoying his company, I know I can't allow anything to happen.

He's my student. What I'm doing with him now is forbidden, let alone if I was to take it any further.

"So how come you've gone back to school?" I ask, trying to steer our conversation back to safe ground.

"I fucked it up first time around. Believe it or not, I was a bit of a nightmare teenager."

"I don't believe that for a second," I say with a laugh. He's got the bad boy image now—I can only imagine what he was like as a kid.

"I didn't care back then. My only focus was pissing my parents off as much as possible. But now, I want more."

"Good for you. There are so many people who just put up with what life dealt them. Not everyone has the guts to admit they might have screwed up and do something to better themselves."

"I've got balls, don't you worry about that." He winks, and I can't help but laugh. This guy does something to me, something I've never experienced before, but the world seems that little bit better when he's by my side. It's crazy. Unbelievable. But true.

"So what's the plan then?"

"Oh god, you're one of those, aren't you?"

"One of those?" My brows draw together as I wait for him to explain.

"Control freak. I've got a couple of friends like you."

"Guilty."

"Well, switch it off. Tonight, you follow my lead and do as you're told."

"Okay, lead the way."

He takes us back to the tube, thankfully, remembering the slow pace I need with these damn shoes on. I guess I could take them off now I won the bet and he had to pay for dinner, but I quite like them. They give me confidence that I'm not used to by standing a little taller, and that's something I need seeing as I'm walking around practically topless.

He takes me to a comedy club on the outskirts of Camden Town and, unlike Eddie, when he goes to the bar he orders us two pints.

I know it's not really anything in the grand scheme of things, but sitting there drinking a pint when a lady doing such a thing was so frowned upon where I came from, I feel like I can take on the world.

"What are you smiling at?" Joe asks when there's a break in comedians.

"Nothing. Everything."

"Okay. Care to explain?"

Shaking my head, I take another sip of my beer. "I just really needed this."

"Yeah, me too." He lifts his drink and takes a sip. He winks at me over the rim, telling me that he knows he's giving me an out from having to explain anything.

I've opened up more to him than I have anyone ever—and that's saying something, because he doesn't really know anything. Eddie knows the most about my life, but that's only because he experienced some of it first hand, one thing I never forget every time he looks at me.

The next comedian up on stage is a woman, and after only two minutes I've got tears streaming down my face. She's by far the funniest person I've ever heard, and the more I laugh the more I forget about the skeletons in my closet and just enjoy my new life.

"You're beautiful when you smile," Joe says, leaning over and whispering in my ear.

I'd felt him staring at me as I laughed at her dry, witty jokes, but I wasn't able to pull my eyes away.

"Even with the tears?"

"Even with them, babe."

"Uh..." Warmth spreads through my body, desire that I'd managed to dampen down erupting as I turn and take in his soft eyes and smile.

"Ready to move on?"

Hand in hand, we walk towards the centre of Camden Town. Joe drags me into the first place that has music pounding out of the doors.

"Drink?" he asks, although I can barely hear him over the live music coming from the stage at the other end of the bar.

"Um..." I grab the menu, but it's plucked from my hand.

"I'll choose. Go grab that seat." Unlike when Eddie ordered for me, frustration doesn't bubble up within me. Weirdly, I trust Joe to get something I'm going to like, not just something he thinks will impress me.

I hover as the couple vacating the table leave, grateful not to have to stand up in these shoes for much longer.

"What's this?" I take a sip of the drink.

"Slippery nipple."

"I'm sorry, what?" I almost spray him with the creamy liquid.

"It's a cocktail called a slippery nipple. You made out earlier that you'd lived a sheltered life, so I assumed you'd not had one before. The drink, I mean," he adds when my cheeks flame.

Why is it that the second he says that, the only thing I can see is him sucking my—no. Totally inappropriate.

As if he knows exactly where my head's at, his eyes drop to my chest. "Although, I could certainly arrange for the other kind, if you fancy it."

A bolt of lust hits me so hard I think I'd be on the floor if I wasn't already sitting. My lips part as my breathing increases. A wicked smile twitches at his lips as his eyes bounce between mine and my lips. I really should do something to stop this. My thoughts vanish when he reaches across the table and tangles our fingers together.

Thankfully, the music starts again, cutting off any more inappropriate comments that might be on the tip of his tongue. I can tell by the darkness of his eyes and the twitching muscle in his neck that he's thinking of plenty.

Turning my focus away from him, I look at the band up on stage and try to ignore the need sitting heavy in my stomach. He, however, doesn't turn away from me throughout their entire set.

Needing a little space to breathe, I excuse myself to the bathroom. The music is still loud as I do my business, but even though I wanted some space, the second I'm away from him, I find myself looking over my shoulder once again before rushing back to the safety of his side.

I find two fresh drinks waiting for me at the table when I retake my seat.

"Should I ask?"

He chuckles as he goes back to the bar to grab his beer, but instead of taking his seat, he comes up behind me and whispers, "The clear one with the olive is a martini—dirty, of course. And the other, that's something else I think you might be in need of."

"Oh?"

"A screaming orgasm." My breath catches as his nose—or lips, I'm not really sure—runs around the shell of my ear. My wanton moan only serves to prove to both of us that that could possibly be exactly what I need.

It doesn't mean you're going to allow it to happen, a little voice screams inside my head. I just about manage to hear her over the blood racing in my ears as I wonder just how good he'd be at giving me a real one of those and not just the cocktail.

He's gone as fast as he appeared, and by the time I look up he's sitting in his seat, sipping on his beer like those few seconds didn't happen.

"What?" he asks when he places his glass down and finds me staring at him with my mouth still agape.

"N-nothing."

"Good, drink up. I've got plans."

"More?"

"Didn't you tell me that you wanted to stay up all night and experience London?"

"I guess."

"Well, what kind of friend would I be if I didn't make that happen?"

Friend. *Friend.* The word feels wrong, but the reality is that even being friends is against the rules. And I know for a fact that wanting more, like what he just whispered in my ear, would smash all the rules to smithereens.

CHAPTER SEVEN

I have no clue what the time is, and quite frankly I don't care. That could be due to the amount of alcohol I've put away tonight, or it could be the company, I've no idea. But as we dance together in the basement of a club that I can't for the life of me remember the name of, I realise that I feel more alive than I have done in...forever. And it's not just this place that does that, it's him. He makes me feel like the woman I've always wanted to be. He makes me feel whole, and I've only just met him.

"Stop thinking," he whispers in my ear, his hands finding my hips and pulling me back into his body.

He's been fairly well behaved since he whispered naughty things about screaming orgasms in my ear at the bar. I must admit that I expected him to pull me to him the moment he dragged me onto the dancefloor. I'd witnessed him dancing before, and I'd be lying if I said I didn't want to experience what it would be like to move my hips in time with his like the girls that night.

"Sorry, just trying to process everything."

"Well, stop. The only thing you should be doing right now is feeling. Feel the music. Feel your body moving in time to the beat, and feel the tension that's pulling your shoulders tight wash away."

"O-okay," I stutter as his groin rolls against my arse. A tremble races through me, and my body follows his lead.

"Better," he whispers when I relax against him. "Just go with the flow."

Something about those words make me tense again. I've gone with the flow my entire life—that's how I ended up stuck where I was. But I soon realise that this is different. Joe's version of going with the flow doesn't involve some of the things my previous life did. His version is about letting go and having fun. Exactly what I told him I wanted.

His fingers dig into my hips a little more, forcing me to shut down my thoughts and just move.

I press back into him, our bodies lining up perfectly. His movements are perfectly in sync with the music. The bass pounds so loud that the floor beneath me vibrates, and it only adds to the tingles that are already surging around my body at being so close to him.

Resting my head back against his shoulder, my eyes fall shut and I soak up the moment. There's every possibility that I might not get this chance again. I could be found and dragged back to face the music at any moment. It's a fact that I can never forget as I constantly look over my shoulder, waiting for an unwanted familiar face.

I've no idea how much time passes or how many songs play while we stand in the exact same position, moving against each other. My aching feet seem to vanish along with the hundreds of people around us. The only thing I notice is that the more I rub my arse against Joe, the harder his cock presses into me. The knowledge that I'm the one doing that fills me with so much delight I can barely wipe the smile off my face. I'm not sure I've ever really turned anyone on before. I can say with absolute certainty that I've never experienced the tension that's sizzling between us right now.

My pulse thunders through my veins and the unmistakable throb between my legs intensifies. I've no doubt the man behind me could help me experience things I've been missing out on, but as incredible as this feels right now, I still can't forget the reasons why it shouldn't be happening.

A growl rumbles up his throat before his breath tickles my ear. "If I didn't know better, I'd think you were doing that on purpose. I didn't think you wanted that tonight, Miss Smith."

I have no words, so when I open my mouth, the only thing that comes out is a needy moan.

"Jesus. You have any idea how badly I need you right now?" My chest heaves as excitement explodes in my belly.

Those few words should be enough to make me step away, to put the space between us that there should be, but in reality, they do the opposite. With his scent surrounding me and the effects of the alcohol controlling my body, I want everything he has to offer.

"Joe," I moan, turning my head so my nose runs along the skin of his neck. I breathe in his woodsy scent, and it only makes my need for him stronger.

He looks down at me. The moment our eyes connect, I think he's going to take everything he wants, and a slither of terror runs through me.

But he doesn't.

He doesn't drop his head. His lips don't find mine. His hand, however...that does move. The rough skin of his palm scratches up the smooth skin of my stomach until his fingers slip inside the fabric of my top.

He reaches my ribs, and I swear I stop breathing. My breasts swell with the need to be touched, my nipples pebble against the heavy fabric hanging over them, and heat floods my core in anticipation.

Time stands still as his hand continues to move. The second his thumb brushes against the underside of my breast, I suck in a huge breath.

"Oh god," I moan, pressing back harder into him as I almost lose the use of my legs.

His hand cups my breast, and I swear I nearly fall apart from that alone. He pinches my nipple between his thumb and forefinger, and my eyes flutter shut so I can focus on the sensation racing through my body.

My chest heaves, my heart races, and my head spins. He's barely touching me, but I'm falling apart at the seams.

"You think I can give you that screaming orgasm from this alone?"

My response is a whimper.

His hips keep moving against my arse, his cock now impossibly hard against me. My core clenches with need to feel him inside me.

"I bet you taste so sweet. If we were anywhere else, I'd rip that fabric from your body and find out. Would you want that?"

Whimper.

He palms my breast again. Even the mention of where we are right now doesn't concern me. I'm too lost to him and the sensations he's erupting in my body.

"I'd lick and suck until you were begging for more." His voice is barely a whisper, but the deep, rumbling timbre has heat blooming low in my stomach.

His other hand teases at the waistband of my jeans.

"You think anyone would notice if I were to find out how wet you are for me right now?"

Whimper.

"Are you ready for me, Miss Smith?" He pinches each nipple harder, pulling them harshly, the action sending lightning bolts to my core. A ball of something explosive grows within me to the point that I feel like I'm about to break apart. My temperature spikes, my heart pounds, and then it happens. Lights flash behind my eyes, and something explodes within me. Wave after wave of pleasure so intense hits me again and again, threatening to buckle my knees.

"Holy fuck." His deep, gravelly voice has aftershocks shooting off around my body.

Dropping his hand from my top, he spins me in his arms. I keep my eyes locked on his shoulder as his arms wrap around my waist. I'm too embarrassed by what just happened to risk looking up into his eyes.

If he says anything, I don't hear it, but his fingers press under my chin and I'm powerless but to allow him to tip my head back.

The desire in his eyes has my breath catching in my throat. His tongue sneaks out and captures my attention as it runs along his bottom lip. My mouth waters as he leans in. I expect his lips to press to mine, but he surprises me once again when he moves to whisper in my ear. "I'm pretty sure that was the hottest thing I've ever experienced."

He's clearly got a lot more experience in this stuff than me, so I highly doubt his words are true. If he had the balls to do what he just did to me while surrounded by hundreds of people, then I've no doubt he's done much, much worse. The thought has disappointment cooling the fire that's still burning within me.

I know for a fact that it's the hottest thing *I've* ever experienced. I'm not a virgin by any means, but when I think back to my previous encounters, the term 'lie back and think of England' comes to mind.

My cheeks heat as I think about my first orgasm being delivered in the middle of a night club.

"You're beautiful when you blush." Unable to hold his eyes, I look over his shoulder. The sincerity pouring from them is a little much to take. "You want to get out of here?"

"Sure." *I think that's probably for the best.* Somehow, I manage to keep that last thought to myself.

Joe threads his fingers through mine and, after stopping to collect our coats and my bags, we head out into the night.

"What time is it?"

"Almost four."

"Four in the morning?" I ask, disbelief filling my voice.

"Yeah. How do you feel, having almost done your full all-nighter?"

"Weirdly not tired."

"Good, because we haven't finished yet."

"No?"

"No. You might want to change your shoes, though. We're going for a night time tour of the city."

The moment he mentions my shoes, all feeling comes back to my feet, and they throb.

Joe holds onto my elbow as I pull the sandals off and slip on my much more comfortable flats. Then we set off.

I've no idea if he has a destination in mind, but I don't really care. I'd follow him to the end of the earth right now if it meant I continued feeling the way I am.

Not once do I look over my shoulder to see if we're being followed, and not a second passes in which I think about my past. It's exactly where it belongs when I'm with Joe: in the past.

By the time he pulls me into a twenty-four hour shop and off licence, we've walked miles and the alcohol that was running through my system has long since disappeared—that is, until he purchases a bottle of tequila.

"You're joking, right? We're not drinking that now?"

"Hair of the dog. It'll help set you up for the day."

The thought of a full day at work has realisation setting in. "Fuck."

"Exactly. But I've got plenty of experience when it comes to partying all night. So are you with me?" He twists the top off the second we emerge from the electric lights of the small shop and takes a swig. He winces as it burns but happily hands it over.

"To going crazy and pulling all nighters," I say with a laugh and lift it to my lips. "Ugh," I complain once I've swallowed it, discovering that there's a reason I've never had this before.

"To unexpected all nighters with beautiful strangers."

When he offers me the bottle again, I stupidly take another shot. It almost immediately makes my head spin.

"Right, we need breakfast to soak this up."

"So we're not going home to bed, then?"

He turns his heated stare on me and I instantly regret the question. "There would only be one reason we'd end up in bed tonight, babe, and it wouldn't be for sleeping." My lips form an O, my heart pounding rapidly. If he could get me off as easily as he did in the club when we were both fully dressed, I can only imagine how skilled he might be once naked. "But you said no one-night-stand, so breakfast it is."

With the half-empty bottle of tequila in one hand and mine in the other, we set off once again.

He directs us to a kebab shop and takes the liberty of ordering for both of us. I'm grateful, because I'd have no clue what to order anyway. I'm a kebab virgin, although I'm not drunk enough to admit that one out loud.

CHAPTER EIGHT

J oe drops me off at my building just before sunrise with a sweet kiss on the cheek and a sexy smile.

He was the perfect gentleman, aside from those few moments in the club, and as I climb the stairs to my tiny flat, I can't wipe the smile off my face. Who knew that bad boy who turned up to his first lesson looking so unsure of himself would help me cross a few things off my to do list with such style?

"Shit," I gasp when I see the clock on the oven as I let myself in. I've only got an hour until I need to teach my first class of the day.

I peel my new clothes from my body and step into my shower, needing to wash the scent of last night's alcohol and nightclub from my body. If I'm intending to go to work still slightly intoxicated, at least I can make an effort to smell fresh.

Seeing as I've still not been to the bloody laundrette, I'm stuck with the only thing left in my wardrobe: a baby pink twinset and a grey a-line skirt. I can't help laughing as I pull it on, thinking about what Joe's opinion would be. He'd probably want to rip it from my body if he were to catch me wearing it. Those thoughts have memories of his hands on me last night consuming me as I blow dry my hair and apply my makeup.

I stop off and pick up a large cappuccino with a double shot of coffee in the coffee shop where everything started last night. I can't help wishing that we could do it all over again. It was by far the best night of my life and totally worth the exhaustion that's starting to take over my body right about now.

MY FIRST CLASS of the day has just settled into its first task when my phone vibrates against my desk. Risking a glance at it, my lips twitch into a smile when I see his ridiculous email address.

To: Quinn Smith
From: Tatstwatsandarseholes
Subject: I can show you the world...

Dear Miss Smith
I hope you enjoyed your magic carpet ride and aren't feeling the effects too badly this morning.
If you ask me, it could easily be turned into an epic love story.
I'm ready to analyse the next chapter if you are.
Yours,
Mr. Kingsman

My phone trembles in my hand. I shouldn't be doing this, and I really shouldn't be this excited about it.

I'm still staring at it when a shadow falls over me. "Shit," I squeak, shoving my phone deep into my bag when I find Eddie at the other side of my desk, also looking down at my phone.

"Morning," I sing happily, hoping to cover up the blush on my cheeks and the fact I only drank some tequila a couple of hours ago.

"Is...everything okay?" His brows are drawn together as he assesses me.

"Y-yeah, of course. This class is great."

"I was asking about you. You look like you didn't get any sleep last night." My heart immediately thunders against my chest. Fuck, does he know?

My hands tremble as he continues to stare at me.

"I've...uh...just got a lot on my mind."

"Everything's okay though, with all that? You'd tell me if you needed something, right?"

"Of course. Everything's fine. I've not heard anything."

My words must be sincere enough, because after a couple of seconds Eddie nods and turns to leave.

I push my bag under my desk and attempt to ignore my phone's existence.

Trying to think about anything but him as well as keeping myself awake, I do a lap of my classroom and check in on each student. This class is a little more of what I'm used to, seeing as the majority are still teenagers. That being said, they're still a million miles from the private school kids of my past.

"How are you doing, Jodi?" I ask, dropping down to my haunches and checking on one of the quieter members of the group. There's something so familiar about her. She reminds me of a younger me. There's a sadness in her eyes that only comes with the overbearing nature of my past.

"I'm good, Miss, thank you." Her words are as quiet as a mouse.

"You can call me Quinn, sweetie. If you need anything, please just ask. I'm here to help." I can't help but offer my support, although I'm sure how much I really mean it goes straight over her head.

Thoughts of my past along with memories of last night fill my mind for the rest of the morning.

I grab myself a panini from the coffee shop around the corner for lunch, and by the time my belly is full it's all I can do to keep my eyes open in the quiet of our little staff room. Pushing my diary and laptop aside, I lay my head on my arms just for a few moments to relax.

I awake to the sound of someone clearing their throat.

Lifting my head, I instantly meet the concerned eyes of Eddie, who's down on his haunches looking at me.

"Are you sure you're okay?"

"I promise." I smile weakly, my sleep-fogged brain making any kind of movement hard right now.

"If I didn't know any better, I'd think you went out last night. Have you made some new friends?"

"No," I lie smoothly. "I had a glass of wine too many with dinner," I admit, realising that he's close enough to possibly smell last night on me.

"Be sensible. I know life's different for you now, but please don't go too wild."

He eyes me as I panic. My palms sweat as I think about what could possibly happen to me if he were to find out what I did last night and with whom.

"I won't. I just needed a little help to relax." It's not a lie. It's exactly what last night was.

"Just remember, I'm here for you."

"I know. Thank you."

The second he leaves the room, my head finds the desk again—only this time it's not to sleep, it's out of frustration for what I'm doing.

The last thing I needed when I stepped out of the building to finally head home later that afternoon was an almighty downpour.

I watch as Londoners run past the front doors to the college building, using anything they've got in their hands to protect themselves from the torrential water. A couple of people shelter in the doorway, but I don't have time for this. My need to be at home and in my pyjamas tops my need to stay dry right now.

A shiver runs down my spine as the cold hits me, but it still doesn't deter me. A warm shower will fix everything.

I'm rushing towards the tube station when a white van comes to a screeching halt right in front of me.

I freeze in terror. My heart races and my head spins as memories hit me.

I can't go back.

My chest heaves as I try to drag in some much-needed oxygen and pull myself together. If they've come for me, I need to prepare for what happens next.

I'm busy mentally building the walls back up that had started to crumble last night when the passenger window opens.

"You fucking getting in or not?"

It takes me a couple of seconds to figure out who it is. The voice is so familiar, and the deep timbre to it has tingles erupting within me, but the sight is anything but what I'm used to.

He's dirty—disgusting actually—but he's never looked better.

My muscles still refuse to move as I stare at his messy hair flopping down onto his forehead, the dark smears covering his face from a long, hard day at work, and the dirty, ripped white t-shirt stretched across this wide chest.

I'm in trouble.

"Do I need to come and put you inside myself?" Although the prospect of that happening has fire racing through my veins, I manage to force my legs to work and take a step towards him.

"No, it's okay," I whisper, but with the sound of the rain hitting the pavement and the hustle and bustle of London in the background, there's no way he hears me.

"Hey," he says when I drop down onto his passenger seat and wipe the rain from my face.

"Hey." I risk a look up at him, and my breath catches in my throat. "Whoa," I breathe. If I thought he looked good from a distance, it's nothing compared to him close-up with his scent filling my nose.

"What?" he asks with a chuckle. "Dirty workmen your thing?"

"Apparently so." The words aren't meant to be said aloud, but it's too late now. His eyes darken and drop down to my lips for a beat. My cheeks heat and my thighs clench.

"And here I was thinking women wanted knights in shining armour."

"Nah, a dirty guy in a work van is good for me." I slam my lips shut, praying that I can put an end to the things that seem to be falling from my mouth.

Glancing at him out of the corner of my eye as I buckle up, I find a sexy smirk playing on his lips. Damn him for knowing how sexy he is.

My eyes slowly travel up his exposed arm, taking in all his ink and wondering what the story behind each one is as he pulls away and back into the Friday night rush hour traffic.

"How are you feeling?" he asks, focusing on where he's going and ignoring my attention.

Hot. "I'm okay. I had a little cat nap in the office this afternoon. You?"

"Much better now I've seen you."

I chuckle. "You always this smooth?"

"Always," he confirms. "So no nightmare students to deal with today?"

"Nope. I've only got one. He's in my Thursday night class. Sits at the back with a smirk on his face and feet up on the desk like he owns the place."

"Sounds like a nightmare."

"You've no idea. He drives me crazy."

I don't need to look over to know that he's smiling. I can feel the amusement coming off him in waves. It's almost as strong as the desire coursing through my veins.

Silence fills the small cab of his van until the tension and crackling chemistry between us almost hits breaking point.

I really need to stay away from this man.

"So...was last night everything you hoped it would be?"

I want to tell him that it was that and so much more, but I also don't want him to know just how much it meant to me. I've already shown too much of myself to him. "Yeah, it was good."

"Good?"

"Yeah, it was fun."

"Fun. Huh?"

"What's that meant to mean?"

"Nothing. Just wondering what I should have done to make it amazing."

I pause, because I think we both know that it was amazing, even if I'm too scared to admit it. "Well...it didn't tick off all my crazy to-do list."

"No one-night-stand. Right."

"That wasn't on my list," I protest.

"Sure."

"How was your day at work?" I ask, trying to steer the conversation away from me.

"Long. Boring. Everything that last night wasn't. Plus, you weren't there."

Looking over, my eyes find his staring back at me, and my

breath catches. The sincerity in his stare is a little much to take. I'm not sure anyone's ever looked at me with such honesty and longing in their eyes.

"I don't think I should have got in this van with you."

"Why?"

"Shit," I mutter. The more I try to be unaffected by him, the more he buries his way under my skin.

He turns back to watch where we're going, but I can't rip my eyes away from his profile. His jaw is covered in the perfect amount of scruff, and his full lips are parted slightly, allowing his breaths to pass. His neck and shoulders are pure muscle, and his chest is rising and falling rapidly, showing me that although he seems calm and composed by this situation, in reality it's hitting him just like it is me.

He turns back towards me, his eyes like blue pools of desire that I really shouldn't want to dip my toe into, I'm afraid I might not be able to stop myself. He holds my stare once again, allowing me to see exactly what it is he wants. Memories from the club last night hit me, and I feel it right in my core. What it felt like to have his hands on me. How he so easily played my body until I totally fell apart in his arms.

"You don't need to be afraid to ask me for what you need."

I suck in a surprised breath. Did I just say something aloud again?

His hand lifts from his lap, and the rough skin brushes across my cheek, sending shudders of pleasure through my body.

Ripping my eyes away from his, I take in my surroundings. My building.

My heart drops that our time is over, until I see the movement of a shadow over by the bushes.

The fear that consumed me when Joe's van pulled up in front of me is strong enough to overtake my desire. My eyes dart around, looking for anything else out of place, and it doesn't go unnoticed.

"Are you okay?"

"I...uh...of course. Thank you for the lift." I squash the tremble in my voice, but the concern that twists his face tells me I didn't do a very good job.

My hand shakes as adrenaline races through my limbs when I reach for the door.

"Would you like me to walk you up?"

I should say no. I'm well aware of that. But I'm also aware that if I were to come face-to-face with my past, having Joe standing behind me would be no bad thing. Not that I have any intention of dragging him into my disastrous past life.

"N-no, I'll be fine." My voice cracks, and I hate sounding so weak and vulnerable.

Pushing the door open, I climb out into the rain. A shiver runs through me as the cold surrounds me. I look back for Joe, regretting my decision, but when I look into the van, it's empty.

My brows pull together, but only for a second because the warmth of his arm wrapping around my waist gives me a clue as to where he is.

"Come on. Let's get out of the rain."

The beep of his van locking sounds out behind us as he guides me towards the building. I make quick work of letting us in, and he silently follows me up the stairs to my door.

I come to a stop with my key in my hand, ready to let myself inside, but I don't get to push it into the lock because Joe reaches out and wraps his fingers around mine.

My eyes focus on his cotton covered chest for a few seconds as I try to muster up the strength I'm going to need to look into his eyes. When I do lift my head, I realise that no amount of time could have prepared me for the heated gaze staring back at me.

My mouth waters. I swallow it down as I try to come up with the right thing to say. Unfortunately, when I do open my mouth, the words that come out aren't the ones I should be saying.

"Would you like to come in?" There are so many reasons why he should say no, but him being here feels so right. I feel so safe when he's beside me, and I'm not ready to lose that just yet.

He looks down at himself and pulls his once pristine white t-shirt from his body. "I should probably go home and shower."

He's right. He should. But, fuck if I don't want to demand he stays exactly as he is because he looks so damn hot.

"I've got a shower," I blurt out, then bite down on my bottom lip to stop anything else spewing from my mouth.

"Oh yeah?" He takes a step forward, closing the space between us. His heat burns my front, making my body ache to feel him pressed up against me.

"Yeah, I mean, it's pretty crap and kinda cold but...it's still a shower." His arm lifts and his fingers thread into my hair, pulling me closer to him. There's barely an inch between us. My head's tilted back so I can look up into his eyes as they bounce between mine and my lips. I don't think I've ever wanted to be kissed quite so badly.

I'm a second away from throwing caution to the wind and reaching up for his lips when he pulls away and says, "Lead the way."

I don't hesitate in lifting my arm, unlocking my front door and pushing it open. The sound of his heavy footsteps tells me he's following and taking in the sparse state of my flat.

"I'm sorry, it's not—"

I turn, but the sight of him standing there staring at nothing but me takes my breath. This place is tiny, but with him here, sucking all the air out of it, we could be inside a cupboard, not a studio.

"Don't apologise, Quinn. It's more than I've got, I can assure you of that."

I don't think for a moment that can be true, but I nod anyway.

"The bathroom's behind that door. The washing machine doesn't work, but if you throw your clothes out, I can rinse them in the sink and pop them in the dryer for you."

Without even thinking about it, he reaches behind his head and pulls the fabric of his t-shirt up his body.

My lips part and my eyes drop to take in the skin he's revealed. It's toned and tanned with just the perfect amount of hair covering his chest.

The temperature inside my small flat suddenly feels scorching as he throws his shirt towards me. I just about manage to catch it, unable to drag my eyes from his half-naked body.

His hands drop to his waistband as he toes off his boots, discarding them where they are. He drops his trousers and pulls off his socks. He stuff them back into his boots and throws the trousers on the top.

"Leave them," he says, flicking his eyes to the pile of clothes. "Just do that."

Then, as if getting almost naked in a stranger's flat is normal, he turns and heads towards the bathroom door.

I stay exactly where I am, frozen to the spot as the sound of the water running hits my ears and steam begins to bellow from the room. He didn't even shut the bloody door. As if I need that kind of temptation. My need to strip down and follow him is already quite strong.

CHAPTER NINE

Realising that I can't still be standing in the same spot when he reappears, I squeeze the fabric in my hands and will the image of water cascading down over his muscular arms from my head. I don't need those kinds of thoughts in my mind if I want to get through this evening without making a mistake I can't take back. I throw his shirt into the sink and slip my coat from my shoulders.

Without thinking, I run the water to fill the sink and throw in a scoopful of powder before a shout fills the room.

"Argh, what the fuck? Turn the tap off, it's fucking freezing."

"Shit, sorry." I can't help but laugh as I reach for the tap to stop the water. I live here on my own; I have no reason to know that running the tap makes the shower run cold. I don't tend to do both at the same time.

Making the most of the water that's still in the kettle, I boil it and throw it into the cold water. Forcing myself to focus on the task in hand, I set about rinsing his t-shirt and lose myself watching the water turn a dirty grey colour. When the shower has stopped, I run a clean bowl of water to rinse it out with, trying like hell to ignore the fact that he's about reappear at any moment.

I wring out as much water as I can when a shiver runs down my spine. My muscles ache for me to turn around, but I'm scared of what I'll find when I do.

Sadly, the first words that leave his lips have me moving without any thought.

"What the fuck are you wearing?"

I spin around so fast that water from his still sopping shirt covers me. "Shit," I mutter, turning and throwing it back into the sink.

Heat seeps into my back before his finger runs around the neck of my cardigan. Goosebumps prick my skin as I wait to find out what he's going to do next.

"I thought you wanted to banish the little old lady clothes."

"I-I do. B-but, they're all I had."

"Then I think another shopping trip is in order, because these aren't who you are." He couldn't be saying truer words. These clothes have never been me, just fabric that I hid behind for everyone else's sake. "I think they need to go."

His fingers slip around my waist until he finds the buttons running down my front. As he pops each one open, my breathing increases. By the time he's at the top, my chest is heaving, my breaths coming out in needy pants. Wrapping his tattooed fingers around the fabric at my shoulders, he slowly pulls it down my arms.

"Joe." It's meant to come out as a warning, but it sounds like a needy moan for more even to my own ears.

His heat is almost scalding as he closes the space between us, his front lining up with my back. The obvious thickness of his length presses into my arse, and my teeth sink into my bottom lip to stop me from making any more embarrassing noises.

My heart thunders in my chest, and my veins fill with fire as his lips brush against the curve of my neck.

"Let me take it all away."

"W-what?" I stutter.

"Whatever it is that puts fear in your eyes. Whoever it is you keep looking over your shoulder for. The reason you're hiding."

"I-I'm n-not—"

"Shhh...don't lie to me, Quinn. I can see it all. I can feel it. Allow me to make you forget, just for an evening."

"Oh god," I moan as his lips continue their trail up my neck. How am I supposed to say no to that?

"I haven't been able to forget about you. Just the memory of you melting in my hands last night has kept me hard all day."

"We can't." My words are barely a whisper, showing just how weak my argument is.

"Says who? Mr. Boring?" His hands move from my waist and find the hot skin of my stomach as he lifts my cami. There's no way he misses my body's tremble when our skin connects. "Get out of your head, Quinn. What does your body want? Listen to what your body needs."

"Fuck." As I turn in his arms, he takes one look at my face and his lips are on mine. He wastes no time in sliding his tongue past my parted lips and seeking my own to dance with.

One of his hands splays out across my back and ensures we're pressed as tightly together as possible while the other dives into my hair as he devours my mouth like he'd die without it.

It's the single best kiss of my life. He makes me feel needed, wanted and desirable—all things I've never experienced before on this kind of level.

"I need you so fucking bad, Quinn. You're driving me fucking crazy," he mutters against my jaw as he kisses along it and down my neck.

"So take me. Do what you promised. Make me forget."

He walks me backwards until I bump up against the counter. His fingers grasp the hem of my cami, but before he pulls it up and over my head, he looks to me for permission. My chest swells that he's thoughtful enough to do so, and heat floods my core at the dark and dangerous look in his eyes. But it's not the bad kind of dangerous. It's the incredibly sexy and full of wicked promises kind.

I nod, and he wastes no time in pulling it off me and throwing it over his shoulder. His lips drop to the swell of my breasts and he kisses, licks and nips along the edge of my bra. My breasts swell with my need for more and strain against the fabric, desperate for more attention. Slipping his fingers inside the lace, he pulls the cup down and wastes no time in feasting on my puckered nipple.

My head falls back as sparks of pleasure shoot to my core and threaten to buckle my knees. Sucking my peak deep into his mouth, his teeth bite down so just the right amount of pain mixes with the pleasure. My fingers grip the counter, my nails digging in the underside of the wood.

"More. I need more."

His eyes flick up to mine, desire and delight shining back at me. The fabric around my ribs is released, and in one swift move my bra joins the collection of clothing on the floor.

"You think I can get you off like this again?"

I don't get a chance to respond, because his large hands cup my breasts and he sets to work.

In no time, my core is clenching as his ministrations on my breasts bring me closer and closer to my release. He's alternated between pinching my nipples with his thumb and forefinger and teasing with his tongue and teeth.

"You taste so fucking sweet. I can't wait to discover more."

"Yes," I breathe, desperate for everything he can give me. "Yes,

yes." He ups the ante, pinching harder, biting deeper, and I fall. I fall into a mind-numbing bliss, but it only lasts so long because I need him inside me, surrounding me, everywhere.

Lifting up, his fingers wrap around my neck as his lips land on mine. The move is possessive, and I can't get enough. At this very moment, I can't think of anything better than being his.

His tongue plunges into my mouth as my hands find the sculpted skin of his back. My nails run down until I hit the towel that's somehow still wrapped around his waist. The need to pull it from his body is all consuming, and just as I'm about to do it, his hands drop to the waist of my skirt. The feeling of the zip being lowered has my thighs clenching.

I should be embarrassed about my utterly unsexy underwear, but, just like my bra, Joe doesn't even bat an eyelid as my skirt drops around my ankles and he quickly pulls my tights in the same direction, dropping to his knees before me.

When he sits back on his haunches and looks up at me, all I see is lust and need reflected back at me.

My chest heaves as our eye contact holds, a silent conversation passing between us. I start to think he's not going to move until he quickly stands and lifts me so I've no choice but to throw my arms around his shoulders and wrap my legs around his waist.

His length that's tenting the towel presses between my legs and gives me just a taste of what's still to come. My core clenches with anticipation.

"Bed?" Joe asks, spinning on the spot.

"Sofa. It unfolds."

"Fuck it."

He drops me onto the sofa and pulls me so I'm practically hanging off the edge. Landing on his knees, he drags my knickers down my thighs and throws them into the room. His eyes zero in on my centre and my thighs close under his close scrutiny. If I'd have known this was going to happen, I might have spent a little longer pruning down there.

"Don't," he barks, pressing his large, calloused hands against the soft skin of my thighs and pushing my legs as wide as they'll go. "You're beautiful. Every inch of you."

Heat hits my cheeks and makes its way down my neck and onto my chest.

"Don't believe me? Let me show you." His lips hit the inside of my thigh and he kisses up from my knee until he's at my core. He licks at my seam before finding my clit and teasing it with the perfect amount of pressure. It's like he knows exactly how to play my body, despite this being the first time he's touched me.

My back arches and my toes curl when he dips his tongue inside me.

"Holy shit." Why haven't I experienced this before? I force the thought from my head, not wanting any part of my past tainting this.

His tongue finds my clit again, and his finger teases at my entrance. He circles and dips inside just enough to have me pleading with him for more. I've never begged a man for anything in my life, but this right now feels so natural.

He sucks hard on my clit, his fingers diving inside me until he hits an undiscovered part of me that has me barreling towards the most intense release I've ever experienced. Lights flash behind my eyes as my fingers grip his hair with such strength I swear I'm gonna rip it from his head.

"Joe," I squeal, not giving a crap how loud I am as wave after wave of pleasure takes over my body.

He continues until my body stops pulsating before sitting back on his heels with a smug as fuck smile on his face.

I push up on my palms, ready to say something about it, but my naked body catches my eye and I realise I'm sitting here with my legs spread, everything on show while he's still got that damn towel around his waist.

He glances down at what's holding my attention before standing directly in front of me, his crotch right in my eyeline. His excitement is obvious with the tenting of the fabric, and my mouth waters to see all of him.

"Go on then." One side of his mouth curls up. His arrogance is enough to have me reaching out and wrapping my fingers around the towel.

In one quick movement, I pull it from his body.

My eyes fly to his cock and my chin drops. *Jesus.* My mouth waters, and I'm powerless to stop my tongue sneaking out and licking my bottom lip.

It's not the first time I've seen one, but fuck, it's the first time I've seen one quite like that. He's pierced.

My hand moves to reach out, but my insecurity gets the better of me.

"Uh..." My eyes fly up to his, but I find no hesitation. He knows exactly what he's doing, and I'd be lying if I said that wasn't a turn on.

He lunges forward, his hand cradling the back of my head as he lays me down on the sofa. His lips find mine as his hard cock teases between my legs, making my muscles clench to experience just how he's going to feel inside me.

I might be naive with my lack of experience in this department, but even I know that piercing is meant to feel incredible. He's already proven himself to be way more skilled than my previous partner, so I can't help but hope that it's going to be mindblowing.

"Joe, please," I moan, needing more than this delicious torture.

Reaching over the end of the sofa, he grabs his discarded trousers and pulls a condom from his pocket.

My eyes lock on his cock as he rolls it down his shaft like he's done it a million times. *He probably has,* a little voice says in the back of my mind, but the second he rubs the head through my wetness, all thoughts leave my mind in favour of the pleasure he can bring me.

"Take it slow, yeah?" I whisper, embarrassed that I even need to say it, but it's been longer than I'm willing to admit.

"Shit, are you a—" His eyes widen, although I'm not sure if it's with delight or terror.

"No, no. Just...uh...inactive?" I don't mean for it to come out as a question, but my word of choice sounds weird even in my own head.

"Well, let's put an end to that, shall we?"

He doesn't give me a chance to respond. Instead, he pushes slowly inside me. My walls stretch to accommodate him, my entire body sighing with relief.

"Fuck." His voice is deep and filled with disbelief. His muscles strain as he holds himself back. "So fucking good."

He pushes deeper, and I gasp when he finds the same spot he did with his fingers that made me fly.

"Move, Joe. Please." I'm begging, but I don't care. I need this right now.

"Thought you'd never ask." He winks before slipping his hands under my arse and lifting me just so. The head of his cock and the piercing graze that spot, sending a shudder down my spine.

His hand runs up my thigh, up and over my stomach before pinching my nipples and finally wrapping around my neck.

With our eyes locked, he pulls almost all the way out of me before pushing straight back in. He does it over and over, increasing the tempo every time until I'm clawing at his back and crying out for more.

I'm pretty sure I've never made a noise during sex before, but suddenly it's all I can do to keep my mouth shut.

A fine sheen of sweat begins to bead Joe's brow as his movement gets more and more erratic.

"Come on me, Quinn. All over my cock." His words are no more than a gutteral groan, but I hear every single one loud and clear, and fuck if they don't push me that little closer to finding my release.

His fingers release my neck. I want to complain about the loss, but then his thumb presses against my clit and I lose all train of thought as my release hits me out of nowhere and totally consumes me.

No longer able to keep my eyes open, my lids lower as they roll back in my head in pleasure, my body twitching and sucking him deeper as I ride out the waves.

"Fuck. Fuck. Fuuuuck," he moans before he stills, his cock twitches, and he lets go of his own orgasm.

He drops on top of me, his softening cock still inside me as our chests heave and our increased breaths mingle.

"Fuck, Quinn. That was..." He doesn't finish his thought. Instead, his lips find mine and he shows me just how much he enjoyed it.

Flipping us over, he somehow manages not to allow us both to end up on the floor. He settles back with me on his lap, his cock slipping free at last. As he reaches down to pull the condom off, I attempt to stand.

"Where the hell are you going?"

"To...uh...clean up?" I awkwardly wrap my arms around my breasts in an attempt to hide from him. It was fine when he had his hands on me, but now I feel totally naked.

"I'm not done with you yet."

"Oh?" My eyes widen.

"There's another condom in my pocket. I intend on using it before either of us puts clothes on." Hesitantly, I walk over and drop down beside the fabric. "Go on," he encourages.

With the little silver packet between my thumb and forefinger, I stand and look at where he's fisting his already hard cock.

"Again?"

"Fucking right. Get over here."

As I climb onto his lap, his hands run up my back and pull me forward until my nipples brush against the light covering of hair on his chest.

I shudder.

"So sensitive." His hands slip around to take their weight, and he palms and pinches until my chest is heaving once again.

With his lips attached to the skin of my neck, he rolls on the second condom without even looking.

"Now, ride me."

I look down at the thickness of his cock, standing proud from his body, and my legs quiver.

Scooting forward a little, I lift up until he lines the head of his cock with my very ready entrance.

"Slow," he demands, and I'm powerless but to do as he says.

I hiss as he fills me, hitting all my over-sensitive nerves. My pussy twitches and clenches as another release makes itself known. I knew it was possible, but I never imagined I'd ever be with a man who could drag this kind of pleasure from my body.

"Now, kiss me. I need your lips."

With our tongues duelling, I manage to find my rhythm with the help of his hands on my hips.

It feels like no time before my thighs are trembling, ready for another release.

"Let go," he whispers in my ear. "Let me feel you."

If I thought the last one knocked me for six, then this orgasm tilted my fucking world on its axis. I don't know whether it's the position or what, but before it's even finished, I know it's the exact thing I need in my life right now.

His hips thrusts up into me as my body grows limp above him before he bites down on the skin covering my collarbone and rides out his own release.

I fall forward onto his chest, and his arms wrap around me.

I'm sated, relaxed, and so fucking comfortable.

CHAPTER TEN

It takes me a few minutes to figure out where I am and what's happening when my eyes flutter open. The bulb above my head is on, bathing the flat in light, but I was asleep on the sofa.

The sound of breathing hits my ears, and I panic.

Jumping from the sofa—and from his hold, it seems—I swipe the first item of clothing I find from the floor and hold it against my naked body.

Joe drags his eyes open and looks at me standing in front of him on the verge of a panic attack.

"You need to leave."

"I...uh...what?"

"You need to leave. Right now."

"But—"

"No buts, Joe. This can't happen. This shouldn't have happened. I'm your..." I can't bear to say the word. "I'm your *teacher.*" I've no idea why I whisper it; it's not like anyone's going to overhear.

"Too late now, babe. It's happened, and I'm more than ready for it to happen again."

He glances down, and when I follow his gaze I find his cock, hard again.

Jesus.

"I can't do this, Joe. I can't lose the only thing I have left in my life. I can't and I won't because of some stupid mistake."

"Mistake?" he asks, getting up from the sofa, his eyes hardening at my choice of word.

"It shouldn't have happened."

"But it did, and don't tell me you didn't feel it."

"Feel what?" I feign innocence.

"The connection. Us. The chemistry."

Oh, I felt it all right. I have since that first day he walked into my classroom. I should have been stronger, should have been able to ignore it. But I couldn't, and now look at me—standing with his disgusting trousers wrapped around my body which smells like him and sex.

Touching him was forbidden. I knew that. But I did it anyway. As if my life isn't already one big clusterfuck—I've just added another load of drama to it.

"Quinn, please. Just come back to bed."

"It's not a bed, Joe. It's a sofa, and the fact that I don't even have a bed should prove just how fucked up my life is. Trust me when I say that this is the last place you should want to be."

Standing, he takes a few steps towards me, but I take the same back.

"Talk to me. Tell me. Let me help you, whatever it is. You don't need to fight it alone."

"No. I can't."

"I'm right here, Quinn. Tell me what you need."

Emotion threatens to climb up my throat, but I swallow it

down. I need to be strong if I'm going to convince him that I'm doing the right thing. "I need you to leave. This can't happen again."

"This is bullshit, Quinn, and you know it." His arms fly up in disbelief, and I cower away. "What the fuck? Quinn, I wouldn't...I'd never...Fuck." His eyes widen in shock, his fingers threading in his hair and tugging painfully hard.

"Just get out, please. I need to be alone."

His eyes are wide and focused on me as he debates what to do.

"Please, Joe."

With a regretful nod of his head, he tugs his boxers on before turning to me and holding out his hand. I stupidly think he's asking for me, and I almost cave. My arm twitches to reach out and wrap my fingers around his, but after a second I realise that he just wants his trousers.

I pull the fabric from around me and hand it over. Broken and defeated, I allow my arms to drop to my sides. I'm sending away the one good thing in my life; what more do I really have to worry about?

Once he's dressed in what's available, seeing as his sopping wet t-shirt is still in the sink, he steps up to me. His fingers slide into my hair and his lips press against my forehead.

We stand like that for the longest time with just our breaths filling the silent space around us. He might not be saying any words, but I can't help feeling like he's making promises. I already know they're not ones he can keep.

"This isn't over, Quinn."

With those words ringing in my ears, he releases me and walks from the flat.

The second the door shuts behind him, all the air leaves my lungs.

What the fuck did I just do?

Without even looking at the sofa where only minutes ago I was sleeping in his arms, I run towards the bathroom. I turn the shower on and allow the steam to fill the small room as I rest my palms on the basin and hang my head.

I just sent away the one person with the ability to make me forget. To make me feel safe. To make me feel alive.

I know it might be the right thing to do—I can't lose my career; it's the only thing I have right now—but fuck, this hurts.

I lift one hand to my chest and rub at the ache which is only getting worse the longer I'm alone. My hand trembles, and I try to ignore it. I'm used to the fear. It's what's got me this far, and I refuse to give into it now. I'm not stupid—I know that what I've already been through has been the easy bit. What I've got to come is only going to be harder.

Risking a look at myself in the steamed up mirror in front of me, I let out a sigh of frustration.

I look like the woman I've always wanted to be. I've got the hair, the make up, some of the clothes I've always dreamed of, but still my past holds me back. Will it always be this way? Will they always have this hold on me? Will I always be forced to live by the fucked up rules and ideals even when I'm miles away?"

I stare into eyes I don't recognise and pray to whomever might be listening that after what I did, I'll be free. That's all I want. To be free to live the life I've always coveted. A life in which the decisions I make are mine and mine alone.

I've had a taste of it. *He* allowed me a taste, and now I want it more than ever. I'm like a junkie craving my next hit, only the thing I'm craving is what most other people have. A life of their own.

"Fuck," I bark, slamming my hand down on the porcelain in front of me.

Every muscle in my body aches for me to go running after him, to demand that he returns and holds me, holds my hand through what's to come, but I know I can't. And not just because of my career, but because I can't do it to him. I've no doubt he can handle it, but he shouldn't have to. My past is mine to bear; it shouldn't weigh down anyone else. It's already destroyed too many lives.

I hate to do it, but I step into the shower and allow the water to wash away what's left of Joe. His scent rinses from my body as the tears I'd been holding but refusing to cry stream down my face. I learned years ago that it was safe to let it all go when standing under a torrent of water.

The longer I stand there, the weaker my body feels. I've not nearly had enough sleep in the last forty-eight hours, and I'm struggling, especially after the orgasms.

My back hits the cold tiles behind me, but I barely feel it against my numb skin as I slide down to the shower tray at my feet. The water continues to trickle over me as images from my past that I'd rather not remember run through my mind, reminding me why I ran when I got an opportunity.

MY BODY FEELS like it's going to explode as Joe thrusts inside me, his large calloused hands squeezing my breasts as he demands for me to come. My chest heaves as I race closer and closer to the release he wants from me. I'm just about to fall when another face appears as he relentlessly slams into me, over and over until I'm raw.

"Fucking bitch, why won't you come? Are you fucking broken?"

I fight to keep the tears that are burning my eyes inside as I keep up the facade he expects— that everyone expects—of me.

I moan, hoping it sounds convincing before calling out his

name. Bile rushes up my throat at hearing it, but I've come to know it's the only way to make it stop.

His cock pulses inside me, filling me, trying to force me to give him a son to continue his masochistic ways.

Chance will be a fine thing.

I think of those little pills I keep hidden in the lining of my handbag. There's no way I'll give that man a baby. I'd rather he killed me before I subjected a kid to the kind of life we live here.

I SUCK in a deep breath and sit up. My hand covers my racing heart as the surroundings come into focus.

It was just a dream. *Just a dream?* A fucking nightmare, more like.

Realising it's almost lunchtime, I drag my aching body from the sofa I never bothered converting into a bed when I fell onto it last night. I had plans for this weekend. I wanted to be brave and go out and explore. Joe had given me the confidence to embrace my new city, and I was desperate to see some of the sights I've only been able to enjoy from a photograph, in a magazine or on the TV up until now, but sitting here with the winter sun shining in through my little window, the last thing I want to do is go out.

A tingle of fear races down my spine as I think about my nightmare. I haven't had one since I left. I thought I'd managed to escape that little bit of my past, but it seems that now I've sent away the one thing that made me feel safe, he's going to slip back into my brain to torture me some more. It doesn't matter how many miles I put between us, he'll always be inside my head, and he damn well knows it. That was all part of the game. The game he played with me, and with his students. If only I was brave enough to speak up sooner, to expose him for what he really is.

Heading for the kettle for a very strong cup of coffee, my eyes land on the wet fabric still in the sink, and my stomach twists painfully as memories of his face as I made him walk away fill my mind.

I drain the now very cold water and set about washing it once again, wishing like hell it was last night again and that he's going to come strolling out of the bathroom wrapped in only a towel.

I know it's not going to happen, and disappointment floods me until the back of my throat burns with tears.

I did the right thing. I did the right thing, I repeat over and over, trying to convince myself that it's the truth.

I need to get through this alone, and then, when it's safe to properly move on, I will. I will rebuild my life the way I want, but right now isn't the time to be focusing on my future. I need to focus on the present and what might be waiting just around the corner for me.

Throwing Joe's shirt into the dryer, I find my own dirty clothes, intending on giving them the same treatment seeing as a trip to the laundrette is the last thing I want to do right now. The monotonous task of hand-washing them is actually quite tempting, but when I glance down at the twinset in my hands, something rebellious hits me and instead of dropping them into the warm water I've just run, I ball them up and throw them in the bin.

Instead, I wash the few new bits I've bought and throw what I can into the dryer before grabbing my phone and doing some online shopping.

I plan next week and order the food I need. I keep the purchases to the minimum, knowing that I've got other things I want to splash what little money I have on. God, pay day can't come soon enough.

I get through three cups of coffee, but by the time I eventually put my phone down, I've not only got my food arriving tomorrow but three separate clothes deliveries. I've kept some of the old me hanging around for too long. It's time to banish the weak and pathetic woman she was and finally embrace the life I've always dreamed of, even if it is from the comfort of my studio flat.

I want to be braver than this. I want to be out embracing the city and exploring some of what Joe gave me a taste of on Thursday night, but after what happened with him yesterday and then my nightmare, I'm not sure I can do it. I'll have to leave eventually—I have a job, after all. I tell myself that I've got two days to wallow about the ridiculous mistake I made inviting Joe in here last night and in memories of my past before I take London by storm on Monday morning.

Okay, so that might be a bit of an exaggeration, but it fires me up enough to push my past back behind the trapdoor I thought I'd banished it to.

CHAPTER ELEVEN

I hold my head up high as I walk out of my building first thing on Monday morning. I'm wearing one of the new outfits I ordered over the weekend, I've done my hair and make-up, and I'm feeling good. But that doesn't stop me looking around the second the door slams shut behind me. I pause to see if there's any movement or rustling in the bushes.

I'm being paranoid, I know I am, but I can't help it. Joe pulling up on the curb like he did in front of me Friday night really spooked me.

I tell myself that no one's there, that no one even cares where I am, and I head towards the tube. I feel better once I'm surrounded by commuters and heading to my classroom.

My first lesson of the week is with Jodi. I'm hopeful that her last lesson was just a one off, and I'll find her smiling and more willing to interact, but the second she walks into the room, I know it was wishful thinking.

She keeps her head down as the others chat away and slowly find their seats. She pulls her books out but still doesn't risk glancing up. My heart aches for her. I've no idea what her story is, but there's something so sad and broken in her eyes, ones I recognise from my former life. I desperately want to tell her that it won't last forever, that she is in control of her own destiny, but it's not really my place to just assume. People's lives are often much more complex than we can imagine, and I'd hate to jump to conclusions about what she's dealing with.

The students must have had a good weekend, because it seems to take forever to get them settled. Eventually, I get them reading silently so I can begin catching up with their coursework progress.

Flipping my planner to this class, I start at the top and make my way down the register, talking individually to each student.

"Jodi, you're up," I call.

She pushes her chair out and walks towards the front of the room. No one looks up at her; it's kind of like she's invisible, probably exactly how she wants it.

She sits herself down in the chair opposite and drops her work to my desk. I scan over it, getting a feel for the quality, and I can't believe what I'm looking at.

"Jodi, this is amazing. Your use of language is incredible, and the way you're describing how that sonnet made you feel...it's well beyond the level of this class. You're really talented."

Looking up from the paper, I watch as her sad, lonely face morphs into the most stunning smile.

"Really?" she asks, her voice barely above a whisper.

"Yeah, really."

"I wasn't sure if it was right."

"There's no wrong answer to how a passage makes you feel, Jodi. That will be different for every one of us based on our lives and experiences. It's the way you've described it."

The pure joy on her face melts my heart. This right here is why I wanted to be a teacher. I grew up knowing I didn't really have any other choice, but I truly enjoy what I do. Although I've imagined my ideal life a million times, I was always still teaching. I love giving young people the opportunity to find themselves just like Jodi is right now.

"Have you thought about a writing career?"

She's silent as she thinks, and it's then that she pushes up the sleeves of her jumper. My eyes drop at the movement, and my mouth gapes at the dark blue and purple bruises that encircle her wrists.

"Jodi?"

In a rush, she pulls her sleeves back down. "It's nothing," she mutters. "I...uh...just fell."

I don't say anything. She doesn't need me to point out that she's quite obviously lying.

Pushing the chair out behind her, she grabs her work and races back to her seat, her head back down in defeat.

My heart aches for what she's going through and my hands tremble, having experienced first-hand the fear she must feel. Obviously, I'm going to report it at the first opportunity I get— much to Jodi's horror, I'd imagine—but other than that, all I can really do is be here and help her get the qualifications she needs to improve her life.

Thoughts of Jodi and how I can help her consume my mind for the rest of the lesson. I've refused to look at my phone since I placed my orders on Saturday, but I know there are emails from Joe waiting for me. I'm just not ready to deal with the reality of what I did Friday night.

Thanks to him, my nightmares are back full force. I've had hardly any sleep since I kicked him out. Every time I shut my eyes, *he's* there. It's not bad enough that my memories of him never leave—he's got to disrupt my slumber now, too.

Jodi glances up at me as everyone else leaves the room. Her eyes are begging for me to let this go, but we both know that I can't.

"Jodi, wait," I call and watch her shoulders sink. "I'm here, okay? If you need anything."

"Thank you," she mutters before basically running for the door.

Falling down on my desk, I rest back in the chair, wishing I could just take a little nap before my next class.

A knock sounds out around the room, and I'm forced to drag my heavy head up.

"Yes?" I call, expecting a student to come running back in because they'd forgotten something. But when the door opens, something very different emerges. A wicker basket.

"This was just delivered for you," Caroline, our department admin says, walking over and dropping the basket to my desk. "I'm assuming you're not expecting it from the look on your face."

"No, I'm really not." As I stare at the box, reality starts to find its way through my confusion, and my heart begins to race. Is this a joke? Has he found me? Is it going to explode when I open it? Crazy thoughts start running through my head as Caroline stands awkwardly, obviously waiting for me to open it to discover what's hiding inside. "Thank you for bringing it in for me."

"You're welcome." She rocks back and forth awkwardly on her feet. It's not until I turn towards my computer that she gets the message that I'm not opening it in front of her, and she starts to back away from my desk.

It's not until she's closed the door behind her that I reach out and slide the box across the desk.

I open the folded tag, but inside all it says is *Ms Quinn Smith*. My hands tremble as I undo the buckles holding it closed, and I brace myself for what I find.

"What the hell?" Pulling the lid open, I find it full of luxury girly products. Letting go of the lid, I start taking them out one at a time. Hand soap and lotion, bubble bath, candles, face masks, moisturiser, the list goes on. It's not until I get to the last item that's wrapped in soft pink tissue that I know for a fact who it's from. It's two ceramic signs, one with *No Regrets* and the other *Live Life Your Way* written in a script font across the front.

Tears burn up my throat until they hit the back of my eyes. Without even thinking about it, I know this is the sweetest thing anyone has ever done for me.

My eyes are still full of unshed tears when my next class arrives. I attempt to swallow down the emotion he caused as I slide the basket under my desk. I glance at my handbag, knowing that my phone is right there. I've probably got a million emails from him. I should look and thank him for the gift, but I know that by replying he'll want more. I've already made a huge mistake when it comes to him, and I think I might be safer avoiding him and keeping our contact limited to Thursday nights in class. It might be the last thing I want in reality, but it's all I can do right now.

THE BASKET and my phone taunt me for the rest of the day. I stay a little later than I'd originally planned so that I can report what I've learned about Jodi, and by the time I leave, it's completely dark outside.

The second I was alone, I woke my computer up and found my emails.

I ignored everything in my inbox and opened up a new one. Finding the name of the woman who deals with all the college's safeguarding, I began my email about Jodi.

I hate that she's going to think I'm sticking my nose in by doing this. She's inevitably going to be called in for a meeting following the information I'm about to pass on, and she's going to hate it.

If her home situation is anything like I'm imaging, then she does everything she can to hide and being pulled up and put on the spot is going to be her worst nightmare—aside from whoever it was who put those bruises on her.

I flexed my fingers a few times before they stopped shaking enough to allow me to type properly.

"I really hope this helps in the long run, Jodi," I whispered to myself and got everything I'd seen and felt into the email in the hope that her life can turn a corner because of it.

Pulling my coat tighter around myself, I turn to look to my right. There's a white van idling on the double yellow lines out the front of the building. My heart jumps into my throat. He's waiting for me?

He's staring down at his phone so misses the fact I've left the building. Without putting much thought into it, I bolt left and hope I'm lost in the crowd.

I race towards the tube, my entire body shaking with adrenaline.

The easiest thing to do would be to get into his van again. But it's dangerous. He's waiting for me right out the front of where I work. The very last place we need to be caught together. Not that there will be a chance of us being caught together, because there won't be a next time.

It's not until I'm locked in my flat that I relax. After placing the basket on my coffee table, I shrug off my coat and pull my boots from my legs. I find the spaghetti I ordered over the weekend and set about making myself some dinner.

While I'm waiting for it to cook, I have a moment of weakness and pull my phone from my bag.

Twenty-four emails.

Twenty-fucking-four.

No wonder he was waiting outside. He probably wanted to make sure I was still alive.

I ignore the first twenty-three and open the last one.

To: Quinn Smith
From: Tatstwatsandarseholes
Subject: Juliet, Juliet, wherefore art thou Juliet

Dear Miss Smith
I sincerely apologise if I've done something to upset you.
I want to make it up to you.
Your carriage awaits...
Yours,
Mr. Kingsman

Checking the time of the email, I see that he sent it only five minutes before I saw him. I wonder if he's still there waiting for me? Or worse, would Eddie have seen him, or will he come here next?

Deciding the best outcome would be if I replied and stopped him turning up here, I start typing.

To: Tatstwatsandarseholes
From: Quinn Smith
Subject: Not meant to be...

Dear Mr. Kingsman,
Thank you for the gift basket. It is beautiful. I'm sorry, but this Juliet isn't to be rescued. Best we leave it now before the tragic ending.
Regards,

Miss Smith

I let out a giant sigh and drop my phone onto the sofa beside me. Really, those words are the last ones I want to say to him. In reality, I want to be begging him to come over here and keep me safe, but that's both unfair on him and the beginning of the end of my career.

Maybe he could change courses? I shoot down the little voice in my head who's getting carried away with herself. I've no reason to think that whatever has happened between us isn't more than a bit of fun to him. For all I know, his friends have dared him to bed the teacher.

My cheeks heat at the thought of being nothing more than a pawn in his games, but something tells me it's more than that, which is another reason why I need to stay away. The last thing I need right now as I try to rebuild my life is a serious relationship.

This is meant to be about me.

About me experiencing all the things I never got to, not falling for the first guy I laid eyes on.

After double-checking my phone is on silent, I finish off my dinner. I'm tempted all night to see if he's responded, but I tell myself that I'm not really avoiding him if I'm waiting for a reply.

CHAPTER TWELVE

By the time Thursday rolls around, I'm almost at breaking point. On Tuesday, I had a box of doughnuts delivered to work. Caroline once again hung around a little too long after delivering them—I'm not sure if she wanted to know who sent them or if she just wanted one. Unfortunately for her, I'd overslept that morning and was starving. I'm not even ashamed to admit that I ate the entire lot before I turned my sofa into a bed that night.

On Wednesday, I didn't have any deliveries at work, but just as I was sitting down to eat my questionable looking ready meal, the buzzer in my flat went off and, at the other end, was a man delivering Chinese. The dishes were exactly the same as we had last Thursday, and, when I got to the bottom of the bag, I found a note. *If you need a hand eating all this, call me...* followed by his phone number. I must admit that after reading that, I did go and get my phone. I even got as far as typing his number in and saving it in my contacts. But at no point did I connect the call.

Not only did my fear of another nightmare keep me awake

Wednesday night, but knowing I'd be seeing Joe in mere hours was enough to have my heart racing.

How was he going to act after everything that's happened between us? Would he just let it go, seeing as I've not responded to any of his little reminders that he still exists that he's sent this week?

By the time the clock ticks around to the beginning of his class, I'm a nervous wreck. I've planned loads of group and individual quiet activities so I don't have to talk much for fear of totally screwing it up.

I breathe a sigh of relief when he's not the first into the room. It gives me hope that maybe he won't show, although I know it's only wishful thinking. He might not always act like the most engaged student in the room, but having marked his work to date, I know he's taking this seriously.

I'm writing instructions on the board when the atmosphere changes. I don't need to turn around to know he's just walked in, and that he's looking right at me. I continue what I'm writing, trying to ignore the burning of his stare. Dread knots my stomach that he might not be being all too discrete about what—or who—is holding his attention. As if this week's not been hard enough, I really don't need suspicious students.

I keep my eyes locked on the board for longer than necessary, putting off the inevitable of turning around and finding him looking like the bad boy geek I've always dreamed of.

Blowing out a slow breath, I spin and cast my eyes over my students, who are all sitting in their seats and patiently waiting for class to start. I breathe a sigh of relief that they're not looking between the two of us like they suspect something.

I do everything I can to keep my eyes from the back of the room, but eventually the pull becomes too much and I look over. He's watching me, exactly like I knew he was, and the second our eyes lock it's like a baseball bat smashes me in the chest. His eyes shine with concern as he studies me. Guilt hits me for not thanking him for all the gifts I've received over the last few days. Suddenly, my reasons for staying away from him don't seem all that important as his body calls to mine.

Standing behind my desk and using it to stop me from walking directly over to him, I start the class. Words pour from my mouth, but none of them register in my brain. I could be telling them any kind of crap right now about Shakespeare and I'd be none the wiser.

All sets of eyes but one lower to get started on the task I've given them. That other set holds mine captive, making my heart rate increase and causing my temperature to soar. They drop from mine and take in my new outfit. Desire pulls at his features as he takes in the black prom style dress that clings to my breasts and makes my waist look much smaller than it actually is. My muscles pull tight as I fight the need to walk over to him.

I know I need to break the connection between us before one of the other students notices, we're already on borrowed time, but it's easier said than done—especially when he looks back up to me. Something crackles between us, and it hits me between the legs. Memories of how it felt having his hands on me Friday night slam into me, and my blush trails down my neck and onto my chest.

His lips curl up into a smirk, telling me that he knows exactly where my thoughts are. Anger burns through me that he's so obviously taunting me in the one place he knows he can't.

I turn my back on him and drag in some much-needed air. I'm stronger than to let him break me. Maybe the old me wouldn't have been, but the new me definitely is.

When I turn back around, he's staring down at the pad of paper in front of him. Something still tingles just beneath my skin with him in close proximity, but, without his attention, at least I'm able to get on with my job.

I grab the stack of marked work on my desk, making sure his is at the bottom of the pile, and I head over to my first student to give them feedback.

With ten minutes left of the lesson, the only work I've got left to give feedback on is Joe's. My hand trembles as I glance over at him. He must feel my stare, because he immediately looks up. His eyes drop to the papers in my hand and a knowing grin appears. He knows exactly what I'm avoiding.

Sucking in some strength, I take a step forward and then pull out the empty chair next to him.

"Mr. Kingsman, I must say I really enjoyed marking this. You have a way with words. It flows easily and clearly shows your understanding on the beginning of the story."

"A way with words, huh? I thought my talents lie elsewhere, if I'm being honest. What would you say, Miss Smith?" he leans in and whispers the last sentence.

My stomach knots as I fight for something to say that won't encourage him.

"I think...that if you keep your head down and focus, you'll come out of this with a really good grade that will give you that step towards the career and life you want."

"What if there's something I want more?" He scans my face, committing each of my features to memory.

"Focus on your future, Mr. Kingsman. That's the reason you're here."

"What if she is my future?"

My stomach damn near falls from my body at his admission.

"Sorry...I uh..." I stutter, scrambling to get out of the chair and away from him. There's no doubt in my mind that he was deadly serious, and it scares me more than I want to admit.

This can't happen. He can't happen.

I finish up the lesson for the evening, give the students their homework assignment for the following week and bid them farewell.

Joe's eyes never leave me as he slowly starts to pack away. It's clear he wants to hang back to talk to me, but I already know being alone with him is a very bad idea.

As students start to leave, I push my chair under my desk and follow them out. Just before I round the corner, I look back over my shoulder to find him staring at me with disappointment written all over his face.

As the majority of the students turn left so they can leave the building, I bolt right towards the toilets, but I don't get very far as I crash into a body.

Looking up, I find Eddie staring down at me with an amused smirk.

"I knew you wanted me," he says with a wink. My stomach twists as I pull myself from his grip.

"I'm so sorry, I just…"

I rush away from him, my heart hammering in my chest.

"I'm not that bad, am I?" he chuckles behind me, but I don't stop to say anything.

Lowering the toilet seat, I fall down on to it and drop my face into my hands. My life was meant to get simpler once I was away from my old life, but I fear I've only made it a hell of a lot more complicated and things are only going to get worse. Every day that passes I expect to receive a phone call, but as of yet, there's been nothing. I know these things take time, but for the sake of those I left behind, something needs to happen to stop lives being ruined more than they already have been.

I wait in the toilets long enough that I hope Joe will have given up and left.

I can feel the pounding of my heart all the way to my toes as I make the silent journey back towards my classroom to collect my stuff.

Poking my head into the room, I breathe a sigh of relief when it appears to be empty. I walk inside and head straight to my desk to collect my stuff when a dark figure in the corner, perched against the desk opposite mine, makes me scream.

"Fuck." My breath heaves as my body shakes. My fear is debilatating and renders me powerless for the couple of seconds it takes me to realise who is staring back at me with a deep frown lining his forehead.

It's Joe.

You're safe.

Breathe.

"Shit, Quinn. I didn't mean...are you okay?"

Tears burn my eyes and my bottom lip trembles. I really thought it was *him* waiting for me.

"I'm...I'm f-fine." My voice breaks on every word. "You need to leave."

Pushing from the desk, he stalks towards me. "You need to stop pushing me away, Quinn. Don't think I don't know that that's what you're doing."

"It's for your own good," I mutter, not willing to divulge any information as to why. Looking down at the floor, I try to avoid the connection that forms when we stare at each other. He'll see too much.

"You might think that, but I very much disagree. You're a nervous wreck. What's going on? Let me help." His hot fingers grip my chin lightly, and I'm forced to look back at him. My breath catches when I see the concern in his eyes.

"It's nothing."

"Bullshit," he snaps, making me jump.

"I'm here, willing to do anything to help you. Stop fighting it."

"I can't." Staring down at my feet, I feel myself starting to crumble under his concerned stare, but he's not having any of it.

Bringing my face back to his, he leans down and brushes his lips against mine. I want to fight it—it's what I should do—but the second he touches me, I'm lost to anything but him and I sag into him, totally forgetting where I am.

His lips part and his tongue darts out in search of mine.

I'm just about to meet his when heavy footsteps fill my ears.

Fuck.

I jump back like I've been burned. Hurt covers Joe's face, but he soon looks toward the door when he hears what's stopped me. We can't be caught in here together.

I hold my breath, waiting for my potential visitor to make themselves known and see how this is going to play out. Eddie is already suspicious of the changes in me. The last thing I need is for him to discover that Joe, one of my students, is the cause.

My head starts to spin, but instead of stopping and entering the room whoever it is continues down the corridor.

I fall back against the desk behind me and suck in a few ragged breaths.

"Come on, let's get out of here. You hungry?"

I'm not really, but I'm also not ready to be alone again so I nod, collect up my stuff and follow him out of the building, hoping like hell we're not spotted together.

"Stop worrying. I'm just helping you with your bags." He smiles down at me and everything I've been worrying about, scared of, over the last few days melts away. *Why does he make me feel so safe?*

After dropping my bag in his van, he takes me to a burger restaurant a few streets away.

We're seated in a hidden corner at the back of the restaurant. I couldn't have chosen better seats if I'd tried.

The silence stretches out between us but at no point does he ask me about what's bothering me, and I couldn't be more grateful.

"No twinset today?" he asks with a laugh.

"No, I binned them."

"Oh?"

"They're not me anymore."

"Anymore?"

I shake my head, not willing to say anything else.

"So...have you had a good week?"

I can't help but burst out laughing at his question. "It's been fine."

"Fine?"

"Yeah. I mean, I have this secret admirer that keeps sending me gifts, so that's nice."

"Oh? Tell me about him. He sounds perfect."

"That might be pushing it. He's going after something he can't have. I'm not the person he thinks I am."

"And who's that?"

I sit back and think about his question for a few minutes. "I'm lost, Joe. I moved here not even two months ago with the intention of finding out who I am. Until I got here, all of my life was planned out for me and I followed along like a good little girl. This is my chance but—"

"You're scared."

"More than you know."

"I've been there, Quinn. I've been alone. I've been lost and not had a clue who I am. We're more alike than you realise."

"I don't believe that for a second. You're so sure of yourself. So confident in everything."

"Now I am, but only because I've worked hard to be that way.

Quinn, listen." He reaches across the table and takes my hand in his. "Our pasts don't define who we are. We do that. Only you have the power to determine your future. What do *you* want for your future?"

"To be free." I slam my lips shut. Why is it that everything I'm trying to keep to myself just spews out of me when I'm with him?

"And how do you do that?"

"I don't know," I whisper honestly.

There isn't much more conversation between us as the waitress brings over our burgers. We eat in silence. I mostly keep my eyes down, afraid of how much he can read in them.

"Can I take you home?"

"Uh..."

"I'll just drop you off. I won't even get out of the van. I just need to know you're back safe."

I nod. "Okay."

He leads me back to where he'd parked, and I drop into his passenger seat.

"So what do you do exactly?"

"General builder. But I want more."

"What's more?"

"I'm not one hundred per cent. Quantity surveyor, maybe, but I'd need a degree most probably. I'm not sure if I've got that in me."

"Don't be so modest. Of course you can do it. You're more than capable."

"You've only been my teacher for a few weeks."

"We can pick out the ones who are going to succeed the minute students walk through the door, Joe. You've got it."

He beams at my praise, and my heart turns over. I think back to his question about the future, and I wonder seriously for the first time if there's a space for him in it.

Joe stands by his words and doesn't even switch the engine off, let alone get out of his van.

After thanking him, I jump out and grab my bags. His eyes follow me all the way to the front door of my building, and knowing he's right there means I don't even look over my shoulder before entering. I know I'm safe while he's here.

I give him a quick wave before allowing the door to shut behind me.

The first thing I do when I get up to my flat is to go to the window. Just as I suspected, he's still there. He's too far away to be able to see him, but it's long minutes before his van starts backing out of the space.

I turn my sofa into a bed and settle with a book when my phone rings. My first thought is that it's Joe, but I soon realise that he doesn't have my number. There are only a couple of people who do, and right now I don't really want to hear from any of them.

Pulling it from my bag, I take a deep breath and look at the screen. *Detective Barker*. Fuck.

Part of me doesn't want to answer. That part would rather be blissfully unaware of what might be happening in my absence. But the part of me that's desperate to move on has me swiping the screen and lifting the phone to my ear.

"Hello?" My voice sounds weak even to my own ears.

"Good evening. This is Detective Barker. How are you?" His voice is over-the-top happy, and my stomach drops to my feet. It's all I need to hear to tell me that what's going to come next is going to rock my world once again.

"I'm...surviving."

He clearly misses the hesitation in my tone or refuses to hear it.

"That's good to hear, because I've got some news."

"Go on."

"The story has been leaked to the press." *Shit.* "I thought it was only fair to warn you that it will most probably hit the headlines tomorrow." My head spins, and white noise fills my ears. My chest heaves as I fight to drag in the air I need, but it's no use. Nothing fills my lungs, and I can't catch my breath.

I can vaguely make out the low timbre of Detective Baker's voice in the background, but I hear no more words as I fall onto the bed and count my breaths as a way to try to calm myself before this turns into a full-on panic attack.

Tomorrow morning, everyone is going to know. The lies and scandal I exposed will be common knowledge. That's good, I tell myself. It's what I wanted. But where will that leave me?

"Are you still there?"

"Yeah, yeah, I'm still here," I manage when the fog begins to lift enough to make out his words.

"Did you hear all of that?"

"Yeah."

"Okay, great. Well, like I said. If you hear anything from them, call me immediately, but I'm confident that you're safe where you are. They won't want to bring any more heat on their shoulders."

"Great. Thank you."

I disconnect the call and allow my hand to drop between my knees as I try to process the little bit of what I heard.

I thought it was only fair to warn you that it will most probably hit the headlines tomorrow.

My hands tremble as I think about the consequences of the world knowing about my old life with all its betrayal and misplaced trust. My stomach turns over, and I worry I'm about to puke right here on my dirty floor, but thankfully a few deep breaths make it abate slightly.

CHAPTER THIRTEEN

I don't get a wink of sleep. Every bang and creek within the building has my heart in my throat, thinking that my past is going to come crashing through my door to teach me a lesson of my own for betraying them.

I know the exact words I'd hear. *"We're family, princess. This is what happens when you go against your own."*

Bang.

The sound of someone's front door slamming is enough to have me jumping from the bed and backing into the corner as my heart races.

Tears burn my eyes, but I refuse to give in to the fear racing through my veins. I've made it this far. I've started a new life. They won't ruin it for me now.

I'm hyper aware of everything as I get ready for work, but I fight against my need to hide like a coward. I'm not the one in the wrong. Why should I be the one hiding?

I want to say that I hold my head high and walk from the building like I have no cares in the world, but that's far from the truth. In reality, my entire body trembles as terror takes a tight grip on my lungs.

They won't break me, I repeat over and over as I make my way down towards the tube station.

I probably look like a right nut case as my head darts from side to side and up and down the street, desperately trying to find out if I'm being watched or followed.

My skin tingles with awareness, but I'm sure it's more my own fears that cause it because I see no sign of anyone looking my way, let alone trailing me. I haven't since the day I moved here, but that doesn't mean I'm safe. I thought I was safe in my own home before—I had no idea what monsters I was living with.

Nothing about my day is unusual, but I still find myself looking over my shoulder at every opportunity. I stay as far away from any newspapers, TV and radio as possible. I'm not ready to relive all of that again—not yet, anyway. I'm not stupid, I know I'm going to have to endure seemingly endless court cases about what I exposed, but I'll deal with that when the time comes.

I make the final part of my journey home from the tube station, my paranoia is at an all time high seeing as it's dark. It's so much easier to remain in the shadows out of sight. I reach for my phone to call Joe numerous times, knowing that I'll feel safe if he's by my side. But I need to do this alone.

By the time I push the main door open, I'm breathing like I've just run a marathon. I jog up the stairs, using the last of my energy before pushing the key in the lock and triple-checking that I secure everything behind me.

This place might not be much to most people, but it's become my sanctuary. Do I wish I had more? Of course. I've worked my whole life and saved every penny I could. I never imagined a time where I'd be forced to leave all of that behind. All I can hope is that when this is all over, I might see some of it once again.

My stomach rumbles, reminding me that I've not eaten all day. Turning to the fridge, I pull it open and groan. I could really do with a little comfort food tonight, but all I've got staring back at me is a half-eaten tub of soup, stale bread, and a block of cheese. Not exactly what I'm craving.

The knowledge that my first paycheck hit my bank today rattles around my head, but I fight the urge to pick up my phone and order a takeaway. I've got more important things to buy.

In the end, I begrudgingly pull the soup from the fridge with a sigh.

The steaming bowl in my hands almost crashes to the floor when the buzzer rings out through the silent flat.

"Fuck." My chest heaves, my breaths racing past my lips.

I place the bowl down with trembling hands and hesitate. After debating whether to answer it or not for a few seconds, I eventually walk over on unsteady legs and press down the button. I figure if my past were to come knocking, then it's not likely to be so blatant as to ring my buzzer.

My assumptions are proved correct when Joe's voice fills the tiny space around me.

"Quinn, you there?" The concern is evident in his tone. I must have done an even worse job than I thought of appearing normal yesterday evening.

"Yeah, I'm here. What's up?"

"I was kinda hoping you'd invite me in and I could tell you."

"Oh, um..." I should say no. I should find out what he wants and send him on his way to enjoy his Friday night. I've already experienced his kind of night out, and I know he wouldn't be satisfied with two-day-old re-heated soup in my tiny studio.

No matter what my brain tells my body to do, it seems my arm has a mind of its own because I don't even realise that I've pressed the button down to unlock the front door and allow him entry into the building until he thanks me.

Before long, I hear his footsteps thundering up the stairs. The louder they get, the harder my heart beats.

You're playing with fire, the little voice in my head says.

Seconds before I know he's going to be standing the other side of the door, I rush towards my mirror, wipe the stray make up from under my eyes and run my fingers through my hair.

Even after all these weeks, I still hardly recognise the woman staring back at me. A little rush of excitement tingles through my veins at the reminder that I'm living my own life at last, even if I am waiting for it to come crashing down around my feet at any second.

My stomach tumbles when his loud, manly knock sounds out.

"Get it together, girl."

I shake out my arms and hope my paranoia vanishes along with my nerves.

I quickly unlock all the locks and in mere seconds I'm pulling the door open to reveal the man I can't get out of my head.

Only I've not met this version of him before.

Gone are the braces and crisp white shirt, and there are no dirty work clothes in sight. Tonight, he's dressed more casually in a pair of skinny dark jeans and a white polo shirt, although his glasses remain.

"You approve?" he asks, and my cheeks heat.

"Shit...I..." I stutter, my body frozen solid as his eyes burn into mine.

"Don't apologise. I like knowing what you're thinking."

His words immediately get my back up. I've been controlled my entire life by men who 'think' they know what I want and what I think.

I'm so done with that.

"You don't know me," I spit, much to his surprise if his raised eyebrows are anything to go by.

His hand lifts to rub the back of his neck, and I instantly feel awful for assuming he meant more than he did with his comment.

"Fuck, I didn't mean—"

"I'm sorry, it was my fault. Old habits die hard, I guess."

His brows draw together. I know he's desperate to discover more about my past, but I'm barely able to think about it right now without falling into a panic attack, let alone talk about it.

"Can I...?" he trails off and nods over my shoulder into my flat. My eyes follow, and I hesitate. "I promise I'm not going to jump you or anything. I just have a proposition that might interest you."

I narrow my eyes at him, already interested in his cryptic statement, and stand aside to allow him over the threshold.

"Coffee?" I ask, walking past where he's dropped to the sofa and over to the kitchen.

"Sure."

I put the kettle on and get the mugs out, anything that will attempt to distract me from the pull that's always there when he's close.

Chancing a glance over my shoulder, I find him sitting back, relaxing on my sofa with his eyes locked on me. My need to find a seat on his lap is strong, but I fight to keep even a scrap of my self-control and continue with what I'm doing...but that's not before he graces me with a heart-stopping smile. That alongside the cheeky glint in his eyes makes me wonder what kind of proposition he's turned up here with.

"So?" I ask, placing his coffee down on the table and sitting as far away from him as possible on my small two-seater sofa.

"So..." He leans forward and places his elbows on his knees. His eyes never leave mine. "I get that you don't want to talk about it. Honestly, I do. But I can see you're scared and from the look of your eyes right now, I can tell that whatever it is is keeping you up at night. I want to help."

"How?" I ask, confused as to how he can help when he has no idea what haunts both my waking and sleeping hours.

"Spend the weekend with me?" My eyes widen in shock. "Let me take you away from here and everything you're worrying about."

"Joe, we can't—" All the reasons why he shouldn't even be here right now circle through my head, let alone the million and one reasons why we shouldn't spend an entire weekend together. The knowledge that I feel too connected to him already after the small amount of time we've spent together up until now is only a part of the problem.

"Forget it all. Whatever's in your head right now, forget it. I'm not a student. You're not a teacher. We're just two people enjoying their time off and each other. Let's leave all the stress behind. Just for a few days."

I can't deny that what he's proposing sounds incredible. I'm desperate to scream yes, pack a bag and drag him from the building, but I've got to think of the bigger picture here.

I sit forward on the sofa, my body willing me to get up and get ready to go, but my mind holds me back.

"What did you say to me before our night out? That you wanted to live, you wanted to experience new things. This is just like that night but longer. Let's tick a few more experiences off your list."

"What did you have in mind?"

"I've booked us a hotel in a place I think you'll love."

"You've booked it? A little presumptuous, wasn't it?"

"You're worth the risk."

My chin drops, my heart damn near stopping dead in my chest

at his words. My eyes hold his as I look for any hint that he's joking, but I find nothing.

It's those four little words and the meaning behind them that has me jumping up and pulling clothes from the small wardrobe at the other side of the room and quickly stuffing everything into a holdall.

"Is that a yes?" Joe asks with a laugh as his eyes follow my every move.

"Just because you asked so politely."

"Not sure I've ever been described as polite before. Next you'll be telling me that I'm chivalrous and thoughtful." His words are quiet, like I'm not really meant to hear them. But I do.

I pause and look up. "You are."

"That's because I've only shown you that side of me."

"I don't believe that. I've seen you, Joe." He stands and my eyes drop from his to take in his body.

"So you have." He stalks over, his eyes darkening. I see what he's doing: diverting the conversation to sex, something he's much more comfortable discussing.

I want to argue that I see more than he realises I do, but much like me not wanting to talk about my past, I can tell this is something he's not keen to discuss.

I hold his eyes when they eventually find mine once again, trying to tell him everything I want. His eyes soften, and I wonder if he understands.

"What do I need to pack? Anything special?"

"Whatever you want. You'll look gorgeous, no doubt." Flames lick at my stomach, the darkness in his eyes telling me that he's being totally sincere. Much like him, I wonder what he sees when he looks at me, because the only thing I see when I look in the mirror these days is the woman I've always wanted to be who's too afraid to really go after the life she craves.

I'm avoiding dealing with so much of my past that I've shoved it into the dark corners of my mind when the one thing that I really should be avoiding is standing right in front of me, promising me an escape.

I somehow manage to break our connection to pack my toiletries and zip up my bag.

"Did you want to finish your soup?" Joe asks, a cheeky smile curling at one side of his mouth.

"I think I'm good."

"Right answer. Come on."

Taking my bag, he throws it over one shoulder before sliding his other hand into mine. I tense, knowing that I should pull away, but touching him is just a little too comfortable. After days of looking over my shoulder, waiting for the inevitable, the feeling of safety that washes through me is too much to deny.

I squeeze his hand a little tighter, and together we lock up the flat and head down to his van.

"Doesn't your boss mind you taking the van off on a mystery weekend with a stranger?"

"First, you're not a stranger. I know you better than I know a lot of people in my life." I turn to look at him as he pushes the key into the ignition and starts the engine. There are so many words on the tip of my tongue, but I know he wants to talk about it as much as I do. So instead of asking anything, I give him a small smile when his eyes meet mine. The more time I spend with him, the more I see the shadows in his eyes he tries to cover with his confidence, but as time goes on, the darker they're getting.

It helps explain the pull I feel towards him.

We're the same, both trying to survive with plenty of skeletons hiding in our closets.

"So where are we going?"

"To the home of literature."

My brows draw together as I think about his words, but nowhere comes to mind.

"I don't—"

"I'm disappointed in you, Miss Smith," he says with a chuckle as he heads out of the city.

"I thought we were forgetting about the whole teacher/student thing?"

"We are, although where we're going should be a good field trip for me."

A thought hits me, and excitement bubbles in my belly. "Oh… we're going to Stratford-upon-Avon." I don't even ask it as a question, because the second it occurred to me, I knew I was right.

"We are. I thought we'd get up close and personal to the man himself. Although, I must admit that I'm more excited about the up close and personal opportunities with someone else." He turns to me, his teeth sinking into his bottom lip as his eyes drop to my breasts. "Did I mention how much I like that dress?"

The dress in question is a simple black jersey wrap, cut a little lower than I'd usually risk for work, but the fabric feels incredible and I needed something a little extra to get me through today.

"Thank you," I say, my cheeks heating. I want to look away, but when his eyes lift and capture mine, I'm powerless to move.

"Do you know what's even better about it?"

I shake my head, unable to form any words.

"How incredible it'll be when I get to unwrap you from it later."

Heat races between my thighs and I shift uncomfortably, a move he doesn't miss.

"Motherfucker," Joe breathes, his chest heaving. "You're going to be the death of me."

I don't get to reply, because the car behind us at the traffic lights beeps his horn. We both look forward to see what was the green light turned back to red.

"Whoops," Joe says innocently. "He'd understand if he had you sitting beside him, distracting him."

I really doubt that.

"You act like you never get compliments, which I find hard to believe." Joe speeds up as we join the motorway, which thankfully means he's unable to look my way.

"Believe it. I think I've had more from you in the past few weeks than I have in my entire life."

His fingers wrap tighter around the wheel until his knuckles turn white, and when I glance at his body, every single muscle is pulled tight.

Reaching over, I place my hand on his forearm. "It's okay. Relax. I'm not there right now. I'm here...with you."

He blows out a breath and looks over at me quickly. His eyes show everything he's trying to hold inside. My stomach drops. If he's this angry just because of a lack of compliments, what's he going to be like when he finds out the truth?

A shudder runs through me at the thought, and I push it away. This weekend, my time with Joe isn't about any of that.

"Tell me more about you." He swallows nervously, I assume thinking that I'm going to hit him with some heavy stuff. "Okay, so...cats or dogs?"

A smile lights up his face and the skin around his eyes crinkles with amusement as he barks out a laugh.

"Easy, dogs all the way."

"Correct."

"Oh, I didn't realise this was a test, Miss Smith."

Embarrassment colours my cheeks. "Sorry, habit."

"Don't apologise." His hand sneaks over and rests high on my thigh. Its warmth and size feels too good to push away.

"Pop or hip hop?"

"Hip hop," I say without even taking a breath.

"Really?"

"All day long."

"Go on then, it's all yours." He nods towards his phone that's sitting in a clasp thing attached to the air vents.

Leaning forward, I wake it up and am greeted by his passcode screen.

"Nine seven one two," he rattles off without a second thought.

I stare at him as he focuses on where we're going.

"What?" His eyes flick to me, and I can tell he wants to hold them but he's unable to given his task at hand.

"You just gave me the code. That's like...I don't know. Serious."

"You didn't bat an eyelid about spending the weekend with me but this you freak out about?" His chuckle of amusement warms me from the inside out.

"It just seems so..."

"Serious?" he repeats. "Chill out. I can just change it later, it's not like I've given you a key to my flat or anything."

He's right, I know he is, but I also don't think I believe a word that's just fallen from his lips.

Trying to ignore the tingles racing around my body every time he glances over at me, I scroll through his music. I come to a stop when I find something that looks interesting and hit play on his 'Old Skool Trax' playlist.

He nods his head in approval and turns the volume up slightly, but not so much that we can't still hold a conversation.

"It's your turn." His hand squeezes my thigh, its heat burning my skin and making it hard to concentrate.

"Uh...night in or night out?"

"Is that a trick question?"

"No, why?"

"Wherever you are."

"That's not how this game works," I chastise, trying to ignore the elation that bubbles up within me as I repeat his answer over and over in my head.

"You know, if you want to live a little, you've got to break the rules every now and then, right?"

"Not my forte."

"So I'm learning."

Silence falls between us, but it's not uncomfortable.

"Okay, you want a better answer? Before meeting you, night out, always a night out. The more alcohol and willing bodies the better." I sense him cringe at his own words, but it doesn't stop him. "But now, I'd willingly trade all of that for a night on your sofa."

I'm totally lost for words, and when he glances over at me, his eyes dark and hungry, it doesn't make it any better.

"Pull over or keep driving?"

"Huh, what?"

"Pull over or keep driving?" he repeats slowly. His hand creeps up a little higher on my thigh, and I gasp when his little finger grazes against my core.

Closing my eyes, I rest my head back and try to focus, to attempt to find my sanity that seems to fly out of the window whenever he's around.

"Keep driving," I whisper. It sounds unconvincing.

"Really?" His voice is deep and gravelly, and it hits exactly where he intends. My clit throbs as my body temperature increases another notch.

"Really." When I pull my eyelids open, a sign showing how close we are appears in front of me. I might be all for exploring my wild side, but I'm not sure that goes as far as getting caught for indecent exposure.

Attempting to direct the topic of conversation onto something else before I change my mind, I rack my brain for another question. The silence becomes suffocating; the only thing I'm aware of is his large, imposing body next to me and his manly scent permeating the air. I crack the window slightly despite it being bitterly cold outside.

"Marmite or peanut butter?"

"Pft, Marmite, every day of the fucking week."

"Thank god. I might have made you turn the car back if you answered that wrong."

"Salt and vinegar or cheese and onion?"

Our this and that game continues until he brings the van to a stop outside a huge Tudor building. It's exactly the kind I imagined when I figured out where we were going, and the kind of place I could only dream of staying.

"This is our hotel?" My voice is full of awe.

"Yeah. Is that okay?"

"Okay? Joe, this place is stunning. It must have cost you a damn fortune."

"As much as I'd love to agree, I actually got us an amazing last-minute deal."

"Just tell me how much my half is, and I'll make sure to pay you back."

His eyes burn into the side of my head as I bend down to grab my bag, ready to get out. A shiver runs down my spine, and when I look over at him I understand why. His eyes are full of anger and frustration. The look is one I'm familiar with, and it makes my muscles tense, ready for what's to come.

"You'll do no such thing. I booked this for you, as a gift. I don't expect anything in return." His voice is hard, but it doesn't hold the disgust or vile words I'm so used to following anger.

I open my mouth to respond, but he beats me to it.

"And don't even think about arguing."

"I wasn't," I lie. "I was going to ask if you were sure you didn't want *anything* in return."

His eyes darken further, but it's no longer with anger. They drop from mine in favour of my lips, and I can't help my tongue sneaking out to wet my bottom one in preparation for what I hope is to come. We've been together over two hours and side by side in this confined space for most of that, and he's yet to do anything aside from place his hand on my thigh and look at me like he wants to devour me.

He clears his throat. "Come on, let's check in." It takes him a few seconds to do as he suggested. His eyes are too focused on my lips to move.

Grabbing both of our bags, he takes my hand and, after placing a kiss to my knuckles, threads our fingers together and guides me towards the entrance.

"I've got a room booked for Mr. Kingsman," he says, seemingly oblivious to the girl behind the reception desk drooling over him.

"Oh um...yes. I have some good news for you as well—it seems your room has been upgraded." He looks over at me and winks. I damn near melt into a puddle on the floor.

The receptionist hands over our key and talks through a couple of things, but I don't pay any attention. I'm too busy taking note of the intricate tattoos that cover Joe's arms and hands.

"Your dinner reservation is for nine o'clock. It'll be in our restaurant just behind me," she explains seconds before Joe thanks her and takes my hand once again. "Would you like any help with your luggage?" Joe waves her off, and we head for the lift.

"I think she liked you," I say once the doors have closed us inside the small space.

"Didn't notice."

"How's that possible? She was about ready to jump the desk so she could lick you."

"You were standing next to me, Quinn. Why would I be paying attention to anyone else?"

"I...uh..." The lift opens on the top floor of the hotel, and we walk out hand in hand.

Joe holds the keycard up to the pad, and the door clicks unlocked. Dropping my hand, he reaches for the handle and pushes it open.

"After you."

I step forward and my eyes go wide.

"Wow." I walk into the huge, luxurious room, trying and failing to take it all in. The old beams are through the walls and ceilings, giving it the perfect old and rustic look that's stereotypical of the buildings here. The rest of the room is in keeping with the age of the building, but it's mixed with a few sleek modern touches.

"I was thinking the same." Having dropped the bags, Joe's hands slip around my waist and I'm pulled back against him. His heat immediately seeps into me, and I breathe a sigh of contentment.

I'm safe.

"Only, I haven't had a chance to look at the room because I can't take my eyes off you."

"Are you always this smooth?"

"Honestly?" he asks between light kisses to my neck which have my nipples pebbling behind my bra. "No. Never. I'm not ashamed to admit that I'm usually a fuck 'em and chuck 'em kind of guy."

I'm not at all surprised, but the way he says it so casually makes me wince.

"Don't go thinking that my partners were under any illusion that it was anything other than what it was. Sex. I've never wanted to spend time with someone like I do with you. I've never wanted a repeat like I do with you. I've never wanted anything from any of the people I've slept with before."

"You want something from me?" I ignore my other curiosity: that he only refers to his previous bed mates as partners or people. I pretty much figured the night I saw him dancing with and kissing anyone in touching distance that he didn't discriminate where sex was concerned. I was brought up with the idea that a woman and man meet, get married and give themselves to their spouse and their spouse only. But standing here, knowing Joe as I do, I really don't care about that part of his past.

I hope when my truth comes out, he doesn't hold it against me.

"Everything, Quinn. I want everything."

He spins me so we're face-to-face. The intensity in his eyes as he stares down at me causes my stomach to drop. *He wants things you can't offer him. Not yet, anyway.*

"Joe, I—"

"Shhh. I didn't say that to freak you out or for you to tell me you want the same from me. I just want you to know that this isn't just a bit of fun for me. How I feel about you isn't a temporary thing. I know it's complicated. I know there are a million reasons why we shouldn't be here. But we are. We're here. We're together, and I can't imagine anywhere else I want to be right now."

His lips find mine, and his tongue sweeps into my mouth, searching for mine. Everything he's just expressed is confirmed by the way his lips move. The emotion he pours into it causes tears to burn the backs of my eyes.

What he said is everything I've ever wanted: a man who's

passionate about what he wants...about me. But right now couldn't be a worse time for it.

"Fuck. I want to be inside you so badly."

"What's stopping you?"

"The fact that we've got reservations and that I've been listening to your stomach rumbling the entire journey here."

"It was not," I argue, although it's weak at best. I'm starving. If it wasn't for him and his distraction techniques, the only thing I'd be able to think about would be food.

"I might need you more than my next breath, but I also need you with a little energy. I don't plan on sleeping much tonight, so you're going to need some sustenance."

My lips form an O, and he steps away from me.

"We've got thirty minutes—not that you need it, because you look stunning already—but do what you need to do and we'll find you some food."

I'm rooted to the floor, still reeling from his kiss as he falls onto the sofa and grabs the TV remote, waking it up and finding it on a 24/7 news channel.

I don't think anything of it as I go to my bag and rummage around for something to wear.

It's not until I hear the headlines for the next story that I freeze.

"The latest private school scandal hit the headlines this morning. According to the police, there have been over one-hundred victims in contact to tell their story about abuse at Earlington Manor. The head teacher has been—"

"Turn it off." My voice is barely a whisper, making Joe turn to look at me so I can repeat my words. I do so before his eyes even find mine.

"Okay, okay. Is this okay?" he asks, turning the channel and finding a repeat of an old US sitcom.

My hands tremble, and my cold blood turns my body to ice at just hearing those words from the TV.

"Quinn?" he asks, walking over and placing his hands on my upper arms. "Are you okay? You look like you've seen a ghost."

I have, I think as memories from my past life threaten to surface.

"I'm sorry. I just can't watch that. I've worked with too many kids who've been affected by that kind of abuse, and I can't hear any more of it."

He eyes me curiously, correctly guessing that there's a lot more to this than I'm letting on.

"I'm okay, I promise." It's a bare-faced lie and he knows it, but when I move towards the bathroom with a change of clothes and my wash bag, he allows me the space I need.

CHAPTER FOURTEEN

The meal is out of this world, and it's almost enough to drag me from my nightmare. Joe wanted to bring me here to get me away from what's haunting me, but he managed to bring it closer than it has been since the phone call from Detective Barker.

I force myself out of my own head so I can enjoy what he's done for me, but it's harder than I ever imagined it would be.

He can see it. The concern hasn't left his eyes since he released me to get ready, but thankfully he's given me the reprieve I need and not asked me about it. He wants to, he's practically vibrating with the need to, but he won't.

"Would you like coffee?" our waiter asks once she's cleared our dessert plates.

"I'm fine, but would you?" Joe's heated and concerned eyes turn to me. I ignore the concern and focus on the desire.

"No, thank you. I think I'm done." I rub my hand over my full belly. I can't remember the last time I ate an entire three-course meal. Not so long ago it would have seemed so normal, but now I live on a diet of toast and noodles, it seems like it was in another lifetime.

I swallow down the last of my wine, and Joe's eyes lock onto my lips and run down my neck as I do. His teeth sink into his bottom lip, and his muscles tense.

"I think I'm done too. I'm done with you teasing me from the other side of the table. I'm done with imagining what you're wearing under that sinful little leather dress, and I'm done waiting for another taste of your sweet pussy."

I gasp. "You can't say stuff like that here. Anyone could hear you."

"So? Anyone who's bored enough to be eavesdropping right now will only be jealous."

I glance around the full restaurant and find everyone lost in their own conversations or meals.

"Excuse me," Joe calls out when a waiter walks past. "Please could we have another bottle to take up to our room?"

"Of course, Sir. I'll be right back with it."

It feels like only seconds later that Joe has a chilled bottle of white wine in one hand and one of mine in his other.

My stomach somersaults as we step into the lift alone. The air crackles between us as Joe hits the button for the top floor and turns to me.

I back up. The look in his eyes and the tight set of his shoulders makes my heart race and my skin tingle.

He closes the distance between us and successfully sucks all the air from the tiny space. His body is impressively huge at the best of times, but right now, in such an enclosed space, he looks downright dangerous.

I feel like a little chick being hunted by its prey, but there's not an ounce of fear in my body right now.

I might be scared of many things in my life, but Joe isn't one of them. My feelings for him might be another story, but him, his strength and power, not so much.

He stops when there's barely an inch between us. His breath races across my face. It smells like wine and chocolate from the moose he just had for dessert. It's delicious, making me desperate to know how it'll make him taste.

I expect his lips to land on mine, but much to my surprise, when we connect, it's only our foreheads that are touching.

His eyes continue to stare down into mine, and it's like he can see all the way down to my toes. The weirdest feeling comes over me, the desire to tell him everything. To spill everything I've kept so close to my chest for so long. It's right on the tip of my tongue, even though I know that now is not the time.

He makes me feel safe. He makes me feel strong. Acknowledging both of those means that I know he'll keep my secrets locked up as tightly as I do. He'll accept them and support me without question.

"Quinn," he breathes, making my insides quiver with need. "What the hell are you doing to me?"

I want to respond, to tell him that I really have no idea, but I don't get a chance because the lift doors open on our floor and we're forced to break apart.

The second the door to our fancy hotel room slams behind us, he's on me. My bag drops to the floor with a thud. I've no idea what happens to the bottle of wine, because both his hands grasp my face as his lips descend on mine. He walks us backwards until I bump up against the wall, but he doesn't stop, not until every inch of our bodies that can touch are.

His hard length presses into my stomach and he grinds his hips slowly, ensuring I feel every inch of him.

"I need you so fucking badly," he groans in my ear after kissing along my jaw. A shudder runs down my spine and radiates all the way out to my fingertips and toes. I sag against the wall as his hands skim down my sides and his fingers dig into my hips with an almost painful grip.

Something flashes in his eyes like he's made a decision, and his hands drop lower to push the fabric of my dress up around my waist.

"Fuck," he moans when he gets a look at the small black thong I'm wearing. It's a little different to the boring pair of knickers I had on the last time.

With his hands on my arse, he lifts me and presses me back against the wall. My arms wrap around his shoulders as I seek out his lips once again.

His length presses against my core, and the ball of need that's already consuming me starts to grow even more insistent. I've never experienced sex like this before. Like if we don't have each other right now and sate the desire running through us, then we might explode. I thought this kind of need and passion was something that only existed in movies and romance novels.

Joe's tongue delves deep into my mouth, exploring like he can't possibly live another second without discovering every inch.

Somehow, he manages to slip his hand between us, undo his fly and release his cock.

"Fuck, Joe," I moan when he rubs the head against the damp fabric covering me. My muscles tense and ripple, needing something to grip onto, something to fill me and give me everything I need.

"I've been tested. I'm clean. I want to feel all of you."

My head falls back against the wall with a thud. Joe's tongue licks up the column of my neck as he waits for my answer. It's not that I need to think about it...more that I need my brain to function to be able to form the correct words.

"I'm..." His tongue swirls around the outside of my ear and I lose all concentration. "I'm on the pill."

Taking that as my confirmation, the fabric of my thong is immediately pulled to the side, and he pushes himself into my wetness.

"So fucking wet for me," he murmurs, pushing the head of his cock just inside me, teasing me.

My muscles try to grip onto him to drag him deeper to get what I need. My heels dig hard into his arse, trying to get him to thrust, and he chuckles.

"What do you need, Quinn?"

"You," I moan, arching my back and shamelessly thrusting my leather covered chest at him.

"How? How do you want me?"

My cheeks heat more than they already are, knowing that he wants me to spell it out for him. But if it's what it takes to feel him pressing inside me, I'll tell him whatever he wants to hear.

"I want your cock inside me. So fucking deep my eyes cross," I add as his pupils dilate until they're almost totally black when the word 'cock' falls from my mouth.

"Gonna. Kill. Me." His words are barely loud enough for me to make out.

My lips turn up in a triumphant smile. I've never had a man at my mercy like this before, and the power it gives me makes me feel invincible.

My elation is soon pushed aside as Joe thrusts his hips, simultaneously dropping me a little lower down the wall so he fills me in one swift move.

I cry out at the sudden invasion, my body stretching almost to the point of pain to accommodate him.

"Fuuuuck," he hisses, slamming his palm down against the

wall beside my head. His muscles are pulled tight, and I know he's trying to give me a minute to adjust, but he's dying to move.

Moving my head from the wall, I let my lips brush his ear. "Fuck me, Joe. Fuck me until the only thing I can think about is you. Make everything else go away."

"Motherfucking shit. Where have you been all my life?"

I assume it's a rhetorical question. His fingers tangle in my hair and my head's pulled back so he can slam his lips down on mine.

His hips find their rhythm and, before long, we're forced to break our kiss so we can both suck in some much-needed air.

My head hits the wall, but if it hurts I don't feel it. The only thing I can focus on is the building tension radiating from my core that's sure to rock my world when it explodes.

"So tight. So wet. So fucking good," Joe chants against the hot skin of my neck as he ups the pace, chasing both of our releases. "Fuck, Quinn. Fuuuuuck," he roars so loud that I've no doubt the rooms either side of us heard, but I don't care. All I care about is the twitch of his cock inside me and the hot spurts of his cum that set off my own mind-blowing release. My muscles clamp down around him as fireworks shoot off around me. My body takes on a life of its own as it twitches and convulses, the pleasure he's caused seemingly endless and so fucking needed.

Our chests are heaving and our skin's covered in a sheen of sweat when Joe pulls out of me and drops my legs to the floor.

"Turn," he demands.

It takes a few seconds for me to figure out if my legs will hold me up before I follow his orders. My knees threaten to buckle the moment I move them, but thankfully, I don't crumple to a pile on the floor.

The second my back is to him, his fingers grip onto the zip at the base of my neck and he pulls it down. My breasts swell once again, my nipples puckering against the lace containing them.

Goosebumps break out across my skin when he pushes the fabric from my shoulders.

"It feels like it's been a lifetime since I've touched you." He kisses down my spine until he finds the clasp of my bra. He unhooks it and allows it to fall to the floor.

Descending, he pulls my thong down my legs before helping me slip my shoes from my feet.

"Turn," he repeats.

After sucking in some confidence, I spin. My skin heats under his intense stare, my nipples harden even further, and my core grows hot for him once again.

Reaching behind his head, he pulls his shirt from his body, revealing his rippling muscles beneath before pushing his jeans and boxers from his hips and toeing off his shoes.

I take my time running my eyes over every inch of him, but my ogling is soon stopped when I'm pulled into his arms and thrown onto the bed.

"I hope you didn't think we were done."

"Not even for a second. Sleep is for the weak, right?" He laughs, and it awakens something inside me that I didn't even realise was missing until right now. My heart swells seeing the wide, genuine smile on his handsome face. I want to wrap my arms around him and never let go, and that's a seriously scary thought. I've never wanted anything as much as I want him, and I already know that nothing good can come from being with me.

I'VE no idea what time we eventually fall asleep, but when I wake it's with Joe's arms locked around me. I breathe a sigh of relief when I realise that I had my first peaceful night's sleep (even if it was only a few hours) since he was with me last time. I put it down to my exhaustion, but I can't help hoping it's more than that, because for the first time in weeks, I feel safe. While I'm in his arms, I know nothing's going to happen to me.

Needing to see him, I try to turn in his arms without waking him. I barely move and my muscles pull, a reminder of just how busy we got last night. I'm most definitely not used to that kind of exertion.

His breathing stays steady and he doesn't move so I think I'm successful, but when I look up, I find him staring back down at me, his eyes full of amusement.

"Hey," I say shyly, suddenly very aware of the fact my naked body is crushed up against his.

"Hi." Something wicked twinkles in his eyes, and my stomach tumbles in anticipation of what's to come. "You hungry?"

"Uh...I guess. What time is breakfast?"

"Right now." Before I have a chance to blink, he's thrown the covers off and is trailing a line of kisses down my stomach.

My body immediately wakes up for him, and my veins fill with fire, knowing what he's about to do to me.

It's safe to say I've never had an alarm clock like this before and I'm pretty sure I'd quite happily keep it. The serious thought makes me still for a beat, and he doesn't miss it. He's hovering over my navel when he looks up and his eyes find mine. He doesn't say any words, but I can feel the question in his stare. Forcing a small smile onto my lips, I nod slightly. He holds our connection for a second longer, I guess trying to figure out if I really am okay or not, but before long the soft brush of his lips under my belly button has goosebumps pricking my skin.

"So fucking sweet. I could eat you all day long, Quinn." Heat floods my face at the thought.

"You won't hear me complaining." I'm not sure how I've managed my entire life without this but after just one lick from his skilled tongue and I feel myself becoming addicted to his touch.

His tongue sweeps up the length of me, making my back arch. Needing more of what he's got to give, I thread my fingers into his hair and hold him down. His chuckle only adds to the sensations he's causing.

Sooner than I was expecting, with two fingers deep inside me and his tongue circling my clit, I come all over his face. He doesn't stop until the last tremors of my orgasm have subsided. When he sits up, it's with the smuggest smile playing on his lips.

"Pleased with yourself?" I ask with a laugh.

He crawls over me, holds my face in his hand and stares deep into my eyes. "You just screamed my name over and over. Of course I'm fucking pleased with myself."

I go to laugh, but his lips cover mine. I hesitate because... morning breath, but it doesn't seem to bother Joe as he slips his tongue inside my mouth. I eagerly return his kiss, the fire he'd doused inside me sparking back to life the second I taste myself on him.

Without breaking our kiss, he situates himself at my entrance, and we both sigh when he slowly slides inside me.

Last night we fucked, and we fucked hard. Hence my aching muscles this morning. But this, this is something totally different. It's slower, it's more...sensual, and when he pulls back and looks into my eyes, I can't help but feel like he's trying to tell me something. Something I'm nowhere near ready to accept or deal with. Tears sting my eyes, and I fight to keep them down, but when he drops his forehead against mine, his hand splayed across my throat possessively, I can't prevent one escaping.

His eyes darken the moment he sees it, and he lifts his hand so he can wipe it away.

"Fuck, Quinn." He doesn't say anything else. He doesn't need to. His eyes say it all as he searches mine, I fear trying to find the same things that he's feeling right now.

I've no idea if he finds what he's looking for, but after a second or two, he drops his lips back to mine and kisses me until we find our simultaneous releases. It's different to the previous ones he's given me. It's calmer, slower, but by no means any less earth-shattering.

"Come on, let's shower." He gets up and walks to the bathroom. My heart drops when I see the slight slump to his shoulders. Did I just disappoint him somehow?

He washes me thoroughly, but although he's attentive, I still can't help but feel like he's suddenly holding back. I want to ask, I'm desperate to, but I'm also aware that asking him too many questions will probably come with consequences: him asking some of his own. The thought of trying to explain everything has my heart racing in panic.

"HAVE YOU BEEN HERE BEFORE?" he asks when we step from the hotel hand-in-hand with bellies full of an incredible fried breakfast and fresh fruit.

"Yeah, I think I came here on a school trip years ago, but I hardly remember it. You?"

"No, never. I'm a Londoner through and through."

"You've never left?"

"Of course. I had holidays and stuff as a kid, but they were always abroad."

"That must have been nice," I say, thinking that I'd have loved to get out of our little town and experience some of the world.

"Yes and no."

"Oh?"

"Pass," he says. His hand tightens in mine, and I feel him physically shut down. I hate it, but at the same time part of me feels glad that I'm not the only one holding back. I feel less guilty about hiding my past from my possible future. *My future*, is that what this is?

We have an incredible morning visiting all the sights—Shakespeare's home and his wife's childhood home, along with others that are connected to his life.

The history is incredible, and I find myself picturing what it must have been like for him back then, writing such epic literature in such a stunning place. I don't have a creative bone in my body, but even I feel inspired being here.

We stop in a café for a light lunch before heading for the Church of the Holy Trinity. The building is out of this world. Its age, its history, everything about it just blows me away, and I'm not ashamed to admit that it drags a little emotion up into my throat as I stand and stare.

"Are you okay?" Joe whispers in my ear when he notices the tears threatening to spill from my eyes.

"Yeah. I'm good."

"Do you want to just sit for a bit?"

Nodding, I make my way over to the closest pew and slide along a little so he can sit beside me.

He's silent, allowing me the time I need to deal with my thoughts. I stare ahead at the chancel, taking in the ornate carved wood and the huge stones that make up the building. Suddenly, without realising, words start tumbling from my mouth.

"I'm married." Joe gasps beside me, but otherwise he does nothing other than to continue staring ahead and allow me to speak. "I was promised to him from as early as I can remember. I know that sounds incredibly old fashioned, but my parents were—are—really traditional. There was never any other option for me despite what I really wanted. I had no choice. I went along with the wedding, telling myself that I'd learn to like him, love him even, but it was never meant to be.

"I was terrified of disappointing my father. He...he has a terrible temper, and I could only imagine what my refusal would result in, so I toed the line, kept their secrets and swept their indiscretions under the carpet like I'd watched my mother do all my life. It was normal. It was my life. We lived in this little bubble, and the days just passed while I dreamt of other things.

"I knew from the get go that we weren't a match made in heaven, but there was no way I could shame my parents and leave. But then..." I trail off, not wanting to go into details of the reason I couldn't deal with it all anymore.

Joe blows out a long breath, and I find myself releasing the air I didn't know I was holding. I immediately feel lighter for confessing just a small part of the secret I'm forced to live with.

"My parents disowned me when I was fifteen, after they found out I was bi." His words are flat, cold, and my heart aches for the little boy that's clearly still so hurt by that.

"Arseholes," I mutter, not meaning for the word to come out aloud.

"I couldn't agree more. I mean, I'll be the first to admit that I was an awful teenager, but I didn't mean to make their lives hard. Well...not in the beginning. I was just trying to figure out who I was and where I fit in the world. Then they discovered me and the boy next door at the bottom of our garden, and I became and even bigger threat to their perfect life. The only way to stop me 'ruining everything' was to get rid of me."

We both sit in silence, the words we just said hanging heavy in the small space between us. The last few minutes might have been intense, but I feel better than I have in a long time.

I don't need to see his head turning to know he's looking at me, his intense stare burns into the side of my face.

Closing my eyes for a beat, I turn to look at him. His face is expressionless aside from his dark, haunted eyes.

"Thank you, for telling me. For trusting me."

"I do trust you, Joe. I just...it's hard for me to go back there."

"I get it. Take all the time you need."

"I hope you realise your parents missed out with the choice they made. They should be so proud of you."

He shrugs. "I'm not so sure about that, I've done some pretty fucked up shit over the years. I probably shouldn't even be allowed in a church." He glances around, and I can't help but laugh at the expression on his face.

"Everyone makes mistakes. It helps shape who we are."

"Do you think that when you think of *him*?" The disdain in his voice is clear, and it almost makes me regret telling him.

"I'm not sure he shaped me all that much aside from showing me exactly what I didn't want."

"You've only told me part of the story, Quinn, but I already know that you're one of the strongest women I know."

I shrug and look away. I don't see myself that way. As far as I'm concerned, I'm weak. Weak for living someone else's life for so long, weak for not following my own dreams, and weak for not exposing those around me for who they really were. But I don't voice any of that for fear of what he might say.

"Shall we move before this gets any heavier?" I ask, hoping for a reprieve from the seriousness of our lives.

"Sounds good."

Joe slides from the wooden pew and holds out his hand for me. I don't hesitate in placing mine in his.

Once I'm standing, he leans down and whispers in my ear. "Thank you for not freaking out."

I glance up at him, wondering if the truth about his life has been haunting him as much as my own has been.

"You can tell me anything. I won't judge. Our pasts are our pasts. I'd much rather spend my time looking forward than back."

CHAPTER FIFTEEN

I swear I blink and our weekend together is over. Nothing more is said about our confessions in the church, and I couldn't be more grateful. I'm glad I did it. I wanted to show to Joe that I was trying to let him in, just like he was me, but that doesn't mean I'm ready to spill any more yet. The time is coming. I can only avoid it and the media for so long. With every minute that ticks around, I know I'm a minute closer to another phone call from Detective Barker and reliving my old life in front of a judge. As much as I want justice for the people they've hurt, I also can't imagine explaining what monsters they are to their faces. They're men I should love, men I should try to protect. Not testify against.

A shudder runs down my spine, and I pause my packing.

Joe's hands land on my hips, and he pulls me back into him. His lips trail up my neck until he nibbles around my ear. "I'm not ready to leave this room." He doesn't need to say the words, the feeling of his erection digging into my arse tells me everything I need to know.

"Me neither." My head rolls to the side as his kisses continue.

He parts his lips and his tongue sweeps across my skin. My heart pounds and my temperature soars, despite only having a Joe-induced orgasm less than thirty minutes ago in the shower.

The atmosphere is heavy as Joe drags both our bags from the bed and we walk out of our little sanctuary.

I let out a giant sigh as the hotel room door clicks shut behind us. Joe squeezes my hand a little tighter in support.

We check out, find his van, and almost before I've had time to think we're on our way back towards the city.

"So your boss doesn't mind you taking your work van away for the weekend?" I ask again, seeing as I didn't get an answer when I asked yesterday.

"I sure hope not, because I didn't exactly ask," he says with a laugh. "I'm sure it'll be fine, my boss is banging my best friend. She can help me make him see things from my perspective." He visibly cringes as the words pass his lips.

"Tell me about her?"

"Who? Lauren?"

"Yeah."

"She's..." he sighs, a small smile playing on his lips as he thinks of her. "She's incredible. One of the strongest women I know, and not just because she's put up with my shit all these years. We met at a pretty low point in both of our lives, almost like fate. She's been my rock."

"She really means a lot to you, doesn't she?" I don't know why I ask; it's obvious from his tone how important she is to him.

"You've no idea."

A weird feeling twists my insides. Is that...is that jealousy? The more I try not to think about it, the more it starts to fester.

"Have you known each other long?"

"Six years or so. I turned up at the office of the company I work for and she was there, the boss' daughter."

"I thought she was banging the boss?"

"Long story, but her dad passed away and Ben took over. They now live together, and I'm waiting for a proposal to happen any moment now. What about you, did you leave a best friend behind?"

Sadness washes over me as reality hits me once again. "No. Eddie is actually the closest thing I've had to a real friend in a very long time."

"Eddie?" he asks, his brows drawn together when he glances over at me.

"Yeah. Mr. Boring."

"Oh, him. I wouldn't have put you two together."

"He's a good guy. He set me up with my flat and got me the job. I just have to look past the fact that he's from my previous life and knows things about me that I'd rather no one did."

"Even me?"

I blow out a long, slow breath. "I'll tell you everything, just... just not all at once."

Reaching across the centre console, he takes my hand in his, his thumb rubbing the inside of my wrist. It's a move I've never felt before, and it's more comforting than I want to admit.

The van falls into silence, but it's not uncomfortable. I run the events of the past couple of days around my head in order to keep my past out, and I can't help but wish it was Friday night again and that we were driving in the opposite direction.

We're in the city long before I'm ready, and even sooner Joe is pulling up into my building's car park.

We both remain seated. The only sounds in the van are that of our deep breathing. I don't want to get out and, from the tense set of his body, I don't think he wants to allow me to leave either.

The moment I step out of this car, reality is going to come

crashing back down on me. Tomorrow is the start of a new week. I've got to walk into college with my head held high like I haven't spent the weekend with one of my students. I've got to pretend that I'm not as bad as the people I left behind. That thought has my heart racing.

I'm not one of them.

I'm nothing like them.

This is...this is more than the nightmares and ruined childhoods they caused.

"Quinn, it's okay." Joe's warm palm gently touches my cheek and encourages me to turn towards him.

"We shouldn't be doing this, Joe. It's wrong."

"Nothing, and I mean nothing, about this feels wrong." His thumb brushes over my bottom lip. "If it's too much, just tell me and I'll quit. I'll see if I can find a course somewhere else or something, but I'm not allowing it to come between us."

"You can't do that. This is your dream, your future."

"Bettering myself and improving my career is only part of my future. Right now, there's something else I need more."

His words hang heavy between us. I desperately want to agree and allow myself to see where this thing between us might go, but I'm scared. Terrified actually.

"Joe, I—"

"Let's not do this now. Let me walk you up?"

I should say no, but when I open my mouth, those aren't the words that fall out. "Sure."

By the time I pull myself from the passenger seat, Joe is already walking towards me, having retrieved my bag from the back of his van.

"If you're lucky, I'll give you a little something to tide you over until after work tomorrow."

Ignoring the heat that rushes through my body, I turn to look up at him. "I don't remember agreeing to seeing you tomorrow night."

"I wasn't aware I needed your permission."

I want to argue, but the sight of the front door of my building makes me lose focus. The panels where the glass used to be is now two panels of plywood, and the metal by the lock is very obviously buckled.

My heart jumps into my throat, and my stomach turns over. I don't need any more information to know who it was that caused that.

I can feel it.

As I go to take a step forward, I swear my fucking bones tremble with fear.

Will he be upstairs waiting for me? Was my paranoia warranted? Have I been being followed?

A million and one thoughts and fears hit me at once as I fight to drag in the breath I desperately need while not trying to look like a total head case in front of Joe.

"What the fuck is wrong with people?" he asks, walking us up to the door and giving it no more than a gentle shove to make it open. "Fucking kids."

If I were a little more focused on him right now, I might make a joke about the kind of teenager he was, because from the things he's hinted at this weekend, breaking into a flat building is probably tame for what he got up to.

"They probably just wanted to steal the post or something," I mutter, not believing a word of it. "I'm okay from here if you want to head off home."

"I thought I just promised you another orgasm."

"I know, but I've already taken up all of your weekend. I'm sure you've got better things to be doing."

"Absolutely not. Trust me when I say that there's nowhere I'd rather be, or anything else I'd rather be doing right now than be with you."

I nod but I don't really register the words. I know I should be swooning, but I'm too focused on what I'm going to find on the other side of the door.

"I know what you're trying to do, Quinn, and it won't work."

"What's that?" I ask, feigning innocence.

"You're trying to hide the fact that you're scared by pushing me away."

Damn him.

"I...I..." Sucking in a deep breath, I allow the fear I'm trying to stamp down to rumble down my spine.

"What are you scared of?"

"I'm just being silly. Come on, I'm sure it's just a broken door."

He looks at me curiously, but after pausing for a beat he gestures for me to walk into the building.

Everything looks as it usually does as we climb the stairs. The terrible graffiti is still covering the walls. The same bare patches on the steps stare up at me. Every single thing is exactly the same as every other time I've been here, until we're facing my door.

"Fuck," Joe barks, but I'm frozen in fear at the sight of my door ajar.

He was here.

This isn't some kind of shitty luck that they chose my empty flat to break into. This has been planned. Planned to ensure I'm terrified in the hope that I'll bend to his wishes to retract everything I'd accused him of.

Not happening.

My body rattles with fear, but I refuse to allow him to continue to ruin my life. I muster up some strength from somewhere and take a step forward.

"Quinn, wait."

I ignore Joe's call and push my door open.

Everything looks exactly as I left it.

My only item worth any money, my laptop, is still sitting on the coffee table where I put it after work on Friday night.

"What the hell?" Joe asks, stepping into the flat and casting his eyes around the room.

"Maybe they got scared off after they broke in," I offer as an explanation. He nods, accepting it as a possibility, but I know better.

This wasn't kids, and no one was scared off.

This is a warning.

My stomach turns, bile burning up my throat as I think about him being here. In the one safe place I've got.

"Come home with me tonight."

"What?" I ask, not registering the words he's saying as I stand frozen in the middle of my living room.

"Come home with me. We'll sort out a locksmith from there."

"No, I—"

"No arguing. I'm not leaving you here." His eyes scan over my face, and I hate to think of the terrified girl he probably sees. "Grab what you need for work tomorrow."

I stare at him for a second or two. I desperately want to argue, but when his eyebrow twitches in a 'don't start with me' gesture, I swallow down the words and turn towards the bathroom.

Stepping into the room, I go to gather up a few bits that I didn't take with me this weekend, but I'm frozen in my tracks.

I try not to react, but I can't stop a scream from passing my lips at the sight.

"Quinn?"

"Sorry, spider," I shout back, pushing the door closed so he can't look into the room.

I stare at the mirror hanging over the basin and fight to keep the contents of my stomach where they should be.

*I'm watching you...*is scrawled across the glass in red lipstick. The arsehole's even finished it off with a little kiss.

My fists clench until my nails begin to cut into my skin.

The longer I stare at the words, the more my anger starts to bubble up within me. How dare he? How fucking dare he force his way into my new life in an attempt to scare me?

Racing forward, I grab a packet of face wipes that are sitting on the counter, pull a few out and start scrubbing.

I need him gone. Out of my life and out of my head. I've already spent enough years being controlled by him. I refuse to allow him to continue to do so.

Suddenly, the thought of the court case that's to come doesn't seem so daunting. This man needs putting behind bars—he has done for a long time. How he's allowed to roam the streets after all the evidence that's piling up against him is beyond me.

"Are you okay?" Joe's concerned voice fills the small room and something inside me immediately settles. I need to tell him everything. If that monster's after me, then I need him to know the truth.

"Yeah, just coming." I double-check the mirror to ensure there's no evidence left behind before pulling the door open and stepping from the room.

THE RIDE to Joe's place is in silence. I might have tried convincing him that that was just an everyday burglary, but I'm pretty sure I'm not fooling him. The way his fingers grip the wheel and the hard set of his jaw tells me he's more than suspicious, and

I'm incredibly grateful he's managed to hold off the questions. For now at least.

He pulls up outside a pretty standard looking apartment building and drags our stuff from the back before guiding me towards the entrance.

There's an out of order sign on the lift as we pass in favour of the stairs, and I follow him up to the third floor. This place isn't flashy by any stretch of the imagination, but it's a hell of a lot better than the building I live in. There's no graffiti over the walls, the paint looks relatively fresh, and the flooring isn't chipped and fading.

"Come on, we should have the place to ourselves."

"Oh, you don't live alone?"

"No, this is my friend's place. I'm currently crashing in her spare room, but she's met someone and will be out with him."

"Okay." I nod and follow him into the flat. If he didn't tell me a woman lived here, then it would be instantly obvious. There are candles, cushions, and little girly trinkets everywhere. It's cute, exactly how I'd want my home to look if I actually had one and a little money

I jump a mile when Joe drops the bags to the floor with a bang. I thought I'd managed to put what happened at my place behind me on the drive over, but it seems I might just be lying to myself.

"Fuck." His eyes run the length of me, and for a second I fear he's going to send me away. But when they return to mine a few shades darker, I realise it's not with fear but something else entirely.

He takes a step forward. His hand glides across my jaw and his fingers thread in my hair so he can tilt my head to just the right angle for him to slam his lips on mine and plunge his tongue between.

His kiss is exactly what I need to forget. I lift my arms around his neck at the same time he lifts me and presses me back against the wall.

All thoughts of the man inside my flat this weekend leave as he kisses me like he might die without it.

I moan with desire as he trails his lips across my jaw and begins sucking on the sensitive skin below my ear.

"Let me make you forget."

"Yes."

"Let me make you feel safe."

A noise rumbles up my throat, and when it erupts, I can only describe it as a needy purr. Whatever it is, it makes Joe smile against my throat, his weekend long scruff scratching at my sensitive skin and sending shivers down my spine.

His fingers make quick work of unzipping my coat before his palms cup my heavy, needy breasts. My head falls back and he makes the most of my exposed neck. As good as his hands feel, I need them on my skin.

"More, Joe. More."

He pulls back and his eyes are wild with desire. "I'll give you everything, Quinn." His eyes lock onto mine, and the intensity and honesty within them make me want to look away, to break our connection, but it's too strong. All I can do is stare back, hoping like hell he's not going to break me even worse than my past tried to.

He's totally lost one second and then seems to remember exactly what he's meant to be doing the next.

My skirt is pushed up around my waist, and my boot covered legs loosen around him so he can slip his hand between us.

Like an expert, he pops the button on his jeans and pushes them and his boxers down his thighs before pulling the lace of my knickers aside.

The head of his cock nudges against my entrance. I expect him to push straight inside, but instead I find him leaning forward so he can whisper in my ear. "I don't have all that much to give you. But this," he surges forward, making me gasp, "this I can give you until my last breath."

It's his admission and the uncertainty in his words that make my heart tumble. He pulls back slightly, his hands on my arse squeezing almost painfully. His eyes find mine once again, and I find everything he's not saying staring right back at me. My chest constricts and I'm under no illusion that right there, in the hallway of his flat, is the moment I surrender to exactly how I feel about this bad boy nerd.

"Joe, I—" I start, feeling compelled to attempt to tell him how I feel, but my words are cut off by his lips.

"Just feel," he whispers against me.

I do as I'm told.

My head falls back against the wall, and I focus on where we're connected. Sparks shoot off around my body as he pulls almost all the way back out of me.

"Please, please," I chant, needing to feel him filling me and stretching me once again.

My begging must snap his restraint, because he lets me slide down the wall slightly, allowing him to hit me even deeper when he thrusts.

He grunts when he slams deep inside me but doesn't stop this time. He pounds into me over and over, and I can't get enough.

My thighs tremble around him, my skin flushes, and the tightening of my centre tells me that I'm about to explode. My fingernails dig into his clothed shoulders as I prepare for what's about to hit me when the atmosphere around me shifts.

What the...? Dragging my eyes open, I have to blink a few times before the two figures standing, gawping at us come into focus. Embarassment hits me, knowing we've been caught. I'm mortified to be found in such a position, especially after having to keep what's been growing between us a secret for so long.

"Fuck. I thought you said it would be safe," I whisper, my voice quivering as I try to hold it together while looking at their shocked faces. The guy casts his eyes aside, clearly giving us the privacy we deserve, whereas the woman is looking between the two of us like we're the most fascinating thing she's ever seen.

"I didn't think...fuck. Some privacy?" Joe's eyes don't leave me. I can feel his stare burning into the side of my face as he talks. It's does nothing to quash my embarassment.

"Yeah, shit. Sorry. Let's go to your place," the woman, who I can only assume is Joe's flatmate, says, wrapping her hand around the man beside her's forearm and slowly backing towards the door. At the last minute, Joe turns to look at her and some weird silent conversation passes between them.

Silence hangs heavy between us long after the door bangs shut.

"I'm sorry. I'm so fucking sorry. I didn't think..." he trails off.

"It's okay," I lie. In reality, it's anything but fine. Being caught with my legs wrapped around one of my students was the reality check I really didn't want.

"We shouldn't be doing this, Joe. This is wrong."

He doesn't want to, but when I tense my legs he releases his hold on me. Once I'm on my feet, I pull my dress back down and start pacing.

My life is already one big disaster, and here I am allowing one of my students—okay, an adult student, although I'm sure that won't make much difference in the eyes of my boss—to fuck me against the wall. I need my job. It's the only thing I've got.

"I need...I need...fuck." Just the thought of telling him that this is over threatens to tear my heart in two. It's only made worse when I look up and take in the devastated expression on his face.

"Don't do this, Quinn. Please, don't do this. Erica's one of my best friends, she won't have an issue."

"It's not about her, Joe. I'm sure she's lovely and only wants the best for you but...this is my life. My career is my life, that's all I have right now, and I can't risk losing it for something..."

"For something what, Quinn? This isn't some big game we're playing here. I'm serious about this...about you. And I can say with total honesty that I've never said that to another person in my life. I won't allow what we have here to ruin your career."

"How? How can you stand there and promise me that? I'm breaking the one rule I always said I'd never touch. It's goes against everything I've ever...fuck," I shout, dropping my head into my hands. *You're just as bad as them,* a little voice sings in my ear. "No, no, no."

I lose myself in my panic. I've no idea how long I stand there chanting, trying to convince myself that I'm different, that this is different, but when I come back to myself I'm wrapped in Joe's strong arms.

"It's okay, babe."

"I should leave." My voice is weak and pathetic, and I hate it.

"I'm not allowing you out of here until I know a locksmith has sorted your door out. I need to know you're safe when I'm not with you." I want to tell him that I'm not safe full stop while my past is lurking, but I keep my lips shut.

"Stay with me tonight. Let me order us dinner and you can sleep here. Tomorrow I'll get a locksmith and extra security added to your door, and then if you need some space," he says through gritted teeth, the muscle in his jaw twitching ferociously, "you can take what you need and I'll be able to sleep, knowing you're safe."

I want to argue, but what he's proposing is too tempting. I should walk out of his front door and not look back but...I can't.

"Okay," I whisper, and his arms tighten around me.

OUR NIGHT together is quiet at best. Joe allows me the space I need to try to process everything, but I fear no amount of time is going to help me figure this out. I want him. I want him like I've never wanted anything in my life, but is it enough to give up on the only thing I've got left? The only thing I've ever really had? He keeps saying that he'll quit, but I can't allow that. He deserves this second chance at his education. He deserves to follow his dreams. It's just all so fucked up, and what I'm running from doesn't even feature. When *he* shows his face again, and I know he will if he's gone to the effort of finding me, then shit's really going to hit the fan.

We don't finish what we started earlier against the wall. Joe doesn't even attempt it. Instead, when we fall into his bed, he just pulls me close and falls asleep with his arm locked around my waist and his cock snugly pressed against my arse.

I lie there all night, trying to make sense of everything, but by the time daylight starts to show through the gap in the curtains, I'm no closer to making any kind of decision.

There's a heavy tension between us as we both get ready for work. Joe knows what's coming, and I can't help but think he's trying to put off the inevitable, hoping that I'll have forgotten. Sadly, that's nowhere near the case.

"Can I drop you off?"

"Around the corner, yeah."

I follow him down to his van, emotion clogging my throat, knowing that our time is passing me by too quickly, but I know I'm doing the right thing.

Neither of us says anything as Joe fights with the rush hour traffic to get me to college, and when we pull up at the curb around the back of the building, we both let out heavy sighs.

"When can I see you again?"

"You'll be in class Thursday, right?"

"Let me quit. I'll re-enroll somewhere else. Please, Quinn. It doesn't need to be like this."

"Just give me a few days. This weekend has been...intense. I'll see you Thursday, and we'll talk after."

"Promise?"

"Promise."

I walk away with a heavy heart. I want the promise I made to be true, but really I've no idea. My head's a mess, and as I walk away with his stare making my spine tingle, I fight the need to turn and run back into his arms.

The day drags. Jodi looks like she's not slept or eaten all weekend, although I don't spot any more bruises. I'm not stupid enough to believe that they're not hiding below her clothes. I know she's been in for a meeting, but she doesn't say anything or give away that she clearly must know it was me who reported it.

It's just after lunchtime when Eddie knocks on my classroom door and walks inside with something in his hand.

"Did you have a good weekend?" he asks curiously when he reaches my desk.

Thoughts of my weekend has tears burning the back of my throat. "Y-yeah, thank you. You?"

"Same old, same old. Here, these were just dropped off for you." His eyebrow lifts as he hands me a set of keys.

"My flat was broken into. I've had all the locks redone." *Or Joe has.* I try to ignore the feelings that threaten to bubble up, knowing that he's sorted all of this for me today.

"Oh shit. Everything seemed normal when I popped around on Saturday afternoon. Was anything stolen?"

"Not that I could see, but I didn't stay there long after I

discovered it." I ignore the fact that he was there, hoping he doesn't ask where I was.

"Where did you go if you didn't stay?"

"Oh...uh...a friend's." I say it with a wince, because Eddie knows full well that he's my only friend.

His face hardens. "You know I'm only at the end of the phone if you need anything." There's something different in his tone, and I fear he's already more suspicious about what I'm up to than he should be.

"I do, thank you."

Thankfully, one of my students puts their hand up to ask a question and our conversation comes to an end before he shows himself out. The last thing I need is Eddie poking his nose in any more and discovering what I've really been doing. He found me this job when I needed it the most; I'm sure he could take it away from me just as quickly. He likes to make out that he's my friend, but a huge part of him isn't all that different from those I left behind. His reputation is more important than a lot of other things I'd consider much more important. I can only imagine how he'd feel if I were to bring scandal down on his department after he grovelled to employ me.

I'm a nervous wreck as I make the short walk from the tube station to my building later that night. It's dark and raining too heavily for the fact that I don't have an umbrella or even a hood on my coat. Water is running down my face by the time I get to the still broken front door. I guess that wasn't really for Joe to get involved with.

My heart's in my throat as I climb the stairs.

It'll be fine. I've got new locks. He can't hurt me.

I've got my new keys clasped so tightly in my hand that the metal is cutting into my skin, but I don't register the pain as my eyes dart around to see if anything is untoward.

I come to a stop in front of my door, relaxing a little when I see the two new locks. My hand trembles as I lift it to slide the key in and find out which key is for which.

I just get the key in the second lock and am about to push the door open when a squeak sounds out from behind me.

My body tenses and my spine straightens, but I don't get a chance to turn.

"Good evening, Elizabeth. You wouldn't believe how much I've missed my wife."

My mouth opens, ready to scream, but it's too late because his hand comes down on my mouth, successfully cutting off any chance I had of getting anyone's attention.

He pushes the door open and then forces me through before slamming it behind us and cutting me off from the rest of the world.

"Oh, princess. We're going to have so much fun."

A blinding pain to my head is the last thing I remember before I'm sucked into a blissfully silent darkness.

ACKNOWLEDGMENTS

I've been looking forward to finding out a little more about Joe since I first introduced him in *Losing the Forbidden*. His story has been a long time coming, and for a while it was really up in the air as to who he was going to fall for, but the moment I realised that he craved something more from his life there was only one woman for the job. A woman who possibly has more secrets and a past she wants to keep hidden even more than Joe does.

I hope you've enjoyed the first part of Joe and Quinn's story. There is still so much more to discover about these two before they get the chance at a happily-ever-after.

This series is very quickly coming to an end, but don't worry, I've already got plans for what's coming next. All will be revealed in the next book (I hope!).

As always, I have so many people to thank. My long-suffering beta readers who have been waiting for Joe's story for what must feel like forever, Deanna, Lindsay, Suzanne and Tracy, thank you so much for dropping everything to find out a few of Joe's secrets.

A huge thank you to Samantha for helping make my life so much easier and keeping me in check and organised. I'm seriously not sure how I ever coped without you.

Eyelyn, as always, thank you for believing in my characters and helping me make them as good as they can be.

Paige, for being the final set of eyes and polishing everything up at the last minute.

And last but not least, all my readers for supporting me on this crazy journey and for loving my characters as much as I do.

Until next time,

Tracy xo

CHASING TEMPTATION

CHAPTER ONE

Doing as she asked is harder than I was anticipating. I've never chased a woman in my life. I'm usually the one trying to shake the clingers, but sitting here, waiting for the clock to tick around so I can leave for my class, I wouldn't be opposed to wrapping my arms around her the second I walk into the room and never letting go.

It's been three days since I dropped her off for work on Monday morning, and I've not heard a squeak from her since. I kinda hoped she might at least message me to let me know she's okay, but apparently her need for space meant as much distance as she could put between us as possible.

I can't really argue; she's got shit going on, and this thing between us has been intense to say the least. She's my teacher, for fuck's sake.

The plan was to re-do a couple of my GCSEs, rewrite a couple of the fuck tonne of mistakes I've made in my life, and see if I'm actually competent enough to consider further education and possibly a serious qualification that might allow me to be more than just a builder.

Okay, so I'm not *just* a builder—my job description says I'm a site agent—but I'm under no illusion that I only got that title because I was in my old boss' back pocket.

I was a mess the day I stumbled into Johnson & Son's office. If the boss had turned out to be anyone but my dad's old mate, I doubt that anyone in their right mind would have given me a job. I was seventeen, covered in tattoos, hungover, and I probably smelled like the back end of a rhino, but he gave me a chance.

Or rather, he gave me what I needed in order for me to do his dirty work.

The second I saw him, I should have known he wasn't offering me a job out of the goodness of his heart. The man had been a friend of my father's; anyone who spent any time with that man was obviously of dubious character. I should have known better than to agree to dance with the devil. It was only later that I was to learn that he was probably worse than my father ever was. He was the master manipulator, and I had no choice but to be his bitch. He could take everything away from me in one swift move if I disobeyed him.

Weirdly, he was the only man I'd listened to in my entire life.

But it wasn't through choice.

It was through necessity.

Looking back now, I can't be all that angry. Yes, he played me, but he wasn't hiding it from me; the person he was really playing was his daughter, Lauren. She's the reason I can't be angry about it all, because he gave me her.

I'd had a few friends growing up but nothing lifelong. The guys at the pretentious all boys private school my parents sent me to only wanted to know me because I knew how to get my hands on alcohol and good weed. Then, when my gran enrolled me into her local comprehensive, I was the bad boy all the 'cool' kids wanted to befriend and all the girls wanted to bed. I certainly got an education from that place, although not in the way of qualifications. I learned that girls would go even further out of their way than boys to get what they wanted, and it was where I discovered that really, I didn't care what sex they were as long as they were willing. I'd lose myself and my shitty life in them in a heartbeat.

I've never been embarrassed by the way I've lived my life or the bad, slutty choices I've made.

Not until I walked into her classroom and her dark, innocent eyes stared into mine. In that moment, I wished everyone I'd ever touched would vanish. She was too good for me, and I was desperate to be worthy. The longer she looked at me, the more I wanted her.

I told myself it was lust at first sight, but even in those very first moments I knew it was more than that. Yes, I wanted to bend her over her desk and fuck her until she cried out my name—that was a given—but more than that I wanted to pull her into my arms and tell her that I'd take away the fear that was oozing from her.

My phone buzzes beside me, and I almost manage to crack a smile at seeing my best friend's picture staring back at me.

> Lauren: What time are you showing your face tonight? Erica won't forgive you if you bail.

Tonight's my flat mate's birthday. I do need to be there after everything she's been through recently, but nothing will drag me away from seeing Quinn tonight. I've promised Lauren that I'll get to the restaurant as soon as I can, but I don't think she believes me.

I've kept my Thursday night dalliances to myself. I thought I was crazy when I filled out the application online to go back to school, and I had no idea what those around me would think. Lauren knows about my past, and I've no doubt she'd support me no matter what, but everyone else...I'm not so sure. They don't know what a fuck up I was, and, quite honestly, I'd rather not have to revisit that time in my life.

I reply, promising that I'll be there. What I really want to do is convince Quinn to come with me after class and introduce her to my friends. This thing between us has only been going on for a few days at the most, but already I'm sick of hiding her.

It's still too early to leave but fuck it. I grab my leather jacket and my bag and head out of the flat. I usually take the tube, but seeing as it's pissing it down with rain and with the hope that I'll be able to get Quinn away quicker after class, I unlock the van door and jump in. It's meant to be for business use only, but what's Ben going to do? Fire me? Lauren wouldn't allow it.

One of the benefits of having a bestie who's banging the boss.

I park a little down the street, thinking it'll make Quinn happy later, and slowly make my way inside.

I'm the first to arrive, not that it's a surprise, and her classroom door is shut. I clench and unclench my fists with my need to go barrelling in and pull her into my arms. The fact that she's in the middle of teaching a class is the only thing that stops me. After three days, I'm fucking desperate to feel her body pressed up against mine and to breathe in her sweet scent.

A couple of others I recognise join me. I nod at them in greeting, but no words pass my lips. Befriending my classmates has never been that high up on my to do list. Getting up close and personal with the teacher, though...that one's right up there.

Eventually her class comes to an end and students start filing out of the room. My heart pounds as the anticipation of seeing her gets the better of me.

Shoving my hands in my pockets to stop me from pushing the

students leaving the room aside in my haste to get in, I wait as patiently as possible.

When it looks like the last couple of stragglers have left, I take a step forward, beating anyone else to the doorway. They might be keen to learn or whatever, but my need is much more important.

Walking through the doorway, my heart's in my fucking throat. I need to look at her, to stare into her kind, dark eyes and take in her soft curves. I've missed her so fucking much this week and right now, seconds away from laying my eyes on her, I'm not too afraid to admit it.

Dragging in a much needed deep breath, I prepare to look at her—only when I lift my eyes, she's not the one rubbing writing off the white board.

"Where's Miss Smith?" I demand, walking straight to the front of the room. I was concerned about her going home after her flat was broken into. I told myself that I was just being paranoid, but now with her not here, it's sending my imagination into overdrive.

Eddie spins, his eyes narrowing on me, disgust clear within them.

"None of your business. I suggest you take your seat."

"Bullshit. Tell me where she is."

Something flashes in his eyes, and it's enough to tell me that he doesn't know the answer to my demand.

"If she's in trouble and you've done fuck all about it, I'll—"

"I don't know," he admits quietly, his skin paler than it was just a few moments ago.

"You don't... Fuck. When was the last time you saw her?"

"Monday."

"Fuck." My hands go to my hair as I try not to panic. I'm aware I've got a class full of Quinn's students piling in behind me and that Eddie has no clue there's anything between us—or at least he didn't until a few seconds ago. "Did you know her flat was broken into?"

"Y-yes." Guilt twists his features.

"And you didn't think to check up on her, seeing as she hasn't turned up to work since Monday?"

"I meant to, it's just—"

"I don't want your fucking excuses." With that, I turn and march from the classroom. I feel the stares of everyone in the room burning into my back, but I don't care what any of them think or what they might have overheard.

All that matters right now is Quinn.

Please be in your flat. Please be in your flat, I repeat on the drive over. I don't remember any of the journey; my head's too much of a mess with all the things that could have happened. I don't register any traffic lights or roundabouts as I manoeuvre my way through the London traffic. The only thing I know is that I break every single speed limit in my need to get to her.

The second I pull up into her building's car park, I grab the spare keys the locksmith gave me for her flat and jump from the van without bothering to turn the engine off or shut the door. The only thing I can focus on is finding her, and finding her safe.

She's kept her past so close to her chest, but the fear that was always in her eyes and the fact that she was always looking over her shoulder was enough to tell me that she didn't want to come face to face with it again. She tried to play off the break in, but I saw the terror in her eyes. It's the reason I refused to allow her to stay, but it's not like I could have kept her locked up safe after. She felt the need to come back here, and all I could do was trust her. Fucking wish I hadn't, mind you.

The front door's still fucked when I get to it. I swing it open with such force that it slams back against the wall. If there were any glass still in it, I might be concerned with the force of the collision, but as it is, I don't need to worry.

Taking the stairs three at a time, I race towards her door. I breathe a sigh of relief when I find it closed and locked.

She's just ill inside. She's safe. She'll be there. No matter how many times I repeat those words in my head, I know they're not true. This is bigger than her being so ill she's not phoned into work or let Eddie know. She told me herself that he's her closest friend, so even if she wanted space from me, he should know what's going on with her.

Shoving the first key into the lock, I pray I'll hear her shout, but there's nothing but silence and the sound of the lock releasing. I repeat the action with the other and swing the door open.

My heart's pounding in my chest as I try to make out what's in front of me.

It's pitch black with the curtains pulled shut.

Running my hand along the wall beside me, I eventually find a switch and bathe the small space in light.

I quickly glance around. Everything's normal. But then I notice something.

The soup and now mouldy bread she left out before our trip at the weekend is still sitting on her coffee table.

Surely she'd have cleaned that up.

I walk over, my eyes darting all over the place to try to piece together what's happened. To my left, I spot her laptop bag dropped randomly on the floor, a pile of papers sliding out of it where it's not zipped up. It's only when I take another step forward that something else catches my eye.

Bending, I run my finger over the spots on the old carpet floor. The colour of the stains has my heart threatening to beat out of my chest. It's fucking blood.

Standing, I back away towards the door.

"What the fuck happened here, Quinn? And where the fuck are you?"

Turning, I slam the door shut behind me and race back in the direction I came. Quinn told me that there's only one person in her present who knows anything about her past. He's the only one who's going to be able to help me right now. I just have to hope she was right and that Eddie is as good a friend as she thought.

THE SHOCK on his face when I storm back into the classroom is even more evident than when I confronted him not even an hour ago.

"She's not fucking there." My voice booms across the room, causing everyone to stop what they're doing and turn my way.

"I'm in the middle of something." Eddie winces at my intrusion, but I see that concern in his eyes again.

"I really don't give a fuck. She's in trouble. You know it as well as I do. But the difference is that you're the only one who knows why and where she might be. Now give these motherfuckers something to keep them busy. You need to start talking."

CHAPTER TWO

My body's vibrating with nervous energy and the need to hurt someone as I wait for Eddie to give my usual class something to keep them entertained. He rushes through his instructions, but I'm not sure how much that's due to his concern or the fact that I'm staring at him with my muscles pulled tight and my fists clenched, ready to fight.

He's made no secret of the fact he doesn't like me, or at least the image I portray. I don't fit into his perfect world of designer suits, pocket squares, and tie pins.

After what feels like a fucking year, he's walking towards me and gestures for me to follow him to his office.

"Where's he taken her, Eddie?" I demand the second he has the door shut.

"I don't know what you're talking about."

"Cut the act. I might only know the very basics, but I know that you know everything. She's been terrified for weeks that he's going to find her, and now she's fucking gone. Where has he taken her?"

"How the fuck should I know? She's been the only one I've had contact with since I left that place."

"But you know where *that place* is. Tell me that. It's got to be a good start."

"Earlington Manor. It's a private school." The name sounds vaguely familiar, but the only private school I know is the hellhole my parents sent me to, and that's not it. "Her father was the head and her husband the head of humanities."

"And why would they want her back?" I need him to fill in a few of my blanks if I have any chance of understanding what the fuck is going on right now.

"Have you not seen the news recently?"

I cast my mind back to the image of Quinn freaking out in our hotel room while I was watching the news.

"Earlington Manor," I say out loud, more to myself than Eddie. "Sex scandal, child abuse, massive enquiry—"

"The one and only. She exposed them. Managed to get evidence that her dad covered up one of her husband's most recent indiscretions and went to the police with it. Then she ran."

"Fuck."

I fall down onto the chair behind me as the information sinks in.

It makes so much sense. It's why she was so against us. She thought that by being with me, she was becoming them.

"Fuck," I repeat, not quite believing what I'm hearing but knowing full well that it's true.

"That place was hell on earth. A place full of wealth where money can buy anything and any wrongdoing can be covered up without a second thought."

"Where is it? We need to go there. We need to find her."

"We?"

"Yes, motherfucker. *We.* Don't you care about her? She told me you were her only friend. Don't you want to know she's safe as much as I do?"

"Yes but—"

"But what? Please don't tell me that you're too much of a stuck-up, pocket square wearing prick to get your hands dirty to save her."

"Uh…"

"Fuck this. I'll Google it. I'll get to her with or without your help."

Turning away from him, I wrench the door open with enough force that it could well come off its hinges before running out of the building and towards where I abandoned my van on the double yellow lines out the front of the college.

By some fucking miracle I've not got a ticket—not that it's my biggest concern right now.

Pulling my phone from my pocket, I type in the school name Eddie just gave me and immediately news headlines light up my screen.

Head teacher covering for his own and his teacher's child abuse.
Lies, betrayal, and abuse uncovered.
Hundreds of victims of abuse at Earlington Manor are coming forward.

"Jesus," I mutter. No wonder she wanted nothing more to do with the place.

Eventually I manage to find the school's website amongst all the news sites, and I locate the postcode at the bottom of the homepage.

Lake District. Nothing like making it easy for me.

Plugging it into my SatNav, I wait for it to find the location and balk when I see the estimated time.

Five motherfucking hours.

"Sorry, Erica, but this is way more important," I say into the small space around me before slamming my foot down on the accelerator and flying into the middle lane, much to the other drivers' annoyance.

It takes me forever to get out of the city and onto the motorway. The SatNav's telling me that I won't be there until gone midnight. I desperately want to go storming in and rescue my girl, but the reality of the situation is that the only address I have is that of a school, and the chance of her being there is probably pretty slim.

It's the longest drive of my life. By the time I pass the 'Welcome to the Lake District' sign, my entire body is locked up with tension. I need to let off some steam but anything less than ploughing my fist into Quinn's ex-husband won't suffice. He's been harassing her from a distance for weeks. It's time he got a taste of his own medicine.

The winding country roads are seemingly endless, but eventually, just as I hit the crest of a hill, this huge old manor house comes into view.

"Wow, pretentious," I mutter as I drive through the entrance, surprised that I'm not stopped by giant gilded gates. They'd fit right in.

Parking up, I climb from the van and stretch out my sore muscles. Huge spotlights illuminate the grand building, and I'm under no illusion that I'm probably the focus of a million CCTV cameras right now, but still, I can't help walking up to the closest window and peeking inside. It's an office. A huge mahogany desk sits in the centre with a massive computer screen on the top. There are a few filing cabinets and an antique looking chair pushed behind the desk but nothing that helps me out with my little quest.

The sound of a barking dog forces me back into my van. The last thing I need is to be wrestled to the ground by a guard dog.

Driving away from the school, I do a tour of the local village. The houses are beyond huge; I guess they would be if they could afford for their kids to go to an establishment like that. I wonder how all the parents feel, watching the news stories play out, knowing the amount of money they've spent to send their little angel to be cared for by a bunch of paedophiles. A shudder runs down my spine. I hated my time at private school, but I never experienced or was aware of that kind of treatment from the teachers. The only kind of thing they could ever be accused of would be turning the other cheek at all the things we got up to.

There's no evidence of life or even a bed and breakfast, so when I come to the decision that I'm at a bit of a dead end, I pull over in a dark layby and tip my chair back as far as it will go in the hope that I might get a bit of sleep. I know it's wishful thinking. As I lie there, all kinds of images run through my head about where she could be or what could be happening to her. If her husband, and her dad for that fact, don't bat an eyelid at hurting innocent kids then they're not going to think twice about punishing Quinn for going against them, that I'm positive of.

I tried her phone on the drive up here. I was in two minds in case he's got it and is monitoring her calls, but my need to find out got the better of me. I was proven wrong about him sitting there waiting for it to ring, because it didn't even go to voicemail.

CHAPTER THREE

I'm still awake when the sun starts to rise over the hills in the distance, and I'm still none the wiser as to what to do. I could start knocking on doors, but if this little community is as tightknit as I imagine it to be then I'll totally lose the element of surprise. Quinn can't have been the only one who knew about the goings on inside that school building, so my guess is that everyone around here is either stupidly loyal or as dodgy as the men in Quinn's life.

Putting my seat back up, I grab my phone and find a message from an unknown number.

Swiping it open, I find an address staring back at me. My brows draw together until I see that the address is for a house in this village.

A small smile of achievement twitches at the corner of my lips that Eddie does care after all. Maybe he really is the kind of guy Quinn thinks he is. Putting it into the SatNav, I find that it's only three minutes away.

I'm sitting out the front of what I assume is Quinn's old marital home before I get a chance to blink. It's a million miles away from her flat in London and just seeing the sheer size of the place helps me to understand her that little bit more.

She must have left everything behind when she ran. Well, everything aside from those damn twinsets. Even those make sense now. I bet it's all the women wear around here—that and a set of pearls around their necks while their husbands are up to all sorts.

Disgust curls at my lips at what's been happening here for probably longer than anyone wants to admit.

I sit and watch the house for a while. It's silent. The only clue that someone might be home is that there's a Porsche and an Audi parked in the driveway. I don't particularly want to sit out here all day. It's going to become seriously fucking obvious that I'm watching the place soon.

My stomach rumbles, reminding me that I didn't eat for most of yesterday due to the intended swanky meal for Erica's birthday, so I decide to try to find somewhere to get some food and come back later. Thankfully it gets dark pretty early these days—plus it's grey, raining, and foggy up here. I'll be much more inconspicuous under a cloud of darkness.

<hr>

"WHAT THE FUCK is going on, Joe?" Lauren shrieks at me when I tell her that I'm not going to be at work today. I'm sitting at a table in the first cafe I found about twenty minutes from the village.

I let out a large sigh. I don't have a fucking clue where to start.

"You're really starting to worry me." Her words make my heart hurt. For a long time, Lauren was the single most important person in my life. The day I stumbled into Johnson and Son's offices in the hope of finding a job, I didn't think my entire life would change.

Okay, so her cuntbag of a dad basically blackmailed me into befriending her, but that was never my reason for truly wanting to spend time with her. The second I spotted her sitting behind her desk, looking like someone had just run over her puppy, something called to me. I was drawn to her in a way I've never been with anybody else ever, until Quinn. There was even a time, not all that long ago actually, that I thought there could have been more between us. She was my rock, she had been for years, and my broken heart got a little carried away with itself. Watching her hooking up with the guy who'd put that sad look on her face the day I first met her was a bit of a slap across the face. I was under the stupid illusion that she was mine, and it hurt having the guy who basically brought us together swoop in and steal her from under my feet.

It didn't take me all that long to realise that I was living in a fantasy land. She was never mine to have. She was my best friend, and when I really thought about that, it was exactly what I wanted. What I *needed*. It wasn't until I fell for Quinn that I realised that what I felt for Lauren wasn't real. The love I had for her was as my best friend. It wasn't real love. I was yet to feel that back then.

But now? Now I've had a taste of how incredible that can be, and like fuck am I allowing it to slip through my fingers.

"I've...uh...I've met someone," I admit for the first time. I've kept Quinn a secret, mainly because I knew it was what she wanted. She was right every time she told me that we shouldn't have been doing what we were, because the facts of it are that we're student and teacher, no matter my age. It'll still be seen that she's taking advantage of her position and she'll be the one in the wrong, no matter how much I might have chased her. But also, I was worried that if everyone knew, if I even mentioned it, then it might not be real. Crazy, I know, but I'd found this little burning light, something I didn't know I needed until the moment I laid eyes on her, and I didn't want to ruin it by having my friends nosing in on my business.

A loud shriek comes through the phone. "Shut the fuck up. You have not. Where? Who is it? Name? When can I meet them?" she asks, exactly as I expected her to. In all the time we've been friends and even living together, I've never once mentioned someone of any significance in my life. This must be somewhat of a shock.

"One step at a time, yeah. I'll tell you all that stuff when I'm back—"

"Where the hell are you?" she interrupts.

I let out a long, pained breath. "She's got some shit going on with people from her past. I'm...uh...trying to smooth the situation over."

"You...playing peacekeeper. Now that I'd pay to see." She laughs, and my stomach drops to my feet. If only it were that simple. "I hope they're expecting a bad boy with ink to show up or you could be in trouble."

I refrain from telling her that my art of choice isn't really an issue right now, but I don't want to drag her into this. It's bad enough that Quinn's in the middle of it.

"Things are...complicated. I'd really appreciate it if you'd keep this to yourself for now, but I promise that as soon as I can, I'll tell you everything you want to know and I'll even let you meet her."

"You'll let me? Wow, I feel so privileged." Sarcasm drips from her words, but I can't care right now. I've got bigger issues than pissing off my best friend.

"Listen, I've got to go. I'll call you when I can, just tell Ben I've got the shits or something, yeah?"

"I've got you, just..." she hesitates, and I hold my breath, waiting for what's going to come next. "Just don't make me regret it."

"I won't. Love you."

"Hmmm... You too. Bye."

I hang up just as the waitress I saw heading this way places a huge plate of fried breakfast down in front of me. I thought I was hungry, but staring down at it after having talked about Quinn, even just briefly with Lauren, killed my appetite somewhat.

I waste the day driving around. I fill up the van just in case we need to make a quick getaway and basically just wait until the sun sets. The second the sky turns dark, I make my way back towards the address Eddie supplied me with.

I've not heard any more from him since that message, so I assume he's been busy teaching all day and trying to ignore what could be happening here. He didn't seem all that keen to get involved yesterday, so I don't know why I'm surprised.

It's completely dark when I pull up behind another car that's parked in the layby I found opposite the house earlier. Pulling my black work hoodie from behind my seat, I drag it over my head and keep the hood up before getting out.

The frozen grass crunches under foot and my breaths come out in clouds of white around me as I make my way towards the house. There are lights on inside, but I see no movement.

Avoiding the stoned driveway, knowing the sound of my footsteps could tip off anyone inside, I make my way around the side of the house.

Looking into a small window, all I can see is the hallway and a couple of doors. Really not helpful. I need to know where she is and if she's okay, not how she decorated her old house.

Blowing out a frustrated breath, I continue towards the back of the house until a twig snapping up ahead catches my attention and my heart jumps into my throat, but when a figure steps out from the trees, I realise that I vaguely recognise his stance.

"What the fuck?" I ask, marching towards him.

"You were right. We need to make sure she's okay."

"And here I was, thinking you were a stuck-up pussy."

Eddie fumes at my words but wisely keeps his mouth shut. He must be well aware that's how he came across yesterday when he basically sent me on my mission without even a good luck thrown my way.

"I'm hoping you have a plan."

The light coming on in an upstairs bedroom halts our conversation, but almost as soon as it's switched on, it's off again.

"Not really. If I walk up and say, 'Hello mate, let's go and get a pint,' he's going to see straight through me. I hated him when I was here, and the feeling was very much mutual, especially when he found out I'd befriended his wife. Apparently she was his and his alone. He's a control freak. Whatever he's up to will have been well planned, but—"

"There'd better be something positive coming next," I mutter.

"But it also means he's a creature of habit, so he'll have some kind of routine."

"Like?"

"Like Friday night was poker night at the school."

A smile twitches at my lips. We might have a chance at an empty house.

"What time?"

"Eight, but he always got there early to help set up. Arse licker," he adds, making me want to laugh because I can picture him doing the exact same thing.

"I guess we'd better get comfortable." I rest back against a tree, my eyes locked on the house, hoping for some movement or a clue as to whether she's inside.

"What, you're not going to storm the place anyway?"

"I'm not a fucking Neanderthal. I'd rather find a way to get us all out of this alive if possible." The mention of anyone dying sends a shiver down my spine. The bloke's a paedophile and an abuser... surely he's not a murderer as well, right?

"Do you think he'd really hurt her?" I ask hesitantly when my last comment fades into the darkness around us.

"I wouldn't put anything past him. He's hurt her before."

Something explodes in my stomach and races through my veins. "He what?" I roar, a little too loudly seeing as we're meant to be hiding.

"Look, I don't know any details, and he was always careful to keep the bruises hidden—not that that was hard, seeing as she was expected to dress like a nun." *The fucking twinsets.*

My fists clench with my need to end this man. How dare he lay a hand not only on innocent kids but on Quinn. *My* Quinn.

"Calm down," Eddie demands when he gets a look at my expression and the heaving of my chest. "We need to go about this rationally. You getting all angry and possessive isn't going to help us."

"I'm sorry, I didn't realise you were experienced with this kind of thing." He opens his mouth to respond but obviously changes his mind. "Lucky for us, I know a thing or two about breaking and entering."

"Of course you do," he mutters, but I choose to ignore it. I know how I look, and I know how I'm judged by people like him.

Silence falls around us as we watch and wait. The minutes tick by painfully slowly. The light from the window we saw earlier flicks on and off a few more times before movement downstairs captures my focus. I want to see the motherfucker who's going to rot in jail after this. I want to look him in the motherfucking eyes until he knows that what he tried to ruin is now mine, and like fuck am I ever going to treat her like he did.

"I think he's going," Eddie whispers, his own eyes locked on the house.

"What gave you that idea?" I quip, seeing as we've both just watched him shrug his coat on.

"Fuck off. Do you want my help or not?"

Rolling my eyes, I turn my focus back to the house. We can't see the front door, but we hear it slam and then the engine of one of the cars roaring to life.

"Ready?" Eddie asks, but he's too late. I'm already halfway towards the house.

Pulling my sleeve down over my hand, I slam it through the glass in the outbuilding and reach inside for the handle.

"What the fuck? This place is alarmed."

"That old thing strapped to the front of the house? Please, that stopped working years ago."

I push the door open, and he follows me until we reach another.

"Now what?"

"Do you have any confidence in me?"

He mutters a response, but I don't hear it. I'm too busy backing up, ready to slam my shoulder into the wood and hoping it's as weak as it looks.

"Joe, I don't think that's—" A loud crash sounds out as the door comes free from its hinges and falls into the kitchen beyond.

"Shut the fuck up, posh boy. Are you actually going to help me or just stand there looking like you're going to piss your pants?"

He fumes, looking over my shoulder. "You go. I'll keep watch."

I'm on the move before he even finishes his sentence.

The house is a blur as I run through to find the stairs. I know exactly where I need to go; I just need to find out how to get there.

Taking the stairs three at a time, I race towards the back of the house. Door after door lines the long hallway, making the house seem so much bigger than it looked from the outside.

I throw each one open and find the light, but each one is empty aside from the furniture. That is, until I get to the one at the very end. When I turn the handle, nothing happens.

"Quinn?" I roar, hoping to get a response, but nothing other than the sound of my own erratic breathing fills my ears. "Fuck."

Backing up, I run at the door, hoping it's as useless as the one downstairs. Sadly, it isn't, and it's not until my third attempt that the wood starts to splinter. I put everything I have into the fourth shove, and thankfully, the door swings open at a twisted angle.

The room is in darkness and the windows have been closed up for some time, if the musty smell is anything to go by.

A noise—a moan—breaks through the ringing in my ears, and when I slam my hand down on the light switch, the woman it belongs to comes into focus but only barely, the dim bulb hanging in the centre of the room dull at best.

"Quinn, fuck." Running towards her, I drop to my knees beside her lifeless body. My heart aches in my chest; it damn near feels like it's going to split in two as I stare down at her.

There's a dirty rag wrapped around her face, cutting into her mouth, halting her from speaking. I make quick work of untying it and pulling her weak body into my arms.

Quiet sobs fall from her lips as she shivers against me.

"It's okay. You're safe now. I've got you." Her body is limp in my arms. She's exhausted; clearly she's been locked in here for a few days. "I'm going to get you out of here."

I push to stand with her wrapped tightly in my arms, but I don't get to full height.

Dropping back to my knees, I lift the blanket covering her to find that her wrists and ankles are bound together, the rope around her delicate skin then tied to huge hooks in the floor.

"Motherfucker."

Gently lowering her, I search for something to cut the rope with. Coming up empty, I realise I'm going to have to leave her. My stomach turns over at the thought of her being alone in here once again.

"I'll be right back and we'll get you out of here." As I gently caress her cheek, her tears wet my fingers as I stare into her blue...wait, blue eyes? She moans in pain, pulling my focus. Releasing my hold on her, I race to the door and back to the kitchen. My heart pounds, my legs not able to move me as quickly as I want to go.

Eddie's nowhere to be seen, but his disappearance doesn't even really register. My entire world is tied up upstairs, and I can't think of anything aside from getting her away from here. There's a knife rack on the counter, I pull out what I hope will be the sharpest of the set and race back to Quinn.

"I'm going to get you out of here, babe. It's all going to be okay."

My harsh breathing fills the room as I saw through the rope keeping her here. My heart's in my throat as images of me walking out with her in my arms fill my mind. I'm going to take her home and keep her safe. She's never going to have to worry about this lunatic ever again.

The knife slides through the rope at her feet before I start work on her hands. I'm just about to cut through the last few fibres when a whimper rumbles up her throat, her eyes going wide in fear.

I turn to look at what has her attention before something hard slams into my head and I'm knocked off my feet. The knife falls from my hand, clattering to the wooden floor at my side. Everything goes fuzzy. Darkness threatens to consume me as I look up to the person yielding a baseball bat.

"She doesn't deserve to be rescued. Elizabeth's nothing more than a filthy whore."

"Motherfucker." By some miracle, my body follows orders despite the burning pain in my head, and I jump to my feet. I use his shock to my advantage to get a good look at him. He's dressed like he should be heading to a golf club, not a fucking poker match, with his jumper tied over his shoulders.

He's not expecting me to get up so easily, and his eyes widen in shock. I step towards him, the muscles in my neck straining, the need to feel him break beneath my bare hands all-consuming.

I'm on him before he's even had time to blink, but I'm already on the back foot with my head swimming.

I get a few solid punches in before he manages to duck around the side of me. My vision's still blurry at the edges, and it seems like it takes forever to turn around and see where he's gone. If he's touching her, I swear to god I'll kill the motherfucker.

"Joe," Quinn's bloodcurdling scream fills my ears and makes me move a little faster, but it's too late. The knife I was using to free her is firmly in his hand and he's moving towards me faster than I can compute. I don't feel anything as the cold metal cuts into my abdomen, but I do hear Quinn's continued screams filling the room.

I don't feel anything until he pulls the knife from my body, then the pain hits.

A roar fills my ears, and it's not until I find myself flying at him that I realise the noise actually came from me.

I see red and take him down to the floor, my fists pounding into his face over and over. The need to end this motherfucker is all I can think about. A red haze descends on me like I haven't felt in years, and I find myself totally out of control. I've no idea how much time passes as I lay into him. He has no chance of fighting me off. I'm like a man possessed as blood sprays from his face and his ribs fracture under my force.

It's not until a pair of hands land on my shoulders that I'm dragged from the moment.

I spin, my fist ready to continue fighting, but I falter when I find a copper standing behind me.

"I think you can stop. He seems to have got just a little bit of what he deserves," he says with a wink. More amusement fills his voice than it probably should, given the situation.

Looking behind him, I find Eddie standing in the doorway with blood running from his lip and an already swollen eye. He looks between me and something behind me, and it's then that reality comes back.

"Quinn, fuck." I run over, falling to my knees at her side and pulling her to me. I'm amazed the coppers allow it, but when I look back one of them nods at me, a small smile on his lips. It's only as I wrap my arms around her and the blanket falls away from her trembling body that I realise she's naked beneath.

I don't care that the man who did this is currently unconscious on the other side of the room. The knowledge that he might have touched what's mine makes me want to do it all over again.

She must sense where my thoughts are, because her cold hand lands on the side of my neck.

"It's done. It's over." Her voice is weak at best. She needs a hospital, that much is obvious, but as paramedics rush into the room, the last thing I want to do is let her out of my arms.

I hold her tighter to me as they tend to *his* body and wheel him out on a gurney, although admittedly they don't put a lot of care into their actions.

"Shit." Quinn's soft, concerned voice fills my ears as she lifts her hand from my side. It's bright red and the reminder I need about the knife. The sight of my own blood on her hand makes me feel a little queasy.

"I'm fine. It's just a scratch." It's a lie, and we both know it.

I shift us so I can rest my head back against the wall and keep her tightly in my arms. I'm vaguely aware of voices in front of us, but I can't make out any words.

My limbs feel heavy, but that doesn't mean I'm going to let Quinn go. I've got her back now, and I'm never letting her out of my sight again.

I fight the darkness that wants to consume me, but eventually I lose and everything fades. A weight is lifted from me as I'm totally consumed by darkness. Her blue eyes and soft curves fill my mind, and I just about remember thinking that there could be a worse way to go.

CHAPTER FOUR

Beeping is the first thing I notice before the ache that starts somewhere in the middle of my body and radiates out to the very tips of my fingers and toes. What the fuck is —*shit.*

I can hear movement in the distance, but as I try to figure out what it all means, darkness claims me once again.

I've no idea how much time passes before my senses come back to me once again, but when they do, a few memories hit me.

Quinn.

Before I manage to even attempt to drag my eyes open, I'm out cold again.

The next time I come to, I hear a vaguely familiar male voice.

"I hate leaving you like this, but I've got to get back."

"It's fine, I get it. I'm fine." Quinn. My heart aches at hearing her voice, and I want more than anything to be able to look at her, but my eyes won't cooperate.

"I know you are, and so is he." My skin heats, knowing they're looking at me.

"I-I know." Quinn sniffles, and it breaks my heart that she's hurting.

"You heard the doctor. He was lucky and will be back to his usual self soon. Plus those two dodgy coppers have somehow managed to ensure there's no investigation so he's in the clear." I'm not sure if Eddie is happy about that or not, but as long as Quinn is, that's all that matters.

"I know." Her quiet sobs fill the room, but the darkness starts to claim me once again.

The next time I come to it's quiet, aside from the fucking beep, and I panic.

Quinn.

My need to know if she's okay has me trying to move.

"Argh," I cry as I try to sit up, my eyes flying open for the first time. The electric lights above me burn, making me squint as I attempt to curl myself into a ball in the hope that the pain stops.

"It's okay, just relax." The sound of her soft voice calms me down instantly, and the warmth of her hand landing on my cheek makes every tense muscle in my body relax.

"Quinn?" My throat is so dry that her name is barely audible. My eyes crack open and her blurry face fills them.

"Shhh. I'm here."

Her other hand squeezes mine, and it's enough for me to relax and drift back off to sleep.

I have no idea where I am or how I got here, but she's beside me. That's all that matters.

The next time I come to, the pain has subsided slightly, but the most obvious difference is that there are two female voices softly speaking, both of which I recognise.

"I can't believe he turned up like that expecting just to walk out with me."

"I can. He's pretty hard headed. Once he gets an idea he doesn't generally stop until he gets what he wants."

"Damn fucking straight." My voice is rough and my throat burns as I say the words, but I can't lie here listening to them talk about me.

Silence falls around us, but I'm yet to open my eyes, seeing as my eyelids feel like lead weights, but I know they're there, and I know they're both staring at me.

Both of my hands are grasped.

"Don't you ever do that to me again, you hear me?" Lauren chastises, squeezing my hand tighter.

Mustering up as much strength as I can find, I drag my eyes open to look at her.

Concern and exhaustion covers her face, her brows pulled tightly together.

"If you hadn't just come out of surgery, I'd put you in there myself for scaring me like that."

"Wha—"

"Here, have some water." Looking to my left, I find Quinn holding out a plastic cup with a straw.

She looks beautiful. She always will to me, but it's clear to see that she's been through a harrowing experience. She has huge, dark circles under her eyes. Her skin is a pale grey colour, and her cheeks look a little sunken. But it's the cut lip and the angry bruise high up on her cheekbone that have a burning need for revenge raging through my body. The thought of what he could have done to her in that dark room has the little contents of my stomach threatening to make themselves known.

"Not now," she whispers, her eyes pleading with mine to let it go. She can clearly read my thoughts, making me wish I could read everything she's feeling in this moment, but my head's too fuzzy to know my own thoughts let alone hers.

After drinking the entire cup, I turn back to my best friend. "Not that I'm not happy to see you, but why are you here?"

"Nice," she says with a laugh. "I'm your next of kin. I got a phone call to say you'd been stabbed and I damn near crapped my pants. Why didn't you tell me about any of this?" She gestures to Quinn, and I immediately feel terrible for shutting her out of this part of my life.

"I did. I told you...this morning?"

"Friday morning," she says after looking at her watch. "That was probably a little late though, don't you think?"

I shrug. Quinn was a huge part of my reason for keeping us secret, and I'd go to the ends of the earth to protect her. I hope I'd proved that.

Quinn sits silently beside me. Her hand might be in mine, but with her legs curled up under her in as small a ball as she can manage, she looks more closed off than I've ever seen her. I want to pull her into my arms and never let her go, but even turning to look at her fucking hurts.

A firm knock sounds out in the small room before a young female police officer pokes her head in.

"Good to see you awake, Mr. Kingsman." A small smile twitches at her mouth before she turns to Quinn. "Could we have a chat please, Ms. Davenport?"

My brows draw together. *Davenport?*

Quinn uncurls her legs and stands. It's then that I really see what her few days captive have done to her. The pair of leggings she's wearing are hanging off her, and the hoodie's hanging loosely from her shoulders. How is that possible after such a short amount of time?

I'm too confused by everything as she kisses my forehead and follows the copper from the room. My head spins with the hazy memories of what happened for me to end up here.

"What did she just call Quinn?"

"Ms. Davenport. Why?"

The name Elizabeth pops into my head for some reason, but I can't pinpoint why.

"N-nothing." I'm too confused to even attempt to make any sense of it.

There's another knock on the door and I'm forced to push my thoughts aside as a doctor and a nurse make their way into the room.

"Mr. Kingsman, it's so good to finally see those eyes," the nurse coos softly. Her tone makes my spine stiffen. I don't need anyone to talk to me like a fucking child.

"I'm just going to go and grab a coffee. Let you do your thing. I'll be back soon." Lauren squeezes my hand and mouths 'be good' before slipping from the room. As if I'd be anything but. I roll my eyes at her retreating form before glancing back at the patronising nurse.

She pulls the clipboard from the base of my bed and starts taking notes while the doctor questions me about my pain levels and checks the lines in the back of my hand, which I only now notice are attached to bags of blood hanging above my head.

He must see where my attention is because he starts explaining.

"You lost a lot of blood before you got here, but hopefully by the time this bag is done you won't need any more. The stab wound could have done some real damage to your bowel, so we had to open you up and assess the situation. I'm pleased to say it really could have been a lot worse. You were relatively lucky, Mr. Kingsman."

Lucky? I was stabbed by a psychopath who locked up my girl like his fucking prisoner. The memory hits me like a fucking sledgehammer.

The machine beside me starts beeping incessantly.

"You really need to stay calm, Mr. Ki—"

"It's Joe," I bark, hating being called by my surname unless it's coming from Quinn. It's the only thing I still have that connects me to my parents, and I fucking hate it.

"Sure. Please, try not to get worked up. We'd like to get you out of this place as soon as possible, so just sit back, relax, and let us take care of you."

I've only been conscious briefly, and already I fucking hate this. No one's looked after me since I was a child. Okay, so maybe that's not totally true. I did get the flu a couple of years ago and Lauren played the part of nurse perfectly. She humoured me with my ridiculous demands but drew the line when I asked for a couple of strippers to come and keep me company while she was at work. I thought she was being a spoilsport; she said she was concerned about my blood pressure while being so ill, which seems to be a thing if the nurse's recent words are anything to go by. My granddad and my dad had dodgy tickers, so I guess I should be a little careful seeing as it's hereditary.

I lie there, getting more and more pissed off as they poke, prod, and ask me a million and one questions. Apparently I'm expected to stay in this shithole for a week at least as I recover from both the transfusions and surgery.

There's no fucking way that's happening.

I don't know where I am. I've no idea if Quinn is okay after everything she's been through. Fuck, I don't even really know *what* she's been through. I've got the barest of details about what happened with her dad and ex-husband. I need to get her out of here and somewhere safe so she can recuperate and figure out a way to rebuild her life.

After what feels like a fucking week, the rock hard pillows have been fluffed, the rough bed sheets are neatly tucked around me, and I'm finally left alone with someone else's blood slowly dripping into my body,

I. Fucking. Hate. It.

I lie there alone with only the sounds of the machines around me for company as I try to drag up as many memories from that night as possible. I must try so hard that I wear myself out, because soon everything fades once again and I float off into dreamland.

When I wake again, the lights are dimmed, although I can still see every inch of the room. The first thing I notice is that the beeping is no more. I look to see if I'm no longer attached to the irritating machine, but before I find that my eyes land on Quinn.

She's curled up in the reclining chair with a hospital pillow tucked under her head and her cheek resting on her hand. Her dark hair is all over the place, nothing like it usually is, and her skin is almost grey. I hate that I'm stuck in this bed and unable to comfort her after whatever it was she endured at that monster's hand. She's dressed in the same pair of leggings and hoodie as earlier. The only bit of skin she's showing is her face, and I hate that she's hiding once again.

It occurs to me that that was what the twinsets were. They covered as much skin as possible and made her blend into the crowd, or at least with every other woman I would imagine were in their circle of friends. Her choices of the short leather skirts and the flared dresses make so much sense. *I* make so much sense. She was rebelling from the life she had before, the life she hated. Was she just with me because I was the rebel to help her break free? What happens now? My heart begins to race as I consider that the strength of my feelings might not be reciprocated. I'm not sure how I'll cope if she tells me it was just a bit of fun and that now her ex-douchebag and father have been locked up where they belong, she's going back to her old life, her old job.

I'm on the cusp of what I can only assume is my first ever

panic attack when the door opens and a friendly looking nurse comes walking in. She's slightly on the podgy side, her uniform clinging to her hips and arse a little too tightly, but she has the kindest face I think I've ever seen.

"Good evening, sweetie. I'm Shelly," she whispers, noticing Quinn sleeping in the chair beside me. "How are you feeling?"

"Frustrated. When can I get out of this fucking bed?"

She chuckles at my irritation. "You'll soon be up on your feet like it never happened."

"Not soon enough," I grunt.

"You remind me of my son. He's just as hot headed." She potters around, checking my vitals.

"Yeah? He must be pretty awesome."

"He is. He also wouldn't think twice about running in and saving the girl he loves." Her eyes flick over to Quinn, and I can't help but follow.

Her lips are now parted. She looks so peaceful, and I pray that whatever happened to her escapes her in her slumber. I know it hasn't always been the case.

"She's refused to leave your side, you know? We all thought we were going to have to get her scrubbed up to go into theatre with you." She laughs. "Somehow we managed to convince her to let us see to her while they were working on you. You've got a good one there, boy."

My heart pounds against my ribs. Is what she's saying true? If it is, it makes my earlier concern seem a little pointless. Is Quinn just sticking around because she feels guilty that she dragged me into her mess, or is she really here because she wants to be? I guess only time will tell.

I fall silent, my mind wandering back to the events that put us both in here. I know I can't remember everything, but his face is one thing I'm pretty sure I'll never forget.

"Shelly?" I ask as she wraps a blood pressure band around my arm.

"Yeah?"

"Do you know what happened to the man who put me in here?"

"You mean the man you also put in here?" she jokes lightly. "I'm sorry, Joe. I'm not allowed to discuss other patients' conditions."

"He's alive then. What a shame." She gives me a weak smile, but if she knows even just a little of the detail around what happened, I can't help but think she probably agrees with me. "There was another man too," I say, thinking about Eddie being there.

"He's fine. Sent home with nothing more than a butterfly stitch on his eyebrow." I nod. At least someone got out of this unscathed.

CHAPTER FIVE

When I wake again, the lights are glowing above my head and Quinn is stirring beside me.

I watch as her eyelids flicker open and she stretches her neck, proving just how uncomfortable it must be sleeping in that chair.

"Morning, beautiful," I whisper, not wanting to scare her seeing as she's not looked up at me yet.

Her tired eyes find mine and my heart aches that she feels the need to put herself second right now. She needs to recover just as much if not more than me after everything she went through.

"How are you feeling?" She swings her legs from the chair and leans towards the bed so she can take my hand in hers.

"Ready to leave."

A small smile curls at the corner of her lips, and I will it to continue. Seeing her wide, genuine smile would go a long way to making me feel normal right now. "You're so predictable."

"How's that?"

"I told your first nurse I saw that I had a feeling you'd be a nightmare patient."

"That's harsh, Quinn. Whatever gave you that idea?"

"I just didn't have you down as the kind of man who lies back and takes what's coming to him."

"Well." A suggestive smirk plays on my lips. "That all depends on the situation, doesn't it? I'd gladly lie back and take whatever *you* had to give me."

Her cheeks heat and my cock stirs beneath the thin sheet covering me, despite my slightly broken body. "Joe, you can't—"

"Okay, kids. Stop getting the patient excited," Shelly says with a laugh as she wanders in with a tray of pills for me.

"I'm just going to use the bathroom."

Quinn gets up and I panic, not wanting to watch her walk from the room. For the first time since I woke up, my body responds properly when I try to move, and I manage to wrap my fingers around her wrist before she gets away. Only, her response to my touch isn't what I was hoping for.

She gasps and rips her arm from my fingers, holding it across her body like I just burned her. Her eyes fill with tears before she runs from the room.

"Shit. Fuck." Throwing myself back onto the bed, my hands scrub down my rough face.

"She's been through a lot, sweetie. Just give her a little time. Do you feel up to having a go at getting to your feet? If you are, we could get you into the shower." The image her words conjure up are incredibly attractive because my skin feels disgusting, but I hate the idea of being forced away from Quinn longer than necessary.

"As long as we're fast. I don't want to leave her."

Shelly smiles, biting back the words that are clearly on the tip of her tongue.

I don't think I've ever truly appreciated being able to stand up, but after being in a bed for god knows how long, I'm really fucking thankful as my feet just about shuffle me towards the adjoining bathroom. The fact that Quinn didn't come in here makes me worry even more about where her head's at right now.

The short walk to the bathroom, even with Shelly supporting me, is the hardest fucking walk of my life. My stomach aches where the motherfucker stabbed me. I expect that but not for my legs not to work. It gives me a bit of a clue as to why they want me to stay here for a week. It also gives me even more of a push to prove them wrong and get out of here at the first opportunity. And when I leave, I'm walking out of those motherfucking doors with my head held high and my girl by my side.

Thoughts of Quinn running out minutes ago dampen my enthusiasm, but it'll be fine, right? She's here. Shelly said she refused to leave. She'll come back to London with me. Right?

I hate that I'm feeling so insecure. Until this happened, I didn't once question whether Quinn was in this as deep as I was. Yeah, I knew she was scared, but she never let me see that she wasn't serious. She hasn't now, but with her being home and the two men who were haunting her gone, I just don't know what to think.

"Take a seat on there, young man," Shelly says, walking us towards a little white plastic seat. I couldn't be more grateful to get off my feet.

I moan in relief as the weight is taken off and I relax back, so exhausted I could probably fall asleep right here.

"Okay?"

"Yeah. Do your worst."

"Lucky for you, I've got a gentle touch." She winks at me and I can't help but laugh. I regret it instantly, a sharp pain radiating from my wound and through my entire body. It's all forgotten

"Thank you." The way she smiles at him makes me wonder if she knows him.

Harry drops the tray on the table and, after checking that I'm okay, leaves us to it.

"You know him." It's not a question.

"I do. I used to work with his mother. He was a student at Earlington, but that was long before I was teaching there."

"I see."

She sits forward on the edge of her seat, her eyes narrowing as they study my face. "Is that a little jealousy there, Mr. Kingsman?"

"What? No. I just thought he was a little overly friendly."

She chuckles. "Whatever you want to tell yourself. Shall we see what delights we have tonight?"

"Can't wait," I mutter. Knowing what the other meals have been like, I'm not all that excited.

I poke at the casserole looking thing in front of me, but all I can think about is the way that nurse looked at Quinn.

"I was jealous," I admit. "He looked at you like he knew you, and I hate that there are people out there who know you better than I do."

"Joe," she breathes, halting poking her own food around the container. "You are the only person who knows the true me. My real hopes and dreams. The version of me that lived here, that knew all these people, was a fake, an actress."

"Why didn't you get out sooner?"

She's silent for a few moments while she thinks. "I've been controlled my whole life. It was normal. It was expected of me to just do as I was told. It took me longer than it should have to realise that that control wasn't the love and care I thought it to be. I didn't know any different. The people my parents associated with were the same, but as I grew up and started getting a look at the world around me, I realised my life was anything but normal. By then it was too late. I'd been married off to one of my parents' friends' sons who'd lived the same sheltered and controlled life I had, only he thrived on continuing it. The longer it went on, the more I resented it, but I was in too deep to just walk away. They wouldn't allow that. I had to bide my time, continue to pretend to be her and just hope the time presented itself where I could live the life I'd been dreaming of."

My heart bleeds for her that she's been treated that badly for so long by people who are supposed to love and support her. I can sympathise to a point because my parents are worthless pieces of shit, but at least they didn't keep me locked up. Her story makes mine sound like a walk in the park. Yeah, I've had hard times, really hard, but at least I've always been able to be myself.

"I love the person you are." Her eyes fly to mine at my admission, but she doesn't say anything in response. I want to say more but when her eyes drop from mine in favour of the food in front of her, I get the message that she's done for now.

We finish eating in silence before Harry comes back and does my check-up before leaving us alone once again. There are a million and one questions on the tip of my tongue. I'm desperate to unleash all of them on her to fully understand everything she's been through, but in the end, I go with the most pressing.

"What happens when I get out of here?"

Her eyes meet mine and her lips part, ready to respond, but a knock on the door fills the room. She blows out a long breath. I'm not sure if it's because she's relieved or frustrated that she doesn't get to answer, but the second a head pops into the room all thoughts of my previous question leave my mind.

The woman who comes to stand at the end of my bed is so familiar. Okay, so her hair is blonde, but the blue eyes that are darting between the two of us are the exact blue ones I'm becoming used to.

"Mum." Quinn's voice is so quiet I almost miss it.

"Lizzie. I missed you so much." She walks towards Quinn with her arms open like she wants to pull her in for a hug, but Quinn stiffens, her tray remaining fully in place on her lap as if it's a shield. "Lizzie?"

"Don't," Quinn snaps in a tone I've not heard from her before. "You don't get to come in here after everything and act like all is well between us."

Pain fills her mother's face, and I can't help but feel for the woman. She's obviously gone out on a whim, hoping that her daughter might accept it. I can't really blame Quinn; from the little I know it seems to be that her mother, although not guilty of committing any of the crimes of the men in her life, must have been aware of them.

"Elizabeth, please, just let me explain."

"Explain? Explain how you sat back and allowed Dad and all the others to do what they did to those poor innocent kids? You could have done something about it long before I ever discovered it was happening, let alone before I worked at the same school. You could have—"

"I know," her mother sobs. "I know. But..." she pauses, looking up at the ceiling like she's praying for strength. "You know what your dad was like. You know how controlling he was. I just couldn't risk—"

"You couldn't risk what for all those children they were abusing on a weekly basis? What was so important to you that you couldn't help *them*? Help me? You knew the kind of monster you were marrying me off too. You could have stopped that."

"I just couldn't. I was scared."

"Scared? Scared of what?"

"Your dad," she whimpers. "He may have never laid a finger on you, but it was a very different story for me. If I made one wrong move I'd feel it for weeks. I couldn't risk exposing them and something happening to me. Where would that have left you? He might have...he m-m-might h-have touched you." Her sobs become uncontrollable, but Quinn doesn't move to comfort her.

I don't know the woman from Adam, but even from here I can tell that she's broken. Quinn might not want to hear her out, and that's fair after everything she's experienced, but I do believe there's truth in her mother's words. I've lived with manipulative parents who were only out for themselves, and I don't think this shell of a woman before me is one of them. Her father, on the other hand, is probably up there vying for king alongside my father and Lauren's. The reminder that all the women I care about have been screwed over by men who were meant to love and care for them has fury boiling in my veins. How hard is it to have a normal childhood with decent parents?

"Don't turn this on me. I was strong enough to deal with whatever was thrown my way. The fact we're all here right now should be proof of that."

"It is, baby. I'm so proud of you." Her face is red and blotchy and covered in tears and snot, her shoulders sagged in defeat, but still Quinn stands her ground.

"Why don't you think about all those kids whose endless abuse has hopefully come to an end, and all those adults out there whose lives will always be touched by what Dad did and allowed to happen under his leadership?"

"You think I've thought of anything else over the years?"

Quinn fumes but doesn't respond.

The silence is heavy with unsaid words. It's only her mother's lingering sobs that fill the space around us.

"Did you have anything else you needed to say?" Quinn's

voice is cold and harsh. It's a million miles away from the soft woman I've fallen for, and I'm so damn hot for her right now. My cock swells beneath the sheets as she stands up against her mother, her eyes daring her to say something else.

I'm amazed that this strong woman before me endured everything she did for so long, but I do understand that bad situations aren't always the easiest to get out of.

"I just need you to know that I'm here for you, for whatever you decide to do next."

"Well, that's big of you, seeing as you've not cared since the day I walked out."

"Elizabeth, that's—"

"That's what? Not fair? How would it be, because you knew exactly where to find me. You were the only one who knew where I was going; I hoped that you'd have the strength to follow me, to find a better life for yourself as well, but just as I feared, you were too weak. You were too weak to stand up for what was right and too weak to give yourself the life you deserve."

"I couldn't. You've no idea what it was like after you left."

"Nor would you if you'd followed."

Her mother pales even further but nods in agreement. "You know where I am if you need *anything* when you both get out of here." Her eyes hold her daughter's a little longer before she turns to me. "I'm sorry we had to meet in these circumstances, but thank you for being there for my baby." She gives me a small smile before backing out of the room.

Having got a good idea of the life Quinn left behind and the fact that her mother turned up wearing a twinset and pearls, I was expecting judgemental eyes when she looked at me and found tattooed arms resting over the top of the sheets, or what's quite obviously not a posh boy face despite this morning's shave.

The sound of her footsteps fade, and, with a huge huff, Quinn falls back onto the chair and lifts her hands to cover her face, successfully cutting herself off from me.

It takes everything I have, but I swing my legs from the bed, ignoring the searing pain that shoots out from my belly. She's more important right now.

My legs feel a little unsteady as I push to stand, but they're not going to stop me. I shuffle towards her. She must know I'm coming, but that doesn't stop her flinching the second I wrap my hands around her wrists and pull her to stand before me.

Every muscle in her body is pulled tight, but she needs this. Gently, I close the space between us and wrap my arms around her. At no point does she relax in my hold, but eventually her trembling reduces.

"Everything's going to be okay. What you did was incredible." I want to tell her that I wish she'd told me, but I don't need her feeling any worse than she already is. I know that if she felt she could have told me, she would. I truly believe that if we had more time she would have opened up more, like she did in the church in Stratford-upon-Avon. She trusted me enough to begin her story. I have to believe that she would have trusted me with the rest.

"I promise I'll tell you everything," she whispers, "just not here, okay?"

I nod, my chin nuzzling against the top of her head as an idea forms in my mind. She wants to tell me everything but not here, and I don't want to be here.

We're forced apart when another knock sounds out, only this visitor is much more welcome than the last.

I release Quinn and scoop Lauren up in my arms. The fact that she made the trip up here for me means everything, especially after how selfish I've been, keeping this part of my life to myself.

She wraps her arms around me gently as I kiss the top of her head and breathe her in. She's always been my safe place, the rational head to my hot one, and I hate that since Ben came back into her life we've grown apart. There was a time not so long ago that I thought it would be Joe and Lauren forever, even if it wasn't romantically. But it seems life had other plans for us because she now has Ben and I've got Quinn...or Elizabeth. Jesus, this is such a fucking mess.

"Feeling better, I see," Lauren comments when I release her.

"Like a new man," I lie. In reality I feel like shit, but if I'm going to convince them to go along with my plan, I can't allow them to see that. "So good, in fact, that I'm discharging myself."

"No you're fucking not," Lauren barks while Quinn stands, her hands going to her hips.

"You're staying exactly where you are until a doctor discharges you." Quinn's lips are pressed into a thin line, her blue eyes ice cold as she stares me down. She looks so cute being angry that I can't help but laugh.

"I'm fine." Summoning up every ounce of strength I have, I make a show of walking back towards my bed and pulling the cupboard open to get my clothes.

Pulling the items out, I find my jeans, boxers and shoes, but nothing to cover my top. I look up at Quinn, and she must sense where my thoughts are at.

"They had to cut them off you."

"I'm sure I rock the hospital gown anyway."

With both Lauren's and Quinn's concerned eyes on me, I pull my boxers on without groaning in agony and have my jeans halfway up when we're joined by Harry.

"Fantastic. Talk some sense into him. He thinks he's discharging himself."

Harry opens his mouth to do as he's told, but the second his eyes find mine, I think he appreciates that it's not an argument he's going to win.

"Obviously, my advice is that you stay as per doctor's orders, but—"

"See, it's fine. Even Harry thinks I should leave."

"Now, that's not exactly what I was getting at."

"Maybe not, but you also didn't tell me to get my arse back into bed. So, if you'd kindly remove this thing from the back of my hand, I'll be off."

Harry's chin drops as he looks between Quinn and me. I feel for the guy. He wants to do the right thing, but like fuck am I staying here any longer, getting poked and prodded and fed shitty food. It's time for me to take my girl for some alone time.

"I'm not happy about this," Quinn huffs as Harry does as he's told and removes the tube from the back of my hand.

"You'll need to be checked over by a doctor before you walk out, but I can get the paperwork for you."

"Thank you, I appreciate it."

He does his job and leaves as quickly as he entered.

"Why aren't you saying anything to try and stop this?" Quinn snaps at Lauren.

"Because there isn't a single thing I can say to him right now that will change his mind."

"This is bullshit."

"Your dumb arse decision aside, I was coming to let you know that I'm heading home. Ben and Erica need me back at work. I'm going to drive your van back and leave you two my car. Hopefully it'll be more comfortable for you to travel home in. That's assuming you're coming home." Lauren chews on her bottom lip as she waits for my response.

My eyes fly to Quinn, because she's the one to hold the answer to that question. Finding out where her head's at is part of the reason I'm getting the hell out of this place.

"He'll be coming home," she confirms, but in no way does she give me any clue as to whether she'll be coming with me or not. After watching her interaction with her mother earlier, I want to say that she has no intention of staying here, but I could be very wrong.

It wouldn't be the first time.

CHAPTER SIX

I t took a hell of a lot longer than expected, but eventually the doctor begrudgingly allows me out of my little hospital room.

Quinn insists on finding me a wheelchair but like fuck am I leaving this place in a set of wheels. I'm walking out of this motherfucking building with my girl by my side and the world at our feet.

The reality of it is much more painful—and slower—than I was expecting, but eventually we make it down to reception and the electric doors slide open for us.

That first breath of fresh winter air is the best one I've ever had. The cold burns my lungs and the pain in my abdomen almost has me doubling over, but I fight it. It's going to take more than Quinn's psycho ex to break me.

"What car's Lauren got?"

"That white BMW," I nod to where it's parked and slowly Quinn helps me get across the road and to the passenger side of the car.

"For the record, I think this is a really bad idea."

It's not the first time she's expressed that, but just like all the times she's said the same thing, I ignore her and wait for the car to be unlocked so I can figure out a way to get inside.

Biting on the inside of my cheeks, I fold myself into the passenger seat, knowing that if I show even an ounce of how painful this is then she'll demand we go straight back inside.

I don't tell her where to go; I've got no idea where we are, but she doesn't ask, she just reverses out of the space and pulls out onto the main road.

"I'm assuming you've got a driving licence," I say with a laugh once the pain's subsided enough to be able to form words.

"Yes. I can legally drive, I'm even fully insured. You're in safe hands."

"I didn't doubt that for a second."

Silence falls around us. It's not uncomfortable, but it's equally not really all that comfortable either. A million and one questions swirl around my head, but I know I need to wait. It's clear she has a destination in mind so I need to sit back and trust that she has a plan.

The motion of the car eventually forces me to put my head back, and, before I know it, my eyes have shut and I'm fast asleep once again.

I don't wake until I sense the car slowing to a stop.

"What's this place?"

"It's somewhere I've always wanted to stay. I thought this might be the perfect time to try it out."

"Looks expensive."

"You got your credit card on you?"

"Yeah, but—"

"This is on my husband. I think he owes us."

I think he owes us a little more than a fancy hotel stay, but I keep my mouth shut for now.

The second Quinn comes around to my door to help me out, I wonder how good a job I did at the hospital of looking like I wasn't in agony.

"I can see it in your eyes."

"What?"

"The pain. You're fooling no one, Mr. Kingston, but I know better than to argue with you."

She leaves me on one of the giant sofas in the entrance while she books us a room. The hotel is stunning, but my eyes don't leave her for a second. I want to think this a good sign, that she hasn't sent me straight back to London alone but wants me to stay here—for a while at least.

She smiles the second she turns around and finds me staring at her. She still looks like she's been through the mill, but she's starting to resemble the Quinn I knew before. Her skin is brighter and her eyes are beginning to get their usual sparkle back.

"Come on, they've got the most incredible room for us."

I expect us to head towards the lift at the other side of the vast room, so I'm a little shocked when she walks us right past it and out of a huge set of doors.

We make our way down a path as the countryside opens up before us, revealing a huge lake surrounded by mountains.

"Whoa, this is kinda nice."

"Kinda nice? Is that what you city folk call the countryside?"

"Something like that. If this is a joke and you're expecting me to refuse to stay in a tent in favour of the hospital, then it's going to backfire on you. I'm not going back."

"I'm not expecting you to go back, or sleep in a tent. This is where we're staying."

She comes to a stop and waves her arm in the direction of a

cosy little cabin with huge windows that overlooks the lake. The lighting on the inside looks warm and inviting, and I can see the flickering from a fire even from this distance.

"Just a slight upgrade from the hospital room."

"Come on." With her arm around my waist, we walk into the lodge together.

It's stunning, by far the most luxurious and expensive place I've ever stayed. If I knew this was where we were heading next, I'd have got myself out of that place even sooner.

"I'm pretty sure this is going to max out my credit card."

"I've got it covered, don't worry."

I stay quiet until she's got me settled in the chair in front of the fire. She steps away, but I catch her hand in mine, stopping her.

"Quinn?"

"Do you need anything? Are you hungry or..." she trails off, sounding totally unsure of herself, and I hate it.

"I just need you." She releases a huge breath and turns to look at me. I hate the empty, haunted look in her eyes. I'd do anything to take all the terrible memories away.

"I'm here, Joe. I'm just..."

"I know, babe. Take as much time as you need. I'm here for you, don't forget that."

"Can I use your phone? I'm going to place some orders."

"Orders?"

"We've got no clothes. Toiletries. Anything. I've already spoken to a lawyer about a divorce—there's plenty of money that should come out of it. Well, if he agrees to it," she says sadly. "Financially, I'm okay. We can stay here as long as we need to, we can spend as much as we need to. You don't need to worry about that. Just...just get better, yeah?"

"It's just a little scratch."

Tears fill her eyes as I try to brush aside the seriousness of what happened. "I...I thought I was going to lose you. When I saw that knife go in...shit." A sob erupts, and when I pull her to sit on my lap, she doesn't deny me. She's been so strong while sitting beside me in hospital. She needs this.

I wrap my arms around her as she cries on my shoulder. Her tears continue for the longest time, but she can stay right here for a long as she likes. She's not the only one who had a fleeting fear that the other night might have been it for us.

Her sobs eventually fade, but she stays exactly where she is. "Babe?" I whisper, thinking she's fallen asleep. I don't expect her to move, but she pulls her head from my shoulder and looks up into my eyes. Her blue eyes hold so much within them. There's still fear, but there's also hope.

"Your eyes are really beautiful." She tries looking away, but I catch her cheek and bring her head back to me. "You really were hiding, weren't you?"

"It was stupid. He'd probably have recognised me from a mile away, but it made me feel better. I so desperately wanted to be someone else."

"Not at all. It was brave, Qu—what am I meant to be calling you?"

Her bottom lip trembles as she realises what I'm asking her. "Elizabeth is technically my first name, but I hate it. My dad chose it and I mostly despise everything he's ever touched. Quinn is my middle name. I didn't want to be a totally new person, so I went with that. I've always preferred it. It was my grandma's name."

"And what about Davenport, *Miss Smith?*" I give her a smile in the hope it shows her that I couldn't really give a fuck what her name is—it's the person she is that I've fallen for.

"Davenport is my married name. My maiden name is Montgomery. I used Smith because I thought it would help me blend in. Like I said, it was stupid."

"Quinn, you're anything but stupid. You're incredible. Everything you've done, everything you've been through. I'm blown away and I don't really know any of it." Guilt fills her face. "Don't give me that look. Take as much time as you need."

She nods but gently gets up. "Please can I use your phone?"

"Eat your heart out."

She takes my phone from my hand when I hold it out for her. I've no idea if it's got any battery or not; it's not exactly been my biggest concern the past few days.

She turns it on and then starts tapping at the screen. "Do you want to pick yourself some clothes?"

"Nah, you do it. I trust you." She smiles at me before looking back down. "I know one thing you can add though."

"Oh yeah?"

"One of those little nurse's outfits. You know the ones, nice and low, short, with some white stockings." I nod as the image of her wearing it appears in my mind. My cock swells and my heart rate increases as I imagine her giving me a one of a kind bed bath. *Oh yeah, maybe being a patient isn't so bad after all.*

The second I take in the panicked look on her face, all the images in my mind fade.

"What's wrong?"

"It's just...you wouldn't want that."

"You're joking, right? I want that more than anything." A smirk curls at the corner of my mouth, but it doesn't affect her.

"No, I'm not. You...you don't want that."

Faster than I can figure out how to respond, she's up and out of the chair and running towards the back of the lodge. A door slams shut, putting an end to our conversation and breaking the connection between us.

"Fuck," I mutter, rubbing my palm down my face. *What did I say that was so wrong?*

It takes longer than I'd like to get myself out of the low chair I'd all but fallen into, but eventually I'm following her tracks and come to a stop outside the door she disappeared behind. Her quiet sobs sound out and my heart breaks. My girl's much more affected by everything that happened than she's allowing me to see, and I hate that she's trying to deal with it all alone.

"Quinn?" I knock gently but there's no response. "Can I come in, babe?" Again, nothing but the sound of her cries.

I fucking hate this. I should be the one protecting her, drying her tears, not stuck on the wrong side of the fucking door. It was only a few days ago I smashed down a few to get to her—I won't bat an eyelid about having to do it again if necessary. Fuck the stitches in my stomach, I need her, damn it.

Taking a chance, I wrap my fingers around the handle and push. I'm amazed when it twists and the click of the latch moving fills my ears.

A knot of dread forms in my stomach at what I'm going to find on the other side. Ignoring it, I push the door open and step inside.

My breath catches when I find her sitting on the cold tiled floor beside the bath with her arms wrapped around her legs and her head resting on her knees. Her shoulders shake with her cries, and I want nothing more than to scoop her up into my arms and carry her to bed so I can hold her until she forgets. It kills me that I'm not able to do just that. Instead, I rest my back against the wall she's sitting in front of and slide down until my arse hits the floor beside her.

She stiffens when she realises I'm next to her. It's physically painful, but I just about manage to keep my hands to myself. I can practically feel the walls she's put up around herself, and I've got to respect that she needs some space right now.

The silence stretches out, and I start to think she's not going to say anything, let alone register that I'm sitting here with her.

"There was never any question that I would follow in my parents' footsteps and become a teacher. I never questioned it because as a child I idolised both of them. They were both intelligent, hard-working, and what I thought were the perfect parents.

"Dad was just a maths teacher when I was a kid. It wasn't until the year I left that he was promoted to head. Mum was only working part time by then, but she soon gave up. I assumed it was because they didn't need the money anymore, seeing as they'd moved into a school owned property. I was only to learn a few years later that my dad basically told my mum that she was done.

"I went to university, did my degree and my PGCE. My dad ensured I did my placements either at Earlington or at another local private school of his choice. I was still totally in the dark as to what he was really like. I assumed he just wanted the best experience for me to start my career off properly. I had no idea he was keeping me close, stopping me from seeing how different Earlington could be to other schools that would have alerted me to issues earlier on.

"It was a good school when I was there as a student. As far as I knew, the teachers enjoyed working there, the students were happy, and I never heard of anything untoward aside from the kids usual breaking of the rules.

"Dad ensured that I got a job with him. I didn't want to work there. I wanted to spread my wings. I also wanted to experience a state school to see what the differences would be. He told me that it would be hard work, that I'd regret it, a million and one excuses that I believed, and eventually I agreed and accepted the post he offered me as a newly qualified English teacher.

"That was probably his biggest mistake. He thought he could control me, make me believe that some of the accusations that started appearing were nothing more than lying, pissed off, privileged kids. He wanted me around to tell everyone else what an upstanding citizen he was and how trustworthy he was. But those accusations just kept coming. I could only defend him so many times before I started questioning him.

"By this time, Jeremy and I were already engaged. We'd been together a few years and friends, thanks to our fathers, since we were in nappies. It was almost expected that we'd end up together. I was naive. I thought he was cute. I thought he was caring in a similar way that my dad was. It was only years later that I'd discover that 'caring' was actually controlling. But it was all I'd ever known."

I blow out a slow breath as her words register within me. My fists clench as the level of passive-aggressive, controlling behaviour she's been subjected to her entire life becomes clear.

"Don't get me wrong, I loved—love—my job. It might have been expected of me but I truly can't imagine doing anything other than working with kids. But as the accusations started getting stronger, I started to resent everything.

"Jeremy and I got married and that was a serious turning point. Rumours started, accusations got more and more serious, and names started to be revealed. It seemed to be getting to the point that Dad couldn't sweep it all under the rug or pay off whoever it was who felt brave enough to poke their heads above the parapet.

"Somehow, no one ever went to the police. I assume because they didn't believe they'd win. My dad was an enigma, a power that no one thought they could touch. He controlled every inch of that school with a strength that appeared unbreakable."

"Until you broke him."

She nods, her hands trembling as she twists her fingers, lost in her memories.

"Jeremy's name started to be brought up and it coincided with him getting angrier and rougher with me at home. Since the day we got married he wasn't exactly pleasant to me, but he turned into a monster. I hated going home to discover what kind of mood he'd be in and what he thought I'd done wrong that day.

"He got the idea in his head that I should stop teaching and be a housewife and mother to our kids." She laughs, but the sound is anything but joyful. "He was delusional. I was never going to allow him to bring another person into our fucked up world. It got the point that he assumed something was wrong with me because I couldn't fall pregnant. That only made his attitude and behaviour towards me even worse. I was pointless to him if I couldn't give him a son."

"Jesus," I mutter, trying to put myself in her shoes.

"I refused to give up my job. There was no way I was agreeing to basically have myself locked in that house like my mum was. I hardly ever saw her, and when I did it had to be meticulously arranged. She convinced me it was because she was busy with friends and bake sales for the church, but I soon discovered that was all a cover up. She was hiding. Hiding from my dad and his anger.

"I started digging into the accusations more. I'd talk to the kids, listen to all the rumours, but I wasn't getting anywhere. So I made a drastic move. I bugged Dad's office. Two days after I snuck in and hid the microphones, a fifteen-year-old boy accused Jeremy of sexually abusing him in his classroom.

"He was ignored, of course, brushed under the carpet like all the other indiscretions. Until I listened back to the recording from Dad's office. It got everything from Jeremy talking about the incident, as he called it, and Dad reassuring him that it could never be proved and he'd do whatever it took to keep his name clear.

"That Friday night, while they were all playing poker—if that's even what they actually did—I packed a small bag, said goodbye to my mum, took my recording to the police, and ran.

"Jeremy had kept me locked up to a point that I'd made no friends over the years, apart from one."

"Eddie," I add.

"I either went to him or...well, I didn't really have any other option. The streets, I guess. I left with only a bit of cash, leaving behind anything I thought could trace him to me. I dyed my hair, got new contacts that changed my eye colour, and I turned up at Eddie's door, hoping that our friendship was strong enough for him to help me. It had been two years since he'd got a job in London and left. He'd hated Earlington almost as much as I did. We connected immediately. By that point in my marriage, I was aware that Jeremy was doing his best to keep me locked up so I knew a friendship with another man was a sure fire way to set him off. We kept it on the down low for months before Jeremy made a surprise visit to my classroom one afternoon and found us laughing together.

"I could see the fire burning in his eyes and I knew I'd fucked up. That moment was where it really all changed for me. I knew I needed to find a way to get out. If me having a friend outside of our marriage was too much, then I knew it was time to end it. I just knew that wasn't going to be easy, and it was another two years before I found my way out.

"Thankfully, Eddie recognised me the second he opened his front door, and I guess the rest is history."

She falls silent. The words she just said to me hang heavy in the air between us. I've still got so much more that I want to know, but I keep my lips sealed. If I've learned anything about Quinn over the past few weeks, it's that she opens up when she's ready. I'll just have to wait for her, even if I want to shake her to find out the real reason she ran in here in the first place.

After dragging in a long, shaky breath, she pulls her head from her arms and turns to look at me.

My breath catches at the exhaustion in her eyes. Reliving all that really just took it out of her. I'm just about to tell her that we need to go to bed when she beats me to it.

"You need sleep. You shouldn't be sitting down here on the hard floor with me."

Reaching out, I take her hand and lift it to my lips. The split is well healed after that arsehole punched me, but the roughness of the scab scratches against her soft skin as I kiss the back of her hand. "I'll sit anywhere you need me to."

Her eyes fill with tears once again, but she doesn't respond. Instead, she stands and reaches out to help me from the floor.

Getting up and to the bedroom is harder than I want to admit, and I'm in agony by the time Quinn's helped me drop my jeans and slip the damn hospital gown that I'm still wearing from around my shoulders.

I almost sigh when my skin connects with the soft cotton of the sheets after being stuck between scratchy hospital ones for the last few days, but I'm too exhausted now I'm down.

Quinn makes sure I'm comfortable before pulling the sheets back and climbing in. She doesn't even attempt to undress; instead she lies beside me fully clothed, leaving too much space between us.

Rolling onto my side and breathing through the pain, I reach out and pull her into my body. She tenses the second I touch her, but she doesn't do anything else. I'm not awake long enough to know if she relaxes under my touch, and I fucking hate it.

CHAPTER SEVEN

Something drags me from my sleep and I lie awake for a few seconds before I realise what it was when Quinn flinches beside me again.

"No, no. Don't touch me."

My stomach turns over at what she must be reliving.

"Shhh...Quinn. It's okay. I'm here, you're safe." I gently stroke her cheek, the roughness of my thumb scratching lightly at her delicate skin.

Her head thrashes from side to side and I expect her to wake, but after a few more seconds, her breathing slows and she falls back to sleep.

Seeing the evidence of what she experienced first-hand is enough to have me wanting to go back and finish the job I started on that motherfucker. There might not have been any charges after I assaulted him, but I'd happily take whatever I'd get if I were able to get my hands on him again.

When I wake again, the bed beside me is empty and the sheets are cold. The ball of dread that's still sitting heavy in my stomach after her admissions last night grows. She's not okay right now, but I'm at a total loss for what to do to help. Without knowing what happened, I don't even know what I'm dealing with.

The sound of water running fills my ears and I push myself up so I'm sitting. My need to go to her is too much to ignore, and before I know it I'm making my way towards the bathroom. I'm expecting the door to be locked, her way of keeping her distance, but I'm pleasantly surprised when I find it once again opens when I push the handle down.

Taking it as an invitation, I walk inside to find her.

Her back's to me as she stands under the waterfall shower. My eyes should be locked on where the torrent of water runs down over her back and onto her arse, but instead my muscles lock, my fists clench, and by some fucking miracle I manage not to growl like a feral fucking beast at the sight of the bruises that cover her body.

Blood rushes past my ears as my need to find that motherfucker and end him consumes me. I've no idea that I make a noise, but Quinn spins, her eyes wide as she tries to cover her body with her arms. But it's too late. I've already seen that that motherfucker's had his hands on what's mine.

The image of her running panicked in here last night hits me. She told me that I wouldn't want her in the sexy nurse's outfit I was joking about. This was why. The state of her body is why she tried to tell me that I wouldn't want her.

I've closed the distance between us before I've registered that my feet have moved.

"Joe?" Her brows draw together, her body trembling as I step up to her and under the water, still wearing my boxers.

It takes every single bit of self-control I possess to push down the images that are racing through my mind as to how he could have made these marks on her perfect skin as I lift my hand to her cheek and stare deep into her eyes.

The love I feel for her mixes with the raging inferno racing through my veins, and it allows me to focus on her, on the person who deserves everything I have, not the cunt who should be rotting in a cell for every single person he's hurt.

I drop my forehead to hers, our eye contact holding although hers is glassy with her unshed tears.

She wants to pull away from me and hide. Her body is locked up tight and she's trying to build her wall up so I can't climb over, but I won't allow it to happen.

"You never have to hide from me, babe. You're fucking beautiful."

A tear drops as she shakes her head so slightly that if we weren't touching I might miss it.

"H-He—" she sobs.

I take her face in my hands to stop her looking away from me. "He doesn't change how I feel about you. He doesn't stop this..." Taking her hand, I place it over my heart so she can feel it racing beneath my chest.

Her breath catches but she relaxes slightly, and I breathe a sigh of relief.

"Whatever happened, whatever comes next, we'll deal with it together. I'm in love with you, Quinn, and nothing about your past, no matter how recent, is going to change that. I promise."

Another sob erupts from her throat and I pull her body into mine. She winces as I wrap my arms around her and hold tight, and I suck in a breath as she presses against my wound. We're both in pain, both broken, but neither of us attempts to move as the hot water cascades over us.

I've no idea how much time passes and, quite frankly, while she's in my arms I couldn't give a fuck. I've needed this since before I first opened my eyes and knew she was sitting beside my bed. Knowing she'd been taken from my arms inside that bedroom and having no idea what had happened to her was the worst thing I've ever experienced. Yes, her body is showing the evidence of her ordeal, but that'll fade soon. The wounds on the inside might take a little longer to lessen, but I'll do everything in my power to make it more bearable for her.

Eventually, Quinn moves her head. She twists slightly and reaches up on her tiptoes so she can drop a kiss to my neck.

A shudder runs through me before she lifts higher, her breath tickling my ears. Goosebumps prick my skin as I wait for her to say something.

"I keep remembering how his hands felt on my body." My heart thunders at her admission, and my hold on her tightens. "How badly I wanted to pull my own skin off to make it stop, to make all of it stop." She pauses, and I wonder if she has a point or is just trying to tell me what happened, but then she makes a request she knows I'd never be able to deny. "Take it away. Make me forget. Replace it with your touch."

"Fuck."

Dropping my hands to her hips, I force her to take a step back. My eyes skim down her body, taking in her curves and the angry welts and bruises that cover them.

My teeth grind to the point I fear I might break one at seeing the evidence of his abuse so clearly in front of me. Listening to what kind of a monster he was, the hints of things he might have done to her in the past was one thing, but this... The kind of anger this drags up is like nothing I've experienced before. I've hated my life and those around me with a passion but never to quite the level I feel for *him*.

"Joe?" Her voice is a soft plea as her fingertips brush my chest. It brings me back to what she's asked of me.

Taking a small step towards her, I lift her hand and bring her wrist to my lips. I kiss the delicate bruised skin that's been marred by the constraints he tied her with.

Her body trembles as I kiss all the way around, but she doesn't once try to pull her arm back.

My eyes find hers. If I'm going to continue, I need to know she's with me.

Her eyes hold fear, more than I ever wish to see within them again, but the blue I'm still so unfamiliar with also holds fire. My girl wants to fight, and I couldn't be prouder of her, knowing that she's taking control of what she needs to rid herself of him, of the past, of her memories.

I trail a line up her arm, kissing and licking at her sweet skin as I go. Goosebumps erupt the higher I get, and the fire in her eyes begins to win out over the fear.

I nip across one collarbone and then the other, her body trembling beneath my lips, but it's with need, not fear.

Sliding my fingers into her hair, I tilt her head back to give me the access I need to her neck as I make my way up to her lips.

"Joe," she moans as I suck on the sensitive skin beneath her ear. Hearing my name falling from her lips is like fuel to the fire that's already raging inside me. My need for her is all-consuming, but this isn't about me right now.

I kiss across her jaw before my lips find hers. As I suck her bottom one into my mouth, her eyes flutter shut.

"Look at me, babe. Let me see your beautiful eyes." Guilt fills them as she realises what I mean, but that wasn't why I said it. I thought she was stunning with her dark eyes; I hadn't been prepared for what these big blue ones would do to me, but one look into them and I'm on my fucking knees for this woman. I'd give her the fucking world if I could.

Not allowing her to dwell on her choices, I slam my lips down to hers and plunge my tongue into her mouth. She wastes no time in allowing hers to join and soon she's sucking it deeper. My cock throbs painfully behind the wet fabric of my boxers, wishing like hell it was that that was being sucked on.

My chest burns for air and I'm forced to pull back. Her breaths race out over my face and a smile twitches at my lips that I'm able to make her breathless from one kiss alone.

"Ready for more?"

She nods, her teeth sinking into her bottom lip, but the second I pinch her nipples between my thumbs and forefingers, her chin drops and her gasp of shock sounds out over the running water. I love how responsive she is to my touch. I'm pretty sure I'll remember the night in the club when I'm on my deathbed. Feeling her coming apart beneath me while we were surrounded by all those people from my simple touch alone was hands down the hottest experience of my life. My need for her after that was off the charts, but she wasn't one of my usual hook-ups. I knew that the minute I laid eyes on her, and I was going to do everything in my power to do things the right way.

Her head falls back as I continue to tease and pinch her sensitive peaks. Her hips writhe as she tries to find some friction, and I can't hold back any longer.

Dropping to my knees, I ignore the pain radiating from my surgery and focus everything on Quinn and giving her exactly what she needs.

My eyes run over the marks he left on her stomach before they drop to her thighs. What I find has my movements halting and something wild exploding inside me. Pushing her legs wider, I find the rest of his handprints that are bruised into the soft skin of her inner thighs.

Everything around me fades as I stare at those marks. Images play out in my head of her lying on that cold, hard wooden floor as he...as he...

"Fuck," I roar, unable to keep a lid on my emotions. My hands tremble, my stomach twists, and my head spins as I sit there under the torrent of water, staring at what he did to my girl. *My* girl. I'm the only one who should be touching her. I should be the only one able to be in this position. "Quinn?" I ask, my voice weak and shaky as I try to prepare to hear the words I know that are to come. "D-did he..." I trail off, not even able to ask the question.

I can feel her stare burning into my top of my head as I focus on his fingerprints.

"Quinn, I need to know if—" My words are cut off when her fingers twist into my wet hair. She tugs slightly and I'm powerless but to look up at her.

Her eyes are full of unshed tears, her face pale and terrified. It's all I need for her to confirm my worst suspicions. She swallows, the muscles in her neck quivering with her uncertainty. She thinks I'm about to back away. She thinks I can't handle this. But everything I said to her earlier was true. Nothing about him or what happened will change how I feel about her. It won't change us. I refuse to allow it to.

She opens her mouth to say something. Knowing her, it's probably to apologise for something she had no fucking control over. Before a word passes her lips, I force her legs wider, part her, and lick up the length of her pussy.

If she needs to forget, then I'll damn well give her everything she fucking needs.

"Joe," she cries, but I don't react other than to up my tempo. Her fingers tighten in my hair and the pain is a welcome relief to the insistent one in my abdomen that won't abate.

"Oh god." Her hips flex, allowing me more access, and I thrust my tongue inside her as her legs tremble with the strength it takes her to stay upright.

She needs a distraction? Fuck if I'm not going to give her one.

I replace my tongue with two fingers and thrust them deep inside her, bending them so I know they'll hit the exact spot she needs. Her cries and mewls for more get louder and louder, encouraging me to push her higher.

Her body twitches and pulsates with the impending release, but I don't let her fall, not yet. I slow the pace, circle her clit with the tip of my tongue, and her entrance with my fingertip as she pants and demands more.

"You want more?" I ask, my voice deep and husky, showing my own hunger for her.

"More. Everything. Please, Joe, please."

Sliding two fingers back inside her, I lift my other hand and begin teasing her arse. She tenses for the briefest of seconds. I've no idea if this is what she had in mind when she said everything, but I trust her to tell me to stop if she doesn't want it.

But she never does. The water running down her back is enough to allow me to push my finger inside her, and she howls with pleasure as I stretch her open.

She's unbelievably tight, her muscles clamping down on my finger as my cock weeps to feel that kind of pressure. I suck her clit into my mouth, grazing it with my teeth, and with her full of me, her hips buck violently as she screams out my name, her pleasure racing through her body, making her legs go weak. Her fingers grip once more as she tries to stay upright as she rides out the pleasure.

Watching her come apart above me, even as broken as she is right now, is one of the most beautiful things I've ever seen. My heart damn near burst out of my chest for this incredible, brave woman before me.

Once she's ridden out every wave of pleasure, I pull my fingers from her and sit back on my heels. My cock's trying to rip through my boxers as I watch her chest heave as she tries to catch her breath.

Without thinking, I press my hand to my side, where the dressing is coming undone with the amount of water that's soaking into it.

"Shit, you shouldn't be getting that wet."

"I don't give a fuck. You needed me. I'm here." I climb to my feet and take her face in my hands. I want to say it's smooth, but the reality is anything but.

"But—"

"No buts."

"Okay, but I really think you should go and lie down." I want to argue and tell her that I'm fine, but I think we'd both know that would be a lie. "I'll order us some breakfast and we can see what's on the TV." It's her way of putting off the conversation from last night that we need to continue. Although our impromptu shower has answered quite a few questions I had about what happened while she was locked up in that bedroom, I won't be happy guessing based on her injuries. I need her to tell me. At least that way it'll stop my imagination going wild.

With Quinn's help, I drop my sopping wet boxers to the tiled floor and wrap a fluffy white towel around my waist. I want to stay and make sure she's okay after everything that just happened, but I'm struggling to hold myself upright.

Using the wall for support, I make my way to the living room and lie back on the sofa to the sounds of her faffing around in the bathroom.

Ignoring the TV for now, I focus on the scenery outside. I love London; it's the only home I've ever known, but I can't imagine wanting to move there after living somewhere as beautiful as here. I always thought I'd be a Londoner forever, but just my short time here is giving me ideas about my future that have never been there before. Suddenly I'm seeing a life in a house in the country with Quinn and a couple of kids. My heart races, but it's not with the panic I thought it would be with the images that are playing out so clearly in my mind.

I've always said point blank that I've never wanted to settle down. Never wanted to have kids and subject them to even an element of what I've had to suffer during my life, but suddenly none of that matters because I know that, with Quinn by my side, I'd never need to worry about our children suffering because they'd have the most incredibly supportive mother. We've both been screwed over by bad parents, and I can't help but wonder as I lie here with the winter sun streaming in through the huge windows if all of that bullshit was just preparing us for our future as parents ourselves. We've both experienced how bad it can be; we know exactly what not to do.

"What's put that smile on your face? I thought you'd be frustrated with blue balls," she says with a laugh. My heart drops slightly when I see she's totally covered up again in those damn leggings and what I've realised is Lauren's hoodie.

"Just thinking about our future," I admit.

"Our future, huh?" She comes to sit on the free bit of sofa beside me and places her hand on my chest.

"Yep. Wondering what our kids might look like."

Her eyes widen in shock, but she doesn't look totally opposed to the idea. "You're not serious?"

"Deadly. I thought I'd lost you, Quinn. When I turned up to class and found Eddie standing at the front of your classroom, I thought that was it for us."

"I'm sorry." She looks away as if she's ashamed of everything that's happened.

"Hey, don't do that." Lifting my hand, I cup her cheek and

turn her back towards me. "Don't apologise for anything you didn't have control over. The only thing I wish was different is that you'd told me what kind of danger you were in. I'd have done anything in my power to protect you."

"I didn't want to drag you into all this."

"How'd that work out for you?" Her eyes fill with tears.

"You're not the only one who thought they'd lost something. I'll never forget that moment as I watched him slide that blade into your stomach."

"I'm fine."

"Just—"

"Ah, come on, babe. It'll take more than a little knife wound to kill me off."

"Little? You saw the size of that thing, right?" Of course I had, I was the one who grabbed it from the kitchen to free her from her restraints. "I need to change this dressing," she says. Clearly her previous question was rhetorical.

She's up off the sofa and at the other side of the room, rummaging through the bag of stuff we left the hospital with, before I have a chance to blink.

She lines everything up on the coffee table in front of us before turning back to me, ready to start picking off the wet bandage that's still attached to my stomach. She starts scratching at the corner, trying to lift the sticky stuff, but it hardly budges now it's dried.

When she does eventually manage to get enough up to grab, she pulls it and I cry out.

She damn near jumps a mile, her wide, panicked eyes turning to me. She's totally horrified that she hurt me.

"Shit, I'm sorry. I was trying to be gentle."

I try to stop my lips twitching, but I lose the fight and a wide smile tugs at my mouth.

"You little shit." She swats my shoulder gently as she realises that I'm having her on. Okay, it hurt a little where it caught my hair, but it wasn't a pain worth crying about. Who am I kidding? She's got her hands on my bare skin. I'm not going to do anything to put an end to that.

She goes back to the task at hand and gently pulls the bandage from my skin. I'm fascinated by the sight of her delicate fingers touching me so softly.

"It looks like it's healing well."

"Good." I don't look at my wound. Instead my eyes lift to her as she works. Her dark, wet hair is falling like a curtain around her face as she studies my stomach. Every time her skin connects with mine, my muscles twitch, but at no point does it distract from how beautiful she is.

My cock stirs once again behind the towel, and she doesn't miss it. Her eyes drop lower and a small smile curls at her lips.

"I'm pretty sure you should be focusing all your efforts on getting better," she whispers.

"Not possible when you're touching me."

"Even after—"

My fingers circle her wrists, stopping any more movement and cutting off her words.

"I meant what I said. I'm in love with you, Quinn. What you went through and what he did doesn't affect that. I want to kill that motherfucker with my bare hands for ever thinking it's okay to lay a finger on you, but it'll never stop me wanting you."

Her eyes hold mine. It's as if she's waiting for me to tell her that I'm lying, but she's going to be waiting a long time if that's the case. My heart pounds against my ribs as I wait for her to do something, my cock pressing against the towel, hoping to get some action.

"You need to rest."

Tugging on her wrist, I pull her so she's hovering over me. "What I need is you." Her eyes bounce between mine as she tries to figure out what to do for the best.

"If it hurts, at all, tell me and I'll stop." Her face is totally serious, and I find myself agreeing even though I already know that once she touches me, nothing will make me stop her.

She finishes reapplying my fresh bandage before dropping her lips to my abs. She kisses along the indentations until she finds the top of the towel. My eyes follow her every movement, my body desperate for her to unwrap the fabric and touch me after being away from her for so long.

My fingers dig into the sofa as I attempt to fight my need to flip her over and fuck her six ways from Sunday. I need to give her the space to do this at her own pace. I've no real idea where her head's at right now. I don't want her to feel like I'm pushing her into anything.

She glances up, wraps her fingers around the fabric at my waist, and smiles. It's wicked and full of promises, and excitement explodes in my belly. After everything, my Quinn's still in there somewhere. I can't deny that it's not a relief to see that little sparkle in her eyes.

Slowly, painfully fucking slowly, she pulls the towel from around my waist and allows it to fall to the sofa. Her eyes burn a trail down my torso before she finds my cock. She bites down on her bottom lip as she watches it twitch with need.

I wait. It's hard as fuck—pun intended—but I'll wait forever if I have to.

Her eyes flick to mine, but unlike what I'm expecting, there's no hesitation in them. Finally, she reaches for me and wraps her slender fingers around my solid length. My hips buck from the sofa and I groan. It's a mixture of delight and pain, but thankfully from the way her eyes shine with achievement, she only hears the lust.

"Fuck, Quinn," I moan as she slowly moves her hand up and down. I've not come since we were in Stratford. I was fucking desperate after we were interrupted by Erica, but I told myself that the next time I got off, it would be at her hands because I was determined to ensure that things were far from over between us—whatever it took—when I saw her again. I just never could have imagined the situation that was about to unfold.

"So fucking good."

She leans forward and licks the tip of my cock. I damn near come on the spot.

"Jesus."

Running her tongue around the top, she then lowers her mouth down my length. Threading my fingers into her hair, I help to guide her. My balls draw up all too soon and tingles erupt in the base of my spine.

"Quinn, I'm gonna—" I don't get a chance to finish my warning because she takes me right to the back of her throat and I explode.

My chest heaves, my body tingling with the aftershocks of my release, but as it begins to fade, the pain begins to make itself known once again.

My hand moves to rest on top of my fresh bandage. Quinn follows its movement and the blood drains from her face.

"Shit, did I hurt you?"

"It was so worth it."

"Fuck." She jumps up from her spot perched on the edge of the sofa and backs away like being close to me might be causing me pain. "Have you had your meds yet?"

"No. How about I take them, we wait an hour, and we can crack on with round two?" I lift a brow in the hope she agrees, but when hers pull together I know it's not going to happen. Shame, I could really do with being inside her right about now.

She rushes over to the bag she got the bandage from and pops out the pills I need before bringing them over with a fresh glass of water.

"What do you fancy for breakfast?" I open my mouth to respond, but I don't get a chance to say anything. "Don't say me. It's not happening. Not until you're healed."

"Spoil sport." I sulk.

CHAPTER EIGHT

We end up staying in our little lodge for five days before Quinn decides I'm allowed out into the world again. As much as I'd like to re-join real life, I'm also a little sad to leave our haven behind...although I'm hoping that getting back to London and putting some distance between Quinn and this place might help with her nightmares that seem to haunt her each night. I'd do anything to take away her pain, her memories, but I'm powerless to do anything but hold her as she cries. It's been incredible just being the two of us, finding out all the little things about each other that we'd not had a chance to do until this point.

Quinn opened up more about her previous life. Although she was understandably reluctant to tell me some of the darker parts, she managed it. I think she was worried about my opinion, but after telling her for the millionth time that the stuff that's happened in the past doesn't bother me, I think she's starting to believe me.

She makes me sit on the edge of the bed while she packs up

the small amount of stuff we have. Seeing as she was brought here against her will and I arrived in a bit of a panic, all we have is what Quinn ordered for us when we first got here.

Thankfully, her bruises have almost completely faded now. I can see her confidence come back a little more each day, and it's incredible to witness. She's becoming the Quinn I fell for again and somehow managing to put *him* behind her.

"I can help, you know. I'm not completely useless."

"Just chill out. We've got a long journey."

"We're going to London, not Australia. I'll be fine."

"You say that now; you've not experienced my motorway driving."

I laugh at her but stay put as she carries the bags to the front door.

"I'm not sure I'm ready to leave this place in favour of that damp studio flat in London."

Stepping up behind her, I wrap my arm around her waist, drop my head to her neck and breathe her in.

"Move in with me?"

She tenses but doesn't immediately say no. "Don't you live in your friend's flat? I can't imagine she wants me there." Her voice is flat, and it gives me a little hope that she might actually be up for this.

"I've actually moved into her boyfriend's place upstairs so they can be together and there are no more accidental interruptions. Trey said I can stay there as long as I'd like, but if you're up for it, I'd really love to get a place of our own sometime soon."

Turning in my arms, she looks up at me, an unreadable expression on her face. "You're serious, aren't you?"

"Deadly. I don't want our time together to be over."

"But I'll be there every day. It won't be like it's been here. We'll have to work and—"

"I'm aware that I'm not asking you on a long-term holiday, Quinn. I know we're going to have responsibilities and that at times, it's going to be stressful. I've never done it before, but I want it all with you. I want the nights cuddled on the sofa, the lazy Sunday mornings. I want the heated arguments and the hot make-up sex afterwards. I want a future, Quinn, and that's something I'd never thought I'd say."

She's silent for a beat too long, and I almost find myself telling her to forget about it and attempting to convince her that it was a joke, but then she opens her mouth and just one quiet word leaves her lips that makes every part of my life fall into place.

"Yes."

"Yes...as in yes you'll move in with me?"

"Yes." A smile twitches at the corners of her lips as my heart races. "Yes, I'll live with you." It's much louder this time, almost a squeal before she wraps her arms around me and holds as tight as she can without hurting me. "I love you too." She mumbles it against my chest so quietly I almost think I've misheard her.

Pushing against her shoulders, I force her to move back a little. "What was that?"

When her eyes find mine, they're full of unshed tears and swimming with emotion. "I love you too, Joe."

My fingers twist in her hair and I pull her lips to mine. My heart damn near beats out of my chest as I repeat those three little words in my head. I've heard them before. Lauren says she loves me, Erica's even said it once or twice, but I've never heard it in this way, and fuck if it's not just knocked my world upside fucking down.

My cock swells against her stomach, still desperate for some real action, but sadly she takes a step back, putting some space between us.

Her chest's heaving just as much as mine as we stand there

silently for a few moments, absorbing what just happened between us.

"Before we do this, there's something I need to do. You're welcome to come or you can just wait for me. It's up to you."

She looks unsure of herself and I hate it. Reaching out, I take her hand in mine. "I'll follow you anywhere, Quinn."

"I thought you might say that. Come on then, the sooner we get this over with the sooner we can head home."

Home. I've called a few places home in my life, but I can honestly say that this is the first time I feel like I really have one. It doesn't matter that the flat we're going back to is someone else's; all that matters is that she's going to be by my side.

We load Lauren's car, but the second Quinn puts an address into the SatNav I know exactly where she's going.

I stay quiet as she drives the relatively short journey back to her old house.

"I always hated this house," she murmurs as she pulls the car to a stop in the driveway beside the two cars still parked out the front. "It's cold. Unwelcoming. Kind of fitting, I guess."

"Do you own it?"

"No, it's a school property. Dad ensured we got the best one—well besides his."

"It's a nice house."

"Is it?"

I don't respond. She doesn't need me to.

Eventually she climbs from the car and I follow her towards the front door.

There's a little key lock that she quickly opens to reveal a key. She sucks in a large breath before lifting it to the lock. Stepping up closer behind her, I press my hand into the small of her back in support and she unlocks the door.

We step inside in silence and I follow her as she pokes her

head into every room. I've no idea if she's come here because she needs to get stuff or what, but she can have all the time she needs.

I didn't pay any attention to the interior of this place the last time I was here aside from the dark room Quinn had been locked up in, but it's exactly as I'd have imagined from everything she's told me about her previous life. Everything is just so. It's all clearly expensive and has its place. It reminds me of my parents' house, and I hate it.

I follow behind her, taking everything in and fighting the memories from my childhood that keep threatening to pop up. Nothing I ever did in that house was good enough. I was always made to feel like a failure and a disappointment—two things I'd quite happily never feel again.

"Joe, are you okay?" Quinn asks, turning and coming a stop in front of me. She reaches out and takes both my hands in hers.

"Of course, why wouldn't I be? I should be the one asking you that question. Being back here must be—" I trail off, not really knowing the right word to use.

"It's...closure. This part of my life is over. But you look like you're about to throw up."

"I'm fine." She eyes me curiously, but, obviously not wanting to spend any more time here than necessary, she doesn't question me.

Before she takes a step up onto the stairs, she sucks in a huge breath.

"You don't have to do this."

"I do." Squaring her shoulders, she begins to climb and I keep right behind her.

Ignoring most of the doors, she stops at one and pushes it open.

The room is an office, much like the one I saw through the window at the school, with a huge mahogany desk and leather chair sitting behind. It's nothing but pretentious. I can't imagine for a second that Quinn ever worked in here.

She walks behind the desk and takes a seat before looking up at me. "Can you get into this?"

Not knowing what she means, I follow her lead until I'm staring at the same drawers she is.

"It's locked," she adds, just in case I hadn't already figured that out.

"So you think I'm capable of breaking and entering?" I raise an eyebrow at her in accusation.

"How did you get in here to find me in the first place?"

"I smashed your back doors in."

"Case in point. Now..." She waves her hand in front of the somewhat flimsy drawers and waits.

"You got a crowbar or something?"

"What, no lock picking?"

"Nah, I missed that day at school."

"Under the stairs there should be a tool box. See what you can find."

I follow her instructions and am soon standing with my head in the understairs cupboard, rooting through a huge bag.

Crowbar in hand, I head back to find her. She's still behind the desk, but she's now got the computer on and is furiously writing stuff down into a notebook.

The floorboards creak as I step into the room. Her head flies up and panic fills her eyes for the briefest moment, showing me that she's anything but fine being here, but that fear soon morphs into something else. I've seen that hungry look on her face once before. It was the day I unexpectedly picked her up from work and was covered in a day's worth of dirt. I expected her to be disgusted, she didn't seem like a girl who'd be willing to sit inside a dirty work van, but the girl I actually picked up that day was far from what I imagined.

Her eyes darken as she stares at me with the crowbar bouncing in my hand before they drop to my body. I'm wearing a plain black t-shirt and a pair of grey joggers, but the way she's feasting on my body, you'd think I was naked. My cock swells as images of what I'd like to do to her in the place she lived with her cunt of a husband fill my mind.

Taking a step forward, and then another, I delight in watching her chest begin to rise and fall faster.

"Do you have any idea how badly I want to fuck you over your husband's desk right now?"

Her pupils dilate, the blue damn near vanishing as her cheeks heat and she squirms in the seat. It's all I need to know that she's as up for this as I am.

Sadly, when she opens her mouth, she doesn't say what I'm hoping for.

"And do you know how badly I don't want you back in the hospital because you've split your stitches? There will be no desk fucking until you're healed."

"Jesus." I lift my hand to my hair, tugging on the length as I repeat those two words in my mind. *Desk fucking.* Her voice sounds so soft and innocent as she says them, but I know for a fact that she's imagining it just as much as I am right now.

Stalking towards her, she wheels the chair back slightly but doesn't really want to escape. I can see the delight in her eyes as my hands land on the arms, caging her in.

"You do like to pretend to be a good little girl, don't you?"

"I just...d-don't...fuck." Her words falter when I slip my hand up the inside of her hoodie and t-shirt to find her bare breast beneath. Her nipple pebbles against my touch instantly, making my already growing cock solid with my need for her.

"Joe...we...we can't," she moans, the breathy sound to her voice at odds with her words.

"Says who? Your ex-husband? Fuck him. He gave up any right to an opinion the first time he mistreated you."

"Joe, we can't."

"Shhh." Wrapping my hands around her waist, I lift her from the chair and deposit her on the edge of the desk. My stomach pulls, telling me that she's right about the fucking, but that doesn't stop me giving her one final memory of this place in an attempt to erase a few of the old ones.

Gripping onto the waistband of her leggings, she lifts her hips and allows me to slip them from her body. I discard them in a pile on the floor before dropping to my knees and spreading her legs as wide as they'll go.

She stares down at me as I focus on her centre. "Let's show him how it should have been done," I mutter before leaning forward and licking up the length of her. Her legs tremble under my palms and a moan of pleasure rips from her lips.

"Fuck yes."

She watches me the entire time, and my chest swells with the knowledge that this moment is one she wants to remember from this house. Knowing that I might be able to take even a tiny bit of the horror away that went on under this roof is everything to me.

As I slip two fingers inside her, her muscles clamp down, making me wish it was my cock. I'm fucking desperate for her, but I also don't want to end up back on a hospital bed being stitched up.

My fingers curl, hitting her sweet spot, and she cries my name out into the otherwise silent house. Two more licks to her clit and she's falling, pushing out all the old nightmares and allowing this sweet memory to replace them.

I lick at her until she's come back down from her high. Her

chest heaves, her cheeks and neck flushed with her pleasure. It's a sight to fucking behold, and it's all fucking mine.

Sitting back on my haunches, I watch as she drags in some much needed air, her legs still apart, giving me the best view of my life.

"Well…I can safely say that's never happened here before."

"Sex in the office?"

"I was more thinking of me getting a happy ending."

"Wait…he never…?" I trail off, too stunned to finish the question.

"Nope. Never."

"I know he's done some seriously unforgivable shit but not even allowing you that pleasure is up there with the worst of it."

"I'm not sure if it was a case of him not allowing it or him unable to."

"Really?" My male ego swells at her statement. "So am I the only one to—"

"Give me an orgasm? Besides myself, yeah. What?" she asks when I don't say anything.

"Just imagining what that might be like. I think you might need to show me exactly how you do it one day."

She swats my shoulder as she stands and rights her clothing. "Let's get this shit done and get out of here, yeah?"

"Whatever you say. Take whatever time you need." I fall back onto the arsehole's chair. My raging hard-on is obvious beneath the fabric of my trousers. Quinn's gaze falls to it and conflict fills her eyes. "Just do your thing. That'll wait." It pains me to say it, but it's the truth. It'll still be hard once we're back and away from this hellhole.

"I need these open." She points to the drawers we came in here for in the first place, and I'm reminded that she sent me on a mission before I had her legs spread on the desk.

"My pleasure."

It takes mere seconds for the old wood to splinter around the flimsy locks. The drawers slide open, mostly revealing a load of crap, but when she pulls the bottom one out I soon understand why she wanted it all. She pulls out paperwork for multiple bank accounts, her passport and driving licence along with her birth certificate.

"I couldn't get in here for all this before I left. He kept this room secured like Fort Knox."

Her words fade off as I notice one of the figures on the bank statements. "Jesus, Quinn. This all yours?" I don't think I've ever seen so many digits on a bank account before.

"It's a joint account but yeah, that's mine."

"Fucking hell, no wonder you weren't worried about bending my credit card on that luxury lodge."

"The lawyer I've been talking to says that I could probably take him for everything after what he's done."

"No less than you deserve."

"Maybe. I'm not sure I can leave him with nothing, though. He might be a monster, but he has worked for this."

"Fucking hell, Quinn. You're more forgiving than me." She shrugs as she finishes off finding what we need.

"With a bit of luck the divorce papers will be inside my flat when we get back and I can get the ball moving. The sooner I lose my surname the better."

I bite down on the inside of my cheeks so hard that the metallic taste of blood fills my mouth as I attempt to keep the words, 'you can have mine instead' inside.

"You think he'll make it easy on you?"

Her sad laugh says it all, but she backs it up with, "We can only hope, right?"

She finishes collecting everything she needs before we walk

out of the room. She looks down at where the door is still swinging in the wind from where I smashed it down, but she makes no move to go down that end of the hallway. I can't say I blame her; her memories must be enough.

"That was my office. It was all cream and gold. I used to love it in there."

I remember the black walls and hard floorboards from when I found her. Clearly the douchebag did some decorating after Quinn left.

"Are you done?" I ask as we descend the stairs.

"Yeah. Let's get the hell out of here."

CHAPTER NINE

I t's just a simple car journey. It should be easy, but by the time I climb out of Lauren's car outside Quinn's building, I ache like a motherfucker.

Quinn wanted to stop, but I insisted I'd rather just get back so she drove us straight here. In hindsight it might have been a mistake, but at least we're back now. A quick trip up to her flat for some of her stuff and then home. Well...the flat Trey rents, but it's home for the two of us for now. I'm hoping we can start searching for our own place as soon as possible. I'm ready for it, ready for my future with this girl.

"Why are you smiling?" she asks, taking my hand as we walk towards the entrance to her building. The door is still fucked and just another reason why she shouldn't stay here, even if the threats are now behind bars.

"Just thinking about us...the future."

Her hand squeezes mine. "It's exciting, isn't it?"

"I understand it now—how Lauren couldn't refuse Ben when he came back into her life. How Erica couldn't deny Trey when he kept pushing. This thing. This connection. It's...unbelievable." Turning her into my chest, I tuck her hair behind her ears and stare into her eyes. The physical evidence of her ordeal is all but gone now. I'm relieved that she's not reminded of it every time she looks in the mirror. "It's everything. You're everything."

Her eyes fill with tears, but there's a smile on her face. "I don't even know how to thank you for everything you've done."

"No need, babe. I'd go to the end of the earth to find you. Now, come on, I can't wait to take you home."

"Okay," she whispers, excitement filling her voice. Her step is lighter as she turns back towards the building.

Quinn lets out a little squeal when she stops at the post boxes and finds a huge manila envelope with a lawyer's stamp on the front. Her excitement is infectious, and I find myself getting carried away with thoughts of making her mine once again.

"Now we wait to find out if he's going to sign his copy."

"You confident?" I ask as we climb the stairs.

She hesitates, but after a second she turns to me, a wide smile on her face, and says, "Of course. We're done. What's the point in refusing now?" I don't point out that her ex-husband is quite obviously a control freak and will probably want to manipulate her any chance he gets, even from behind bars.

We fill a couple of black bags with her few belongings and she finally gets the chance to put the old soup and very mouldy bread in the bin.

"It might sound odd," she says as we head back down the stairs, "but I think I'm going to miss this little flat."

"That's not odd."

"I'd dreamed about what this place might look like for years. The place that I'd escape to. My sanctuary away from my past. It might not have been much, but it's everything to me."

"Plus, it's where you were living when you found me."

"I'm pretty sure *you* found *me*. You were the one who walked into my classroom looking all bad boy nerd. I didn't stand a chance."

We've steered clear of talking about the whole student/teacher issue while we've been away, but as she says the word 'classroom' her voice drops and I'm reminded that we've got some hard conversations ahead of us. *She's moving in with me.* That's all the reminder I need to know that whatever comes next doesn't matter. I'll forget all about qualifications and a better job as long as I have her by my side. That's if Eddie would even let me back after everything.

I'm desperate to ask what she wants to do, but I keep my mouth shut until we're settled and less exhausted from the journey.

"Ready to go home?"

"So ready."

I direct her to my building and in no time we're pulling Lauren's car into my parking space out front.

By some fucking miracle, the out of order sign on the lift is nowhere to be seen. I breathe a sigh of relief that we don't have to carry the contents of the car up four flights of stairs to Trey's flat.

"Wow, this place is nice," Quinn says, walking in ahead of me and placing the bags on one of the sofas.

"Yeah, I could have found myself in a worse place, that's for sure."

"You go sit down." I turn to her to argue, but she doesn't allow it. "I know you're struggling. Just go and sit down and I'll get the last of the things."

"No need," a very familiar voice says from the doorway. When I turn back I find both Erica and Trey with armfuls of our bags.

"Stalking much?" I ask with a laugh, assuming they heard our footsteps and ran to find us.

"I'm so glad you're okay." Erica's eyes are a little wet as she runs at me and wraps her arms around my waist.

It hurts, but I don't give a fuck. Returning her hug, I drop a kiss to the top of her head.

"Okay, enough of you. I need to meet your girl properly." She wipes the tears staining her cheeks that are probably courtesy of her pregnancy hormones.

Erica turns to Quinn and none of us miss the redness of her cheeks as she's reminded of the first time they met. Quinn might be embarrassed, but I know Erica better than that and she won't give a fuck about finding us mid-fuck. It won't faze her in the slightest.

She opens her arms and Trey and I watch as Erica pulls Quinn into her embrace. She says something in Quinn's ear that we're too far away to hear, but whatever it is has Quinn looking up at me over Erica's shoulder. Her eyes are soft and her smile is easy, and I relax for the first time since she walked away from me the morning she claimed to need space. I didn't realise it was still eating at me, but having her here, in the arms of one of my best friends, it really settles inside me that this could be it.

"We should leave you to get sorted," Erica says, releasing Quinn. "I just needed to see for myself that you were okay."

"Stay for dinner?" I ask without thinking. This living with someone and having to ask their opinion is going to take some time to get used to. It's just that now I'm surrounded by my people once again, I'm not ready for them to leave quite yet. My eyes fly to Quinn—I'm about to apologise when she nods.

"Yes, I'm starving. What about Lauren and Ben, should we ring them?"

There's a moment of silence as all eyes turn on me. Quinn's just curious about inviting more of my friends while both Erica and Trey smile at me with knowing eyes. They've both realised just how far gone I am for this girl. She gets me. She knows that the only thing missing right now is my best friend and that, after everything we've just been through, I need this. I need my people, and I need to be normal. More than that, I need her to be part of my normal.

"I'm on it," Erica announces, pulling her phone out and turning away slightly.

I reach my hand out, and Quinn walks over and gently wraps her arms around my waist. "Thank you."

"I know how much you missed them. It's nice to see you smile like you did when they turned up."

"I smile more than I ever have with you."

"I know, and I love it. But they're your family. I get it."

"And what about yours?"

"My family? I don't have a lot of that these days." The sadness in her voice is like a physical pain to my chest. I want to talk to her about her mum but right now is not the time for that. Once the dust is settled, maybe I'll bring it up.

"I was thinking of Eddie. You want to invite him to join us?"

"Really?" Her brows draw together in confusion. "I didn't think you liked him."

I think for a moment to find the right words to describe my feelings for Eddie. Is he a judgemental prick? Yes. But he's helped Quinn out when she's needed it the most, and he had my back when we went after her. Kind of. But if he means something to Quinn, he's important to me. End of.

"I don't really know him, but I know you, and if you say he's a good guy, then I'll give him all the time in the world to try to prove it."

"Thank you."

"If it wasn't for him, I'd never have found you." A shudder

runs up my spine as I wonder what might have happened had that been the case.

Quinn goes over to find her phone, which is dead after being abandoned in her flat for over two weeks.

"You want to use mine?" Taking it from my hand, she finds his number and lifts it to her ear. "You think he'll be able to cope with all the ink?" I nod over to Trey, although most of his is hidden beneath his shirt. Ben's, however, will be very much on display for Eddie to disapprove of.

"I'm hoping you might have smashed a few of his preconceived perceptions after saving my life."

I swallow down the emotion that statement drags up. Is that what I did? Would he have gone that far?

Seeing where my thoughts are, Quinn places her hand on my forearm and gives me a little smile as the sound of the call connecting fills my ears.

Not more than thirty minutes later Eddie follows Lauren and Ben into the flat. Thankfully, Trey and Erica ran downstairs to get everyone something to drink seeing as our kitchen is basically empty. Before long we've all placed our food orders and are sitting back on the sofas with drinks in hand. Erica sulks as she looks at the glasses of wine in both Quinn and Lauren's hands seeing as she's unable to drink and has to put up with a glass of cloudy lemonade. Eddie looks surprisingly at home with a beer as he talks to Trey about the education system. It's not something I thought Trey would be all that interested in, but I guess he needs to be seeing as he has two teenage daughters who'll be going through it all soon.

"So, are you going to be leaving us for better things once you've got a few certificates behind you?" Ben asks. He doesn't look as happy about the idea as I'm sure he would have done not so long ago. He hated me when he first came back, and rightly so.

Lauren made it look like I'd stepped into his place when the side of the bed he abandoned was barely cold, but we've managed to build some kind of friendship now that Lauren's in his arms once again.

Thinking about reality is a sobering thought, one I'm not ready for. "I've no idea what I'm doing, man. It seemed like a good idea, and I guess it was because I met this one." I wrap my arm around Quinn's shoulders and pull her into me, kissing the top of her head. "But I've no idea what comes next."

"Well, we'll support you whatever you decide. If you want to go part-time so you can study or anything, all you need to do is ask. There are definitely opportunities for progression as long as the work keeps coming like it is if you'd like to stay in the industry."

"That means a lot. Thank you. But we'll see. I've got more important things to worry about now."

"I get that, man. I really do."

The evening is just like so many we've had in the past, aside from the obvious additions of Quinn and Eddie. I feel more like myself than I have in a long time. I hadn't realised the strain keeping my evening school and Quinn a secret were, but now it's all out there I feel like I can breathe again.

Once we've eaten, the girls insist on cleaning up, leaving me alone with the guys. While Eddie sits sipping on his beer, probably wondering what his life has become—at least he didn't turn up wearing his tie pin and pocket square—the three of us watch our girls as they clean, chat, and laugh. Quinn seems to have fitted in perfectly, and I couldn't be happier. Stories of her past are depressing at best; having a couple of girlfriends is exactly what she needs. I'm busy scheming up things I could plan for the three of them to do when Ben drags me from my thoughts.

"I never thought I'd see the day, you know?"

"Sorry, what?" Turning to look at him, I find amusement written all over his face.

"The day you looked at a girl like that." He nods over to where Quinn is and I can't help but follow his gaze. I just can't get enough of her. Her dark hair's been pulled back from her face with a couple of clips, and she's still wearing one of my hoodies over a pair of leggings. It's so fucking sexy. I look away as she goes to bend over to load the dishwasher because I don't need my boner trying to break through my joggers while I sit with these dickheads.

"You're just still shocked that I didn't fall for a guy. Don't even try to tell me you lot didn't have bets going on."

Ben holds his hands up in defence as Eddie blanches beside him. He clearly wasn't expecting me to openly announce that I've swung both ways in the past. My sexuality isn't something I'll ever hide, and I smile thinking that it'll just give him something else to judge me for, but all he does is shrug his shoulders and take another sip of his beer. Maybe I've proved that no matter who was in my past, Quinn's it for me now.

Quinn laughs at something, and my head snaps around to find her once more. A smile twitches my lips and my chest swells with everything I feel for her.

"Fucking hell, he's gonna beat us to it, isn't he?"

Turning back, I find Ben elbowing Trey in the ribs. Trey laughs, clearly having a better idea about what Ben's talking about than I do.

"You bought the ring yet?" I damn near spit out the beer I'd just tipped into my mouth.

"Ring? No."

"You've thought about it though, right?"

"I...uh..."

"You're so fucking whipped, man."

Ben and Trey joke about me falling for the teacher while Eddie sits nervously playing with his can. I'd figured out the first time I saw him with Quinn that he wanted her. I've no idea how he's feeling now aside from knowing that anything between the two of them is never going to happen. Or maybe he's just worrying about having a member of staff shagging a student. Who the fuck knows? He's so stiff and unreadable it's hard to get much from him.

"So what about you then?" Ben asks turning to Eddie. "Got a girl on the scene?"

"No, not currently." Ben's eyebrows rise at his posh tone.

"You're into girls though, right?"

Laughing to myself, I watch as Eddie's eyes almost pop out of his head at the suggestion.

"Yes. I'm very much into girls."

"You should come out with us sometime. I'm sure we'd find you a few willing candidates, right Joe?"

The image of some of the women I've met on nights out come to mind. They'd eat Eddie alive.

"No, no, I think I'm good," he says, sounding horrified by the suggestion.

"We'll see. You can't be the only single one in this little group."

The way Ben's accepted him kind of surprises me. Eddie's not really our kind of guy, but I guess he's thinking the same as me. If he's important to Quinn, he's just been baptised into this crazy little family we've got going on.

***

BY THE TIME we say goodbye to everyone and Ben's adamantly told us both that we've got to be at the work Christmas do he's organised next weekend, I'm so ready for a bit of one on one time with my girl.

"Your friends are—"

"Crazy, weird, completely fucking nuts?"

"I was going to say awesome, but yeah, I guess those work too." While we were locked in our little lodge, I'd given Quinn the rundown of each of my friends and how they got to where they are now so she'd have a little inside information ready for when she met them. From how well she got on with the girls, it seems my plan worked.

"Lauren and Erica invited me out for a shopping trip at the weekend, if you're okay of course," she adds quickly.

"Quinn, I am more than okay and perfectly able to look after myself for a few hours. You should go, get your new life started with a bang."

"I thought we'd already done that when we pulled my first all-nighter."

"Oh yeah, that night went with a bang all right."

The image of her falling apart beneath my hands once again fills my mind and my cock swells. Lifting my hands so my palms cup her breasts, I squeeze until she lets out a little moan of pleasure.

"But your—"

"I'm fine, Quinn. Stop worrying and let us take what we both need. Plus," I add, a salacious smile forming on my lips, "you can do all the work."

"Oh, can I?"

"Fuck yeah. I wanna watch you ride me." My heart pounds and my blood reaches boiling point as it all heads south. "Come on. Let's christen our new home." Taking her hands in mine, I pull her down to the bedroom.

The second we're in the room, I reach for the hem of my hoodie and pull it up and over her head, revealing her thin t-shirt. That soon follows and lands in a pile on the floor so I can suck her nipples into my mouth. Her taste explodes on my tongue, and I'm reminded once again that I'm probably never going to get enough.

Kissing down her stomach, I push her leggings from her legs before standing and making quick work of my clothes. The second I'm naked, I fall down onto the bed and stretch out, waiting for her to do her worst.

"You sure about this?" She chews on her fingernail as her eyes run the length of me. They linger on my cock, telling me that although she's questioning this, she wants it just as badly as I do.

"Get the fuck up here."

She crawls onto the bed, going to settle herself over my waist, but that wasn't what I had in mind—not yet, anyway.

Wrapping my hands around her waist, I lift her until she's straddling my face.

"Oh."

"Oh fucking right." I pull her hips down so she's at the perfect distance to be able to tease with the tip of my tongue, but I don't allow her to fall. It's been forever since I was inside her, and the next time she comes she's going to be full to the brim with my cock.

"Joe, please," she begs when I pull my fingers from her just before she reaches the point of no return.

Unable to wait any longer, I allow her to crawl down my body before resting my arms out and allowing her to take control. She wastes no time in wrapping her hand around my cock and guiding me to her entrance.

We both gasp as we connect for the first time in weeks. My entire body locks up with pleasure as she slowly sinks down onto me, her pussy clenching tighter with every inch she takes.

"Fucking perfect," I moan as I watch her start to move. She's slow and gentle. I know she's worried about hurting me and splitting my stitches, but I'm determined to drive her so crazy that she forgets.

Unable to only watch, I grab on to her hips and force her lower so I can grind into her. She cries out my name, and, exactly as I intended, she ups her tempo. Her tits bounce as she drops down harshly on me, desperate to find the release I kept her on the edge of all this time.

Just before she falls, her hands lift and she takes her breasts, squeezing her nipples between her fingers.

"Fuck, Quinn. So fucking hot. So fuck—" I don't get to say any more because her pussy squeezes me so fucking tight that it sends me over the edge with her.

She rides out every last second of our pleasure before falling down onto me. Our chests heave, our hot skin sticking together, but I couldn't imagine anything better. Her weight gets heavier as she relaxes and I have to shift slightly when my stomach starts to ache.

"Shit, am I hurting you?"

"I'm perfect. You're fucking perfect."

She shifts her weight off me but we don't lose our contact as we both drift off to sleep.

I want to say that being back in London means Quinn gets a full night's rest, but it's far from that. If anything, her night terrors are worse. She's refused to talk about her nightmares, but I don't need to hear her words to know what they're about. If things don't start improving then I fear I'm going to have to push her to talk— whether that's to me or a professional. Only time will tell.

CHAPTER TEN

The smile that lights up Quinn's face when she fights her way into the flat, laden down with bags after her shopping trip with the girls, is everything.

She walked out of the house this morning leaving me with a raging hard on after she got herself all dressed up for her day out. Her excitement was infectious and her joy now is exactly the same. Anyone else would think she has nothing to worry about, but I see her concern when she thinks I'm not looking. I recognise the extra makeup she's using to cover the dark circles under her eyes.

"I'm assuming you've had a good day."

"It's been incredible. My feet hurt!"

"Sit down and I'll get you a coffee."

"Wine?" she asks with a laugh.

"Sure thing. Wine coming right up."

Hearing that my suspicions were correct about her never having had a girly day out before confirmed what I was thinking about ensuring she gets to do it all now. She might have given me her London bucket list the night I took her out, but I think in reality there's a lot more that needs to go on it.

Taking her glass over, I fall down onto the sofa next to her and allow her to show me everything she bought.

By the time she's been through all the bags, there's a towering pile of clothes, shoes, and handbags, not to mention lingerie that I'm dying to see her in, on the coffee table in front of us.

"Whoa, how much did you spend?"

"I've no idea. Do you have any idea how good it is to say that?"

Having lived quite a bit of my life with absolutely nothing to my name, I agree, knowing exactly how she must be feeling.

The solicitor Eddie set her up with to deal with her divorce proceedings came over yesterday seeing as they'd only been speaking on the phone the last couple of weeks and explained the process, and if everything goes as he's planning then she shouldn't need to worry about money for a very long time. Which brings us to the elephant in the room.

Her job.

As if she can read my mind, she rests back on the sofa, takes a sip of her wine and turns to me.

"I don't think I want to go back to work." She says the words in a rush like she's not sure what my response is going to be. "I mean, I want to work, but I don't think I want to go back to my old job."

"Okay."

"Okay?"

"Of course. We've got a place to live, I've got a job that pays pretty well, and you've got some money. Why would it be an issue?"

"I just—" Her face pales.

Taking her free hand in mine, I stare into her eyes to ensure she hears every word I say. "I'm not him, Quinn. My priority is you and your happiness. I don't care if I have to work double to allow you to do whatever it is you want. I'll do anything it takes to make you happy."

Tears fill her eyes and I catch the first one that falls with my thumb. She nods but doesn't say anything for a minute or two.

"What about you? You're going back to school, right?"

"I'd like to, but like I said, it's not my priority right now. Anyway, Eddie might not even have me back."

"I'm sure he will. Let's invite him round for dinner and we'll sweet talk him into letting you back. Probably best to do that before I resign. I'll help you catch up on what you've missed while I look for a new job."

"What do you want to do?"

"I still want to work with kids, but I'm not totally sure."

"We'll figure it out."

She relaxes into my side and breathes me in. I want to bite my tongue and follow her lead, ignoring the elephant in the room, but knowing it's in her best interest, I sit up and look down at her.

"W-what's wrong?" Her brows draw together, sensing that I'm about to say something that she's not going to like.

"I think...I think you should see someone about what happened."

"I'm fine, Joe. This isn't the first time I've had nightmares. They'll get better."

"But what if they don't? I'm worried about you."

She blows out a long breath as I stare at her, pleading with her to do the sensible thing. She keeps playing off what happened like it was an everyday thing, but it wasn't. It's something she needs to deal with before it takes over our lives and he continues to have control over her.

"Okay," she whispers. "Okay. I'll look into it."

"Thank you," I say, a huge wave of relief washing through me. I want us to start our lives together properly, not with him hanging over us. We've still no idea if he's going to grant her the divorce she deserves; he shouldn't take her sleep too.

WE HAVE the most surreal week. Well, it's surreal to me because I've never done the domesticated thing before. Together we clean the flat and move the furniture around a bit to make it less Trey's place and more ours, and we go shopping for some little trinkets and cushions that Quinn says will make the place more homely. After being cooped up for the past week, it's incredible to get out of the house and get some exercise and fresh air. We fill the cupboards full of food and spend our nights cooking together. Quinn escorts me to the doctors to have my stitches out and to hear that I really am okay and should be able to go back to work soon, although only on light duties at first. I also hold her hand while she registers and books an appointment to get the ball rolling for her to get the help she needs. Her entire body trembled with fear, telling me that she was doing the right thing. She needs to deal with this properly, and as much as I wish I could be the one to fix everything, I know I'm not capable of it.

By the time the weekend rolls around we've fallen into our new life in our new home easily.

I leave Quinn to sleep in on Saturday morning seeing as she had a particularly bad night, and make our morning coffee. I tidy up a little from the night before, and when I walk back into the bedroom with steaming mugs in my hand her eyes flutter open.

"Good morning," I sing, my excitement getting the better of me.

"What's that smile for? Should I be scared?"

"Not at all. I've just got a surprise for you today."

"Oh?"

"I'm not telling you yet. It's a surprise."

"Fair enough." She pushes herself up the bed, the duvet falling to her waist and revealing her perfect, naked tits to me.

"On second thought, I might keep you in bed all day." Even though I was given the full go ahead from the doctor, Quinn is still keeping me on light duties in the bedroom it seems, despite the sexy lingerie that I know is hiding in her drawers. I'm fucking dying to take her exactly as I need her.

I hand her coffee over before climbing in beside her. She's silent for a few minutes as she chews on her bottom lip, deep in thought.

"What is it?" A small ball of dread fills my stomach. I hate it when she's obviously concerned about something, and this is most definitely one of those times.

Turning to me, I can see the tension in her features. Reaching out, I grab her free hand and squeeze in what I hope is support.

"Am I enough for you?" she asks quietly, casting her eyes away.

"What?" Grasping her cheek, I pull her back so she has no choice but to look into my eyes. Her blue ones start to swim with water as she waits for my response.

"Quinn," I breathe. "You're everything to me."

"But you used to—"

Guessing where she's going with this, I cut her off. "I was lost, Quinn. I went after whatever I could to try to find a place I belonged. It's the only way I knew. But it wasn't until you that I found where I was meant to be."

Her lip trembles as she reaches for me. "But the girls said—"

I laugh. "I should have known they were behind this."

"It's not their fault, they were just filling me in on some of your past...conquests."

"I'm not proud of my past, but I won't apologise for it. It was what it was. It distracted me when I needed it, but it's a part of who I am."

"I don't want you to apologise, Joe. I just want to know that you're not going to miss it. The men, the multiple partners."

Taking her mug from her hand, I place it on the bedside table and pull her down the bed, pushing the covers off in the process.

"Why would I miss that when I've got you?"

By the time we're both set for the day, she's running late for her surprise, but at least we're both satisfied—for now at least.

"Who's that?" Quinn asks when the buzzer sounds out.

"Your surprise."

She quirks an eyebrow but goes for the door when I make no move to do so. She's greeted by Lauren and Erica asking if she's ready to go.

"Where are we going exactly?"

Walking over, I pass her a bag I'd already packed. "You're going to spend the day at the spa so you're ready for our big night out."

"Really?" she asks, sounding like a little girl who's just been told it's Christmas morning.

"Really. Here's everything you're going to need."

She squeals with excitement but ignores the bag I'm holding out in favour of jumping into my arms.

"I love you," she says softly into my neck as I hold her.

"I love you, too."

When I glance up, I find both Lauren and Erica staring at us with soppy smiles on their faces.

Releasing Quinn, I hand her the bag. "You need to get going before these two start crying or some shit."

"It's the pregnancy hormones," Erica protests.

"Yeah, and what's her excuse?"

Lauren's mouth opens, but she doesn't get a chance to say anything.

"Oh my god, are you?"

"What? No! I'm just happy for Joe. I never thought he'd ever find someone to put up with his shit."

"Nice. Well, please try not to turn her off me before the end of the day, yeah?" I'm not really worried—there's nothing in my past that I'll hide from Quinn. There are probably a few things I'd rather explain myself instead of those two, but I trust them to know what to not say just quite yet, although if this morning's conversation is anything to go by it seems they haven't held back with divulging the number of sexual partners I've had.

No sooner have I closed the door behind Quinn after wishing her a good day than I'm opening it again to reveal the guys. The spa isn't the only surprise, although by the looks on their faces right now they're not as excited about this part as I am.

"What? Would you rather have gone to the spa?" I ask as Ben and Trey stomp into the flat carrying everything we're going to need.

"No, a day at the pub would have been sufficient, but oh no, you've got us here fucking decorating," Ben moans, following Trey straight down towards the bedroom. "You owe us for this."

"Whatever," I mutter, going for the kitchen so I can feed the grumpy fuckers.

With their bacon under the grill, I go in search of my decorating party. The furniture is already in the centre of the room and they're putting dustsheets down.

"And you didn't want to just paint, you had to go for the fucking wallpaper, didn't you? Fucking hate wallpaper."

"What's got your knickers in a twist? Lauren refusing to put out?"

"Yes. She decided for some fucked up reason that we'd wait for

Christmas. She read some shit in a magazine about delayed gratification. Fuck knows. All I do know is that Christmas better fucking hurry up and it had better be fucking good," he sulks much to our amusement. That is until I remember something.

"Aren't we all going away for Christmas?"

"Yep." A wide smile forms across his face.

"You'd better have a room at the other end of the house," Trey complains.

"Oh, like you can talk. I have it on good authority that this room's not all that soundproof. Isn't that right, Joe?"

"Correct. Although I doubt you two have heard a peep from us yet."

"You not getting any either?" My fingers twitch to wipe the smug as shit look off Trey's face.

"She's worried about my stitches."

"I thought you had them out?"

"I did," I groan.

"Maybe tonight's the night. Just wait until you knock them up, Erica can't get enough."

"Oh fuck off, you smug shit." Ben throws a paintbrush at Trey. He doesn't see it coming, and it connects with the side of his head.

"Chance would be a fine thing."

Before I know it, the smell of burning bacon filters down to us and two angry sets of eyes turn on me.

"You promised us breakfast. You'd better have more," Ben calls as I run from the room before the smoke alarm starts blaring.

Sadly, I don't have any more, but a quick visit to Uber Eats and I've got a breakfast made for kings on its way to the flat. They've agreed to help me pull a changing rooms job on our bedroom; the least I can do is feed them.

With the three of us barely stopping for breath, we manage to have the room papered, painted and put back into place with an hour to spare to meet the girls.

Ben races off home to get ready while Trey heads downstairs to do the same.

I stand in the doorway to our new bedroom and hope that I did the right thing. I know this place isn't where we've chosen to live, but with Quinn not returning to her job and not really knowing what she's going to do next, it might be where we live for a while yet so I want it to be as homely as possible for both of us.

Hoping I've achieved just that, I head for the shower and attempt to remove any evidence of paint from my body so she doesn't suspect anything.

Lauren's booked us a table at a fancy pants bistro for our work Christmas meal. The place looks like an old warehouse with all its pipework and ventilation being used as part of the decoration. All the fittings are copper and the lighting is a little dark as Trey and I make our way to the maître d'. He shows us to a private function room up a flight of stairs where I find a few of my colleagues who all come over to greet me and see how I am after I disappeared from work two weeks ago.

There are a few wives and girlfriends here already, but the one I'm desperate to see hasn't arrived yet.

"Should have known they'd be late," Ben says, coming over to join us with a handful of pints.

The minutes tick by before a silence falls over the room. Wondering what's going on, I look towards the door where everyone else seems to be staring and my breath catches in my throat.

Standing between Lauren and Erica is my girl, but she doesn't look anything like I've seen before.

Her hair has been styled into an edgy inverted bob, her eyes are dark and smoky, and her lips are fire engine red. But as breath taking as that is, it's the dress that I'm pretty sure has stopped every conversation in the small room. It's leather, low cut and skin fucking tight. It just about hides her breasts, nips her in at the waist and skims down her round hips and shapely thighs until it stops just below her knees, revealing milky calves and one serious pair of strappy fuck-me heels.

"Pretty sure your gentle lovin' is gonna end tonight, man," Ben whispers in my ear, but I barely register the words. I'm too lost to Quinn.

She doesn't look anywhere in the room but at me. A slightly unsure smile graces her lips and I just about manage to keep my feet rooted to the spot and not drag her off home before tonight's really begun. How the fuck am I meant to look at her like that and not do anything inappropriate?

Trey breaks the moment between us by dragging everyone's attention to him and Erica when he pulls her into his arms and slams his lips down on hers. We're in a room surrounded by people who know they're a couple—the public claiming of his girl is a little much, but each to their own.

Lauren disappears into Ben's side, together greeting people they saw only yesterday at work like it was a year ago. All the while I can't take my eyes off Quinn. My mouth waters, my muscles clenching with my need to go over and drag her out of here to be alone.

Eventually she gets impatient and she makes her way over.

"Hey."

"Hey, yourself." My eyes drop from hers, taking in every inch of her and committing it to memory. "Did you have a good day?"

"It was incredible. Thank you so much."

"It was totally worth it. This dress is...fuck, I don't even know what it is. Where've you been hiding it? I'd have remembered if it was in your collection last weekend."

"Erica kept hold of it for me to surprise you."

"Well, I'm certainly surprised. Although I'm not all that impressed that every guy I work with is also seriously surprised by it."

"Better show them who I belong to then."

Challenge shines in her eyes. I wait for a beat until she thinks I'm not going to take her up on it before reaching for her waist. She lets out a squeal as we collide. I wrap my hand around the back of her neck and pull her lips to mine.

Shouts, catcalls and wolf whistles sound out behind me, but I pay my idiot co-workers no attention as I put all my focus into kissing my girl.

When I eventually pull back, her eyes are glistening with lust and her tits are swollen and fighting to get out of her dress. If it wasn't so fucking incredible to look at, I might want to make her change back into a twinset to ensure those babies are for my eyes only.

"Come on, we need to order," Lauren calls out behind me. After another two seconds we make our way to our seats.

I get a few winks and slaps on the back from the guys before they greet Quinn politely. I've known a few of these guys for a long time now. They know exactly what I'm like, seeing as we've been on more than a few nights out and heard me bang on and on about never getting tied down, but they all accept Quinn like she's a permanent part of my life—which I'm grateful for, because that's exactly what she is.

The meal's incredible and the service fantastic, but nothing is more mind-blowing than the woman sitting beside me. She joins in with everyone's conversations like she's known them all her life, she's charming and funny, and she has everyone wrapped around her little finger in mere minutes. It makes me so sad to think that the previous man in her life kept her locked up like she was in a fucking prison and stopped her enjoying herself like this.

"Are you okay? You've got a serious look in your eyes that I'm not sure I like," she asks when there's a break in the conversation.

"I'm good. Just trying to figure out what I did to deserve to have you sitting beside me."

She shrugs. "You decided to better your life and instead you found me."

"There's nothing instead about it. You have made my life better. Fuck it, you've *made* my life."

Her eyes soften as she smiles at me. I'm so close to telling her that we'll sack off the rest of the night in favour of heading home when Ben announces that we're on the move.

Everyone gets up and grabs their coats. A few of the older members of staff bid us farewell as they head off home for a mug of cocoa and their slippers, but the rest of us move to our usual haunt, The Avenue.

The last time I was here it was the night I've since discovered Quinn was watching me. She's told me more than once that she was jealous of the people I was dancing with that night and how we could just forget the world and enjoy ourselves. Well, I fully intend on giving her all of that. It might not be the one night-stand she wanted, but I have every intention of taking her home with me tonight.

After two rounds of shots bought by the boss, we head out to the dance floor. I waste no time in pulling her into me and moving with the beat of the music. She looks back at me and her smile is wider than I think I've ever seen it before. The realisation of how much weight has been lifted off her since the last time we were in a club hits me and I drop my lips to hers.

Turning in my arms, she tucks her hands into the back pockets of my trousers and pulls me tightly to her. I lose myself to her kiss and to the beat of the music.

I've done this a million times before, danced until I forgot the world around me, but having her in my arms feels like the first time I've ever done it. I meant what I said to her earlier: meeting her really did make my life. All the bullshit from my past melts away, my parents, my endless encounters with strangers as I tried to connect with someone in a way I didn't know I needed to. They all fade to nothing, and the only thing I can think about is my future with my girl.

We drink, we dance, and we laugh. Time seems to stand still as I enjoy my evening with my favourite people. At some point Eddie joined us. He was apparently meant to be spending the evening with his douchebag friends (Quinn's words, not mine) in the VIP section but instead decided to slum it with us peasants. At one point he even found himself a girl to dance with. Maybe there is more to him than meets the eye.

I've no idea what the time is, but in the end my need for Quinn gets the better of me. I've no idea what she's got hiding under that dress—if anything, it's so damn tight—but I can't wait any longer to find out.

"We're leaving. I've got somewhere better to be."

"Oh yeah?" she breathes in my ear.

"Yeah. Inside you."

Taking her hand, I lead her away from the dance floor and our friends.

"Shouldn't we tell them we're leaving?" She looks back over her shoulder in concern but everyone's too busy dancing to pay us any attention.

"They'll understand."

She nods slightly and allows me to pull her the rest of the way from the club. As we descend the stairs, I order us an Uber, and as if someone is looking down on us tonight, there's one right outside.

We climb in the second we spot it. If he says anything I don't hear it because the moment I close the door behind me, I pull Quinn into my side and continue what we started in the club.

My tongue slides past her lips and she moans quietly into my mouth, her need for me getting the better of her just like mine is for her.

The journey is over in a flash, although I'm not sure that's really true because the second my lips connect with Quinn's all sense of time seems to vanish.

We're out of the taxi and fumbling our way towards the lift before I've realised we've moved.

I slam my hand down on the button for the fourth floor and together we crash back against the wall. My hands run up her waist and squeeze her breasts, my need to have her naked almost has me ripping fabric from her body. Her fingers frantically pull at where my shirt's tucked into my trousers. The hot skin of her hands meets my abs, and I flinch at the sparks that shoot around my body.

Fuck, I hope I don't ever get used to that feeling.

I'm just aware enough to know when the lift door opens. I swing her up into my arms and carry her to the door. I've got it open and we're on our way towards the bedroom before I have time to blink. In my lust haze I've totally forgotten about her final surprise for the day, until she looks up at me and says, "What's that smell?"

"Just wait."

I drop her to her feet outside our closed bedroom door.

"Go on," I encourage.

She lifts her hand and pushes the handle down. The second the door swings open she gasps.

I left the bedside lights on along with the little fairy lights that are now hanging around the gold-framed mirror above the bed.

"Joe, it's beautiful."

Coming to stand behind her, I nuzzle her neck, drinking in her sweet scent.

"You said your office was cream and gold and that you loved it so..."

"It's perfect."

"I just wanted somewhere that felt like yours. That felt like home."

"This is my home, Joe. It's where you are."

"Fuck." I scoop her up and launch her at the bed. She squeals and giggles as she bounces, but she soon stops when I loom over her.

"You ready to properly christen your new home?" I flip her over before she can even answer and pull the zip of her dress down her back. She arches when my tongue follows its progress and I find exactly what I was expecting: no bra.

Pushing the fabric from her shoulders, I cup both her breasts, making her moan in pleasure.

"I hope you've got plenty of energy because you're not sleeping tonight until I've made you come every way. Starting with these." I pinch her nipples hard and her arse grinds against my erect cock.

I trail kisses down her back until I can't wait to have her taste on my tongue.

Flipping her on to her back, I pull her dress from her legs, leaving her sexy as fuck shoes in place. I have every intention of feeling those bad boys digging in my arse cheeks in the very near future.

Emotion chokes me as I stare down at her before me in just a tiny lace thong and her shoes.

How the fuck did I end up here with this incredible woman waiting for my touch?

"Fuck, I love you."

Ripping my shirt from my body, I toe off my shoes and drop my trousers. I leave my boxers on for now. If my cock touches her then my restraint is going to snap. I need her fucking begging for it before I slide on home.

Crawling up the bed, I kiss up her legs and her stomach before kissing around her breasts, teasing her until she's thrusting them into my face for more.

"Fucking love it when you're like this," I mutter before giving her what she needs and sucking one nipple after the other deep into my mouth.

She moans, her nails clawing at my back, and my control snaps. Finding her wet and needy centre, I thrust two fingers inside her, delighting when she clamps down and arches her back. I find her sweet spot while torturing her nipples with my tongue and teeth and in minutes she cries out my name. Lifting my eyes to her face, I watch as she falls apart. Her lips part, her cheeks flush, and her eyes close as she rides out the waves of pleasure, and my chest constricts with everything the sight does to me. I swear I could do this every fucking day for the rest of my life and it would never be enough. This woman beneath me is everything I had no idea I wanted, but I'm going to fucking well keep her.

CHAPTER ELEVEN

"What's wrong?" I ask the next morning when I emerge from the shower and find Quinn staring down at her phone, her forehead creased and bottom lip trembling, even though she's trying to contain it.

She lets out a sigh but doesn't look up. "He's refusing to sign."

"Fuck." I fall down beside her and pull her into my side.

"My lawyer has booked me an appointment to see him if I want to." I tense. The last thing I want is for her to have to look that monster in the face again.

"Do...do you want to?"

"No," she says, a sad laugh falling from her. "I never want to see him again, but I need to move on. I need to close that chapter of my life and I can't do that while I'm still technically Mrs. Davenport."

I nod, unable to disagree. "Okay, so when are we going?"

"I've got to ring him back."

She stands, her fingers gripping her phone in a death grip. Silently she leaves the room, and my heart breaks for her. Things had just started improving. She's had two sessions with a therapist and a couple of peaceful nights, but I can't help thinking that seeing him will send her back to when it first happened.

She's only gone a few minutes at the most.

"We can go today."

"Today?" I ask, my eyes wide with shock.

"He'll pulled some strings for me. I want this sorted ASAP."

"Wow, okay. Are you sure you want to do this?"

She shrugs. "You don't have to come, I can do this alone."

"Fuck that, Quinn." I push myself from the edge of the bed and stand in front of her. I take her cheeks in my hands and bend slightly so I can stare into her eyes. "You never have to do anything alone again. You need to face him? Then we do it together. This is how things are now, Quinn. Us. Me and you."

She nods, tears forming in her eyes, but she doesn't allow them to drop.

Taking a step back, she turns toward the wardrobe. Wrapping my fingers around her wrist, I pull her back to me. "You change your mind at any point. You tell me and we'll turn around."

"I need to do this. I need those papers signed, but also, I think seeing him locked in there might help give me the closure I need."

"Okay, let's do this."

In only thirty minutes we're on the road. The drive to the prison is long and sadly mostly in silence as Quinn most probably relives her life with the man we're about to see. I hate that she's dealing with this on her own, but I'm confident that she'll say something if she needs me.

The prison itself is a massive red brick building with huge gates topped with barbed wire. After getting through security we find a place to park and sit and stare. Dread sits heavy in my stomach, I can only imagine how Quinn's feeling right now.

Reaching over, I take her hand. It trembles as I hold it tight in support.

"We can go back," I offer.

She shakes her head. "No. I can do this."

She blows out a long, slow breath before unbuckling and pushing the door open. The bitter wind immediately rushes into the car and makes me shiver. This place fills me with nothing but dread, and the dark and cold weather only makes it that much more unnerving.

Getting through to where others are waiting to meet their loved ones is harder work than getting through Heathrow, but after what feels like a year, we find ourselves a seat at a table and wait.

Glancing over at Quinn, I find her as white as a sheet as she worries the sleeve of her jumper, her eyes locked on the door a couple of the inmates have come through as she waits to see him again.

I know the second he appears because everything about her changes. The strong and confident woman I know and love almost vanishes before my eyes. I follow her stare, but if it weren't for her reaction then I never would have recognised him.

He's sporting a shiner of a black eye and a split lip. It's been weeks since I laid into him—that should have healed long ago. This is recent, and something settles inside me that he's not being treated the way I'm sure he expects to be in here.

"Elizabeth," he drawls, making my fingers curl into fists at my sides. "To what do I owe this pleasure?"

Quinn opens her mouth but no words pass her lips. My demand for him to set her free is right on the end of my tongue, but I bite it back. It's not my place to do this for her.

"I see you brought your security again. He should be rotting in here with me after his assault. What did you do? Pay off the cops or something? A thug like you shouldn't be walking the streets."

"That's enough," Quinn snaps, finding her voice at last. "Do not talk to him like that. He's more of a man than you'll ever be."

He laughs. It's bitter and evil. "Is that right?" His top lip curls in disgust as he looks me up and down. It's amusing because where I'm six foot two and built of solid muscle, he's a tall, skinny golf playing wanker. Even if he did stand up to me the day I found Quinn, he never would have won. Sadly, the only people he can beat are women and kids.

"I want a divorce, Jeremy. I need you to sign those papers and get it over with."

"Yeah, about that..." He taps his finger to his busted lip. "I don't want to."

Anger rolls off Quinn in waves.

"You're a fucking arsehole, you know that?" she seethes, careful to keep her voice down so she doesn't alert the guards.

His laugh has a shiver of terror racing down my spine. How Quinn lived with this cunt for so long and came out as stable as she has is a fucking miracle; the guy is nothing less than a total psychopath.

I lean forward, my teeth bared, the muscles in my neck straining with my restraint.

"Give her what she's fucking owed."

"Oh wow, the goon talks."

My teeth grind to the point I fear I might crack one.

"I do a fucking lot more than that. Top of my list is taking care of a woman as she deserves to be treated. Now sign the fucking papers and allow Quinn—Elizabeth—to get on with her life while you rot away in here."

"Never."

"What did I ever do to you for you to hate me so much?" Quinn asks, sounding genuinely curious.

He looks her up and down, making me want to wrap my hand

around his neck. "I don't hate you, Elizabeth. I love you." His brows draw together as if this should be obvious to his wife, his eyes bounce between her like he's waiting for her to return the sentiment.

"Liar. You never loved me. The only thing you love is control. You never wanted me to stand up for myself. You always wanted me weak and put exactly in my place."

He shrugs. "Well, it seems like you've got me all figured out. Which leads me to wonder why you bothered making this trip. You're mine. You'll be mine for as long as I can keep you, so you can forget about your precious divorce. You'll have to kill me before I sign those papers."

"I'm sure that can be arranged," I mutter, barely keeping myself together.

"Fine. Have it that way. Divorce or not, you no longer control me. You no longer have that power. Goodbye, Jeremy. I hope you have a fucking horrible stay and get everything you deserve." With that, she pushes her chair out behind her and stalks towards the exit.

"Sign those fucking papers," I hiss. "I see the guys giving you the eye in here. They clearly haven't held back." I nod at his face. "And that's only from a couple of weeks here. I'm sure I could find a way to make your life a living hell. You're in here with the worst of the worst, I'm sure they'll take great delight in wiping an abuser and paedophile from the planet." I don't hang around for his response. I need to get to my girl.

The second I step from the room she runs at me, tears staining her cheeks. I open my arms and wrap her in them as she cries.

"I knew it was a stupid idea."

"You had to at least try. But like you said, it doesn't matter. He can't rule your life now. We'll just wait him out. Your life can move on with or without his consent."

She nods against me, but I'm not sure if she believes me. We've not really talked about where our relationship is headed, but I have every intention of asking her to be my wife one day. I'd like that to be one day soon, but I'll wait forever to hear her say 'I do' if I have to.

The drive home is almost as silent as the trip up, but Quinn seems different. She might not have got what she needed, but I think she was right. Seeing him in there, without his freedom...it was the closure she needed.

<hr>

OUR NEW LIFE together continues as if the trip to the prison never happened. Quinn doesn't really mention it, but now she's got her answer she's relaxed somewhat. So what if we have to wait five years for her to be a free woman? It'll be worth it.

With only a week before we head off to the Cotswolds to celebrate Christmas as one big, dysfunctional family, Quinn insists on doing something that I've never been all that fussed about, decorating the flat before Eddie comes round for her to admit that she's not returning to work. Lauren used to somehow manage to get me to help her, usually with blackmail of some kind that involved a night out and free alcohol, but this year I'm actually looking forward to doing something so normal.

We spend almost an entire day shopping for everything we're going to need. Quinn oohs and ahhs for hours over what colour theme she wants before eventually deciding not to have one and just going all traditional.

My van looks like Santa's thrown up inside it by the time we head towards home ready to put it all in place. I've got a giant arse tree strapped to the top, which makes everyone we pass look our way.

Even with a working lift it takes us three trips to get everything up to the flat.

"Have you got a Christmas playlist on your phone?" Quinn asks, putting the bag full of mulled wine, mince pies and dinner ingredients in the kitchen.

"Do I look like the kind of guy who has a Christmas playlist?"

"Scrooge!" she calls back while I pull up something along the lines of what she's after and hit play.

The beginning of 'Step into Christmas' fills the flat and she immediately starts wiggling her hips in time with the music.

I think I'm going to enjoy the next few hours.

With the music blaring, we turn the flat into Santa's grotto and by the time we're waiting for Eddie to arrive, lights twinkle, the festive candle Quinn picked up along with her cooking fills the air, and it all takes me back to a time where I was so innocent I had no idea what my life was really like and when I actually enjoyed family Christmases. I was probably four or five, and the thought of it being twenty years since I enjoyed this time of the year sits heavy in my chest.

"What's wrong?" Quinn asks, making me jump as she wraps her arms around my waist and presses her face between my shoulder blades. I instantly relax.

"Just thinking about my childhood."

"Do you have any good memories?"

"A few. Before my parents showed their real colours. You?"

"Same, although I think I had a few more years than you did. But at the same time, I wasn't brave enough to get out when things started going south."

"None of that matters now." Spinning her around so I've now got my arms around her waist and my chin resting on the top of her head, we both stare at the twinkling lights of the tree. "My life started the day I walked into your classroom. The world is our oyster. We can make our own memories, our own families, our own happiness."

"That sounds perfect. This is going to be the best Christmas ever."

"Just the first of many, babe."

She looks back over her shoulder at me and just as I'm about to press my lips to hers, the buzzer goes off.

"Cock blocker," I mutter much to Quinn's amusement as she walks over to the door to let Eddie in.

We're instructed to sit at the table while Quinn finishes off dinner. Eddie chats away about something, probably something boring he read in The Times, but I'm too distracted watching Quinn move about in the kitchen and bending over to pull the chicken out of the oven.

"Are you even listening?" he snaps, dragging my attention back.

"Honestly, no, not a fucking word."

"I hope you're a better student than dinner guest."

"I don't know if my teacher will agree."

"Pain in the arse," is called from the kitchen.

"The woman doesn't lie."

Eddie falls quiet as Quinn brings our plates over and we start to tuck in.

"This is incredible, thank you."

"It's the least I can do after everything you've done for me."

Awkwardness settles as we all avoid the giant elephant sitting in the spare chair.

"So...what are you two planning on doing, because you can't exactly—"

"I'm not coming back," Quinn blurts and then breathes a huge sigh of relief.

"Oh."

"I'm sorry, but after everything, I think I just want to do something different. I love teaching, you know that, but I need a break or something."

"Understandable. And what about you? Am I expecting you to be back in class in the New Year?" Eddie turns his eyes on me.

"If you'll have me."

"I'll certainly consider it," he says, but a smile twitches at his lips as he tries to stay serious.

"You're teaching my evening class?"

"Yeah, I had to shift things around when you didn't come back. I was the only one who could do it. They're a pretty good class. I've picked up a couple of your day lessons too."

"You've been missing the worst student."

"Is this all I'm going to get if I come back?"

"Yeah, probably."

It's nice to see a different side to Eddie, the one Quinn probably got to know all those years ago instead of the judgemental arsehole I first encountered. I'm sure he's got his reasons to dislike how I look, just like I have for how he chooses to dress. Maybe we've even got something in common if I were to press the issue, but that's not something for this pre-Christmas get-together.

The conversation moves on to other things and it's not until we're sitting on the sofas later in the evening that Quinn brings up work again. They start discussing which classes he's taken over and they go through a few students while I refill our drinks.

"Tell me about Jodie Attington." Eddie leans forward, his elbows on his knees, looking more interested in this one than the others they've talked about.

"Oh um... I don't know a lot other than the report I filed. I'm assuming you've read that?"

"I have. She just looks so sad, so lost. I don't know, there's just something about her."

"Watch out, sounds like Mr. Richards is getting a little too interested in a student," I say with a laugh, expecting him to do the same, but instead all the colour drains from his face.

"I'm...I'm just concerned for her welfare."

Quinn gives me a look that screams 'shut the hell up', and I busy myself with my drink while she explains the bruises and suspicions she has. I immediately feel awful for making a joke of the situation when this girl is obviously having a shit time of it.

"I'll miss students like her. Knowing I was making a difference to students whose lives were spiralling out of control around them was one of the things that got me out of bed in the morning."

"I'm sure you'll find loads of opportunities to work with kids like that in this city. Even some voluntary mentoring or something."

Quinn's eyes light up at the suggestion. She nods. "I'm going to look into that. I love the idea of helping students who've not had the kind of upbringing I did—not that it all turned out so great in the end."

"You'll be incredible at it," I say, dropping down and placing a kiss to her temple.

Eddie watches the interaction between us with intrigue filling his face.

"I've got to say that I wouldn't have put you two together in a million years. But sitting here now, student/teacher issue aside, you're kind of perfect together."

"Aw, are you going all soft on us?" Quinn asks light-heartedly.

"Well, obviously I'll never approve. I bet he doesn't even own a tie pin."

"Fucking right I don't, just like I'm sure you don't have any tattoos."

He swallows, a sly smile forming on his lips. "Actually, I do."
We both stare at him, mouths agape. "I am not showing either of
you two though."

"I told you he was a square," I say, elbowing Quinn in the ribs
lightly.

"On that note, I think it's time I left."

We say goodbye and wish each other a merry Christmas and a
happy New Year before Quinn closes the door behind him.

"There's no way he's got a fucking tattoo."

Chuckling, she steps away from me but I wrap my fingers
around her wrist and pull her back.

"The cleaning can wait. I think it's time you taught your
student a lesson," I whisper in her ear. She wants to chastise me, I
can sense it, but her body shudders with desire. "I'll even let you
grade me."

"You're impossible."

"You love it." I throw her over my shoulder and march her
towards our bedroom. I've no idea if Erica and Trey are in
downstairs, but I have every intention of giving them a taste of
their own medicine. Hours of it.

EPILOGUE

Three months later...

Christmas was everything I hoped it would be and more. The six of us ate, drank, laughed, and made memories together. The holidays are for family, and that's exactly how we spent it.

The day before we left the flat, I found Quinn writing a Christmas card. I was a little surprised seeing as she'd quite happily left her old life behind and I wasn't aware of anyone in her new life she'd want to send one to that we hadn't already.

When I peered over her shoulder, a smile curled at my lips. She was writing to her mum. I'd broached the subject a couple of times about her reaching out. There was something that didn't sit right with me after her visit to the hospital, and I couldn't help feeling that both of them were in a similar position and could support each other, build a connection and find some light in the dark situation they'd been in.

"I might not send it," she admitted when she realised she had company.

"I'm proud of you for even writing it, babe." She smiled and stuffed it into her bag before we left the flat. Not ten minutes into the journey out of London and she demanded I pull over. Thinking something was wrong, I turned to her but she was already half out of the van. I left her to it and watched as she ran to a post box sitting on the pavement. She sucked in a large breath before popping the envelope through the hole.

"I've no idea if she even still lives at the house, but I feel better now," she admitted as I pulled away from the curb.

She didn't mention it the whole time we were away, but I could tell it was playing on her mind.

The first thing she did the second we stepped foot back in our building was to check the post. Sure enough, amongst the flyers and crap there was a Christmas card. Clutching it to her chest, I followed her up to the flat so she could open it.

It turned out her mum had moved, but the new residents had forwarded it on to her. She was living with a widowed friend as she tried to figure out what to do with her life now her husband was behind bars and her daughter at the other end of the country.

I'm pleased to say that since then they've been working hard to rebuild their relationship, and Quinn's even convinced her mum to come and stay with us in a couple of weekends' time.

I went back to both work and evening school when the new year started, and Quinn set out on her quest to find her new job and continued her regular therapy sessions. As she predicted, her nightmares had improved but they still happened most nights, and I wasn't letting her get away without the help she needed.

She's had a few interviews but as of yet she's not received the call she's been waiting for. She's got time though and she's got money to keep her going, plus what I'm earning. Things are pretty much perfect; there's only one little thing left to make our lives complete right now, and I intend on putting that straight tonight. And Quinn has no idea.

Quinn

I'm sitting on the sofa looking through job sites, hoping my perfect job will jump out at me and waiting for Joe to come home from his evening class. I was not expecting the manila envelope that arrived this morning. Since our trip to the prison, I tried to put thoughts of Jeremy ever signing our divorce to the back of my mind. Joe was right. He was out of my life and no longer had a say in how I lived. Five years was nothing in the grand scheme of things. It taunts me from the coffee table. My stomach knots as I think about showing Joe. I'm no longer a wife, no longer Mrs Elizabeth Quinn Davenport. I am at last free to live the life I've always wanted. I'm free to consider where my relationship with Joe could go. I never want to forget this feeling buzzing in my veins.

I made sure Joe had caught up on what he'd missed by the time his first class of the year rolled around, and just like I expected he got straight back to it and has produced some great work, none of which I've helped with. I've no doubt that he's got a bright future ahead of him if he keeps his head down and continues working hard.

It doesn't matter how much money I've got sitting in my bank account, I still feel guilty that he's the only one with a job. I've done some voluntary work, but even that didn't quite hit the right mark. I know that job is out there somewhere, I just need to find it.

Looking at the clock, I've still got over thirty minutes until he's back. I've got our dinner prepared but there's not much I can do until he's here. My phone buzzes and I reach to grab it off the arm of the chair.

Joe: There's a box in my wardrobe.

My brows draw together as I stare at his cryptic message. Pushing myself from the sofa, I go in search of it.

Pulling the door open on his side of the wardrobe, I find it immediately with a note on the top.

Wear me.

A little laugh falls from my lips when I remove the lid and find the outfit he bought me the night he took me out to fulfil some of my bucket list. Memories hit and heat blooms in my chest. Even that first night I knew there was something between us, although I never could have imagined what was to come and how close it would bring us.

Pulling out the skinny black jeans and the barely there silver top, I make quick work of changing and doing my hair and make-up. I'm just putting my lipstick on when another text arrives.

Joe: Fancy a coffee?

I can't keep the smile off my face. I know exactly where he's asking me to go. I also know that if Eddie catches him texting in class, he's going to rip him a new one. The most unlikely friendship might be forming between them, but no one stands in Eddie's way or breaks his rules when he's teaching, even his budding new best friend.

Finding my shoes, I book an Uber and race out of the building, now desperate to see him. It seems like a year ago that he kissed me goodbye before leaving for class.

As usual, the traffic is horrendous trying to get across the city, but eventually I make it to the coffee shop. I step inside, expecting to find him waiting for me, but the only people here are busy with their own lives.

My stomach drops with disappointment that he's not here yet and I stand in line to order our drinks.

I'm lost in my own thoughts as a shiver runs down my spine. "Cappuccino, one sugar, chocolate sprinkles," is whispered in my ear, and I step back to lean into him. His warmth engulfs me as his lips find the skin of my neck.

"What's all this about?" I ask once we're seated.

"Thought it was time we had another crazy night."

"I don't need all that now. I've got you to keep me on my toes."

"You might not need it, but you deserve a good night out."

I can't really argue with that so I smile at him and sip my coffee.

"Plus, if I remember rightly there was something on your to do list that you never ticked off."

I laugh. "I'm not having a one-night stand."

"Damn fucking right you're not."

I try racking my brain for what other word vomit fell from my mouth that night, but I don't get the chance to figure it out because Joe stands and hold a hand out for me. "Ready to paint the town red?"

"So ready."

We take the tube into the centre of London, and I'm not surprised when he drags me to the Chinese takeaway we came to last time and orders the exact same dishes. We sit in Leicester Square and polish off every single bit as we sit, people watching.

The little trip down memory lane is exactly what I didn't know I needed.

"Joe, I need to tell you something," I admit, ready to explode with excitement.

"Okay, go on." I hate that there's a little hesitation in his voice.

"I got some surprise mail this afternoon." His eyebrows rise. "I'm free."

"You're what?" His brows draw together, but I can see a little bit of hope sparkling in his eyes.

"I'm free. He signed."

"He signed?" he echoes.

"He did. I'm free."

Joe's up before I have a chance to blink. He pulls me from my seat and spins me around right in front of all the people in the square. I can't help the joy bubbling up my throat and I laugh as he continues. When he eventually set me on my feet, I sway with dizziness.

His eyes search mine, but he doesn't say anything. A little disappointment finds its way in. I hadn't realised that I was hoping he'd drop to one knee instantly and demand I become his, but that's exactly how I feel. Swallowing it down and forcing myself to enjoy the moment, I stare back at him.

"So what's next? Comedy club, live music and getting me off in a nightclub?"

His eyes darken with lust at my last suggestion. "Sounds like a pretty damn perfect night to me."

With our hands connected, Joe leads us in the direction we went that night. We visit all the same places and drink all the same drinks. The whole evening is incredible, just like I knew it would be, and although I have fond memories of the first time, tonight is even better.

The differences are stark.

I'm no longer scared for my life, no longer looking over my shoulder or fighting the growing connection between us. Tonight, I let go. I laugh like I have no cares in the world, and I knock back slippery nipples and screaming orgasms like a pro. And when he pulls me to him on the dance floor towards the end of the night, I don't tense, I don't worry if we're going to be caught, because I know without a doubt that this man is mine and there's not a damn thing anyone can do about it. The only thing I care about right now is being in his arms and making sure he never lets go.

The music pounds around us as we move in time to the music. Our hips roll, our skin is covered in a sheen of sweat and the alcohol we've consumed is making my head spin, but I zone out everything bar him and this moment.

His hands rest on my ribs just inside my top, but unlike last time they don't venture any higher, although it must be killing him to do so. Things are different this time. The lust simmering just below the surface ready to explode within both of us is still there, but we've learned to contain it, if only just. I've no doubt that Joe's restraint is going to snap any moment and I'm going to be dragged home to finish off the night properly. Not that there will be any complaints from me.

It can't be five minutes after I have that thought that he leans into my ear and suggests we leave. Excitement bubbles in my belly for what's to come, and I eagerly take his hand when he offers it, following him from the club.

He helps me into my jacket and together we walk out into the night. It's still dark although there are signs of the approaching morning. London's commuters start a hell of a lot earlier than I was ever used to living in the country. Taxis zip past us, and others pour from clubs and bars ready to head home, probably to get ready for work like Joe's going to have to do in about two hours.

"Where are we going?" I ask when he ignores the cars lining the pavement and heads farther into the city.

"Breakfast," he says like it's the most obvious thing in the world. I try to bite back my disappointment that he's not taking me home to have me for breakfast. We've got the rest of our lives for that, I guess.

He takes us to a 24/7 diner and we fill up on greasy food before he sets off again until he slows in front of a dark building with a pink neon sign out the front.

"What's this place?" I crane my neck to see the sign properly. *Rebel Ink. Tattoo studio.*

"Joe?" I ask, my voice cracking slightly, although I'm unsure if it's with fear or excitement.

"I'm pretty sure this was on your list, and I wouldn't want you missing out on something you've always wanted."

"I was talking crazy that night."

"No you weren't. You want to be a rebel, and this is the place to be. I also happen to know that inside that building awaits the best damn tattoo artist this city has ever seen just waiting for us."

"Really?"

"Well, I think so. You ready?"

"Um...no."

He laughs but presses the bell beside the door nonetheless.

"What fucking time do you call this?" the guys asks even before the door's open.

"Sorry, got a little carried away with ourselves."

"Fucking pain in the arse."

I laugh to myself but follow Joe's lead when he gestures for me to step inside.

My eyes widen slightly when I get a look at the guy who's just let us in. I'd have thought he'd be an older biker type guy with no bare skin on show, a massive beard and a biker jacket, but instead I'm greeted by a young blonde guy who clearly looks after himself. He's wearing a long-sleeved black t-shirt so I don't get a chance to see what ink he's got, if any.

"Quinn, this is Zach. Zach, this is my girl, Quinn."

"Nice to meet you." He nods at me and turns towards a small room the back. I guess we're meant to follow.

"Up you get then," he encourages once we're all in the room.

"Uh..."

My heart hammers in my chest, but excitement gets the better of me. It's helped by the look of awe in Joe's eyes.

"I know you've thought about this more than you've ever let on. So, up you get," he says with a laugh.

He's right of course, not that I tell him.

"What's it going to be then?"

Sucking in a deep breath, I prepare to explain what I've been dreaming about for years. I never wanted anything big or fancy, just something to remind me of the life I made for myself out of the disaster I found myself in the middle of.

"I'd like some flying birds on my wrist. Not big...like this..." Pulling my phone from my bag, I find the image I've had on there for months just in case I ever got brave enough to put myself in this position."

"Consider it done. Lie back."

"Can't say I'm not relieved that you didn't want that somewhere more intimate."

Zach laughs at Joe's alpha caveman appearance. "Nothing fazes me now, man. I've pretty much done and seen everything."

I shudder at the thought while he sets up.

"You still want what we talked about?" Zach asks Joe.

"I do," he states proudly.

Something stirs inside me at the thought of getting to sit and watch Joe get inked.

I'm soon distracted from the thought as a buzzing fills the room and the first scratch of the needle hits me.

"Fuck."

Zach looks at me from the corner of his eye. The words *don't be a pussy* are right on the tip of his tongue, I can practically hear them.

Joe takes my hand and I squeeze it as Zach sets to work.

It stings, but actually it's not all that bad. It certainly wasn't painful enough to put me off considering another.

Once I'm wrapped up, we switch places after Joe's lowered his braces and undone his shirt. My mouth waters at the amount of skin he reveals, my earlier lust hitting me full force.

He lies back like he's done it a million times, which of course he has.

Zach gets himself ready before hovering his gun over Joe's left pec.

I watch, completely fascinated as Zach draws on his skin. His hand in the way means I don't really get to see what he's creating until he's finished and Joe sits up.

They both stare at me as I get my first look at the stunning artwork.

"Holy shit," I screech when it dawns on me what he's just done. "That's my name."

Joe grins while Zach just slaps his shoulder. I'm not sure if he's telling him he's an idiot or not, because it's kind of what I want to do. He's just had my name permanently tattooed over his heart.

"You like it?"

"I'm in shock and feel slightly bad that I didn't even consider your name and just got birds."

He laughs. "There's always time, babe."

Once he's dressed again we say our thanks to Zach, who sets about closing up for the night—or morning—to head home.

Joe still doesn't order us a taxi and we once again walk. Eventually the Thames appears in front of us. I'm assuming that Joe's got a destination in mind but at no point do I ask. I just enjoy his company. The tattoo on my wrist burns but I welcome it, a reminder of everything that got me to this point in my life.

We walk along the west bank until Joe heads towards Millennium Bridge and starts to cross.

"Where are we going?"

"We're nearly there."

I keep walking, ignoring the aching of my feet and wishing I'd thought to bring some flats.

We're halfway across when he suddenly stops and turns to me.

"What are you doing?"

"Enjoying the view."

"You should probably be watching the sunrise over the buildings then," I say with a laugh, but at no point does he take his eyes from me.

He sucks in a deep breath and swallows.

Wait...is he nervous?

I open my mouth to demand he tells me what's going on when he suddenly drops down onto one knee.

My eyes open so wide I fear they might be about to pop out of my head as he reaches into his pocket and pulls out a small black box.

Holy shit.

"Quinn, I never ever thought I'd be doing this. I spent most of my life trying to find a piece of me that I didn't know I was missing, and then when I met you everything fell into place. My past slipped away and the only thing I could see was my future. *Our* future. I don't want to spend another day without you by my side. You've taught me so much more than any English lesson I could ever attend. You've taught me what true love is, what it truly means to put someone else first and to hope like hell they feel the same.

"My life started the day I walked into your classroom, and I don't want to live another day without you.

"So...if you'll have me, will you do me the greatest honour of agreeing to be my wife?"

A sob rumbles up my throat and the tears filling my eyes fall down onto my cheeks. I watch him pull open the box in his hand and reveal the most stunning and unique engagement ring I think I've ever seen in my life.

"Is that a black diamond?" I ask, reaching for it, not believing what I'm seeing. The princess cut black gem is cushioned in a rose gold band. It's breath taking and so Joe. It's just more proof that he gets me. He understands the rebel inside me and allows me to set her free.

"Is that a yes?"

"Of course it's a yes. A million times yes."

He's up from the pavement and has me in his arms in a second. He spins us around, clinging to me so slightly I worry my ribs might be about to crack.

"I love you so fucking much, Quinn."

"I love you, too." His lips find mine and as the sun rises behind us we celebrate the next chapter of our lives. Together.

I never wanted a white knight, and it turns out that the bad boy in the dirty work van was exactly what I needed.

Are you ready for Zach's story?
Hate You is an angst-filled, emotional and steamy enemies to lovers romance.

ONE-CLICK NOW *or continue reading for a sneak peek.*

ACKNOWLEDGMENTS

Originally, Ben's story was meant to be just one standalone to finish off my Falling series, I never expected it to take the turn it did but I'm so glad that it did. I've loved discovering more about these beautifully broken characters, and Joe and Quinn were no exception. I knew Joe would have an interesting story to tell from the moment he appeared in Losing the Forbidden and I was so excited to discover it.

I can't believe at almost eight months after publishing the first book in the Forbidden series that I'm now writing this on the final one. It's sure been a rollercoaster of a few months.

I've got so many people I need to thank. My awesome betas, Deanna, Lindsay, Suzanne and Tracy. Samantha, my PA, who I've no idea how I lived without. Evelyn, my editor, who puts up with my ramblings and makes them make sense. Paige, for proofreading and making sure each book's been as polished as possible. James Critchley and his mouth-watering models, George, Danny, and Daniel for gracing the covers and being the perfect guys for my characters.

And finally, you for being on this journey with me and supporting me all the way. I couldn't do any of this without you, so THANK YOU!

So, what's next? Well, you might recognise Zach the tattoo artist as Harrison's younger brother in His Manhattan. I loved him from the moment I wrote him back in 2017, and he's been nagging me ever since for his own book. Well...that's next. A brand new series focused on his tattoo studio, Rebel Ink. It'll be releasing spring 2020 and I can't wait to share more with you about it. Make sure you're in my reader group and signed up to my newsletter to be first to find out all the sexy details.

Until next time,

Tracy xo

ABOUT THE AUTHOR

Tracy Lorraine is a *USA Today* and *Wall Street Journal* bestselling new adult and contemporary romance author. Tracy has recently turned thirty and lives in a cute Cotswold village in England with her husband, baby girl and lovable but slightly crazy dog. Having always been a bookaholic with her head stuck in her Kindle, Tracy decided to try her hand at a story idea she dreamt up and hasn't looked back since.

Be the first to find out about new releases and offers. Sign up to my newsletter here.

If you want to know what I'm up to and see teasers and snippets of what I'm working on, then you need to be in my Facebook group. Join Tracy's Angels here.

Keep up to date with Tracy's books at
www.tracylorraine.com

<u>Falling Series</u>

<u>Falling for Ryan: Part One</u> #1

<u>Falling for Ryan: Part Two</u> #2

<u>Falling for Jax</u> #3

<u>Falling for Daniel</u> (A Falling Series Novella)

<u>Falling for Ruben</u> #4

<u>Falling for Fin</u> #5

<u>Falling for Lucas</u> #6

<u>Falling for Caleb</u> #7

<u>Falling for Declan</u> #8

<u>Falling For Liam</u> #9

<u>Forbidden Series</u>

<u>Falling for the Forbidden</u> #1

<u>Losing the Forbidden</u> #2

<u>Fighting for the Forbidden</u> #3

<u>Craving Redemption</u> #4

<u>Demanding Redemption</u> #5

<u>Avoiding Temptation</u> #6

<u>Chasing Temptation</u> #7

<u>Rebel Ink Series</u>

<u>Hate You</u> #1

<u>Trick You</u> #2

<u>Defy You</u> #3

<u>Play You</u> #4

Inked (A Rebel Ink/Driven Crossover)

Rosewood High Series

<u>Thorn</u> #1

<u>Paine</u> #2

<u>Savage</u> #3

Fierce #4

<u>Hunter</u> #5

Faze (#6 Prequel)

<u>Fury</u> #6

Legend #7

Maddison Kings University Series

<u>TMYM: Prequel</u>

<u>TRYS</u> #1

<u>TDYW</u> #2

<u>TRYS</u> #3

<u>TVYC</u> #4

<u>TDYD</u> #5

<u>TDYR</u> #6

<u>TRYD</u> #7

Knight's Ridge Empire Series

Wicked Summer Knight: Prequel (Stella & Seb)

Wicked Knight #1 (Stella & Seb)

Wicked Princess #2 (Stella & Seb)

Wicked Empire #3 (Stella & Seb)

Deviant Knight #4 (Emmie & Theo)

Deviant Princess #5 (Emmie & Theo

Deviant Reign #6 (Emmie & Theo)

One Reckless Knight (Jodie & Toby)

Reckless Knight #7 (Jodie & Toby)

Reckless Princess #8 (Jodie & Toby)

Reckless Dynasty #9 (Jodie & Toby)

Dark Halloween Knight (Calli & Batman)

Dark Knight #10 (Calli & Batman)

Dark Princess #11 (Calli & Batman)

Dark Legacy #12 (Calli & Batman)

Corrupt Valentine Knight (Nico & Siren)

Corrupt Knight #13 (Nico & Siren)

Corrupt Princess #14 (Nico & Siren)

Corrupt Union #15 (Nico & Siren)

Sinful Wild Knight (Alex & Vixen)

Sinful Stolen Knight: Prequel (Alex & Vixen)

Sinful Knight #16 (Alex & Vixen)

Sinful Princess #17 (Alex & Vixen)

Sinful Kingdom #18 (Alex & Vixen)

Knight's Ridge Destiny: Epilogue

Harrow Creek Hawks Series

Merciless #1

Relentless #2

Lawless #3

Fearless #4

Ruined Series

Ruined Plans #1

Ruined by Lies #2

Ruined Promises #3

Never Forget Series

Never Forget Him #1

Never Forget Us #2

Everywhere & Nowhere #3

Chasing Series

Chasing Logan

The Cocktail Girls

His Manhattan

Her Kensington

HATE YOU SNEAK PEEK
PROLOGUE

Tabitha

I stare down at my gran's pale skin. Her cheeks are sunken and her eyes tired. She's been fighting this for too long now, and as much as I hate to even think it, it's time she found some peace.

I take her cool hand in mine and lift her knuckles to my lips.

"It's Tabitha," I whisper. I've no idea if she's awake, but I don't want to startle her.

Her eyes flicker open. After a second they must adjust to the light and she looks right at me. My chest tightens as if someone's wrapping an elastic band around it. I hate seeing my once so full of life gran like this. She was always so happy and full of cheer. She didn't deserve this end. But cancer doesn't care what kind of person you are, it hits whoever it fancies and ruins lives.

Pulling a chair closer, I drop onto it, not taking my eyes from her.

"How are you doing today?" I hate asking the question, because there really is only one answer. She's waiting, waiting for her time to come to put her out of her misery.

"I'm good. Christopher upped my morphine. I'm on top of the world."

She might be living her last days, but it doesn't stop her eyes sparkling a little as she mentions her male nurse. If I've heard the words 'if I were forty years younger' once while she's been here, then I've heard them a million times. She's joking, of course. My gran spent her life with my incredible grandpa until he had a stroke a few years ago. Thankfully, I guess, his end was much quicker and less painful than Gran's. It was awful at the time to have him healthy one moment and then gone in a matter of hours, but this right now is pure torture, and I'm not the one lying on the hospital bed with meds constantly being pumped into my body.

"Turn the frown upside down, Tabby Cat. I'm fine. I want to remember you smiling, not like your world's about to come crashing down."

"I know, I'm sorry. I just—" a sob breaks from my throat. "I don't know how I'm going to live without you." Dramatic? Yeah. But Gran has been my go-to person my whole life. When my parents get on my last nerve, which is often, she's the one who talks me down, makes me see things differently. She's also the only one who's encouraged me to live the life I want, not the one I'm constantly being pushed into.

That's the reason I'm the only one visiting her right now.

When my parents discovered that she was the one encouraging my 'reckless behaviour', as they called it, they cut contact. I can see the pain in her eyes about that every time she looks at me, but she's too stubborn to do anything about it, even now.

"You're going to be fine. You're stronger than you give yourself credit for. How many times have I told you, you just need to follow your heart. Follow your heart and just breathe. Spread your wings and fly, Tabby Cat."

Those were the last words she said to me.

HATE YOU CHAPTER ONE

Tabitha

The heavy bass rattles my bones. The incredible music does help to lift my spirits, but I find it increasingly hard to see the positives in my life while I'm hanging out with my friends these days. They've all got something exciting going on —incredible job prospects, marriage, exotic holidays on the horizon —and here I am, drowning in my one-person pity party. It's been two months since Gran left me, and I'm still wondering what the hell I'm meant to be doing with my life.

"Oh my god, they are so fucking awesome," Danni squeals in my ear as one song comes to an end. I didn't really have her down as a rock fan, but she was almost as excited as James when he announced that this was what we were doing for his birthday this year. Although I do wonder if it's the music or the frontman who's really captured her attention. She'd never admit it, but she's got a thing for bad boys.

I glance over at him with his arm wrapped around Shannon's shoulders and a smile twitches my lips. They're so cute. They've got the kind of relationship everyone craves. It seems so easy yet full of love and affection. Ripping my eyes from the couple, I focus back on the stage and try to block out that I'm about as far away from having that kind of connection with anyone as physically possible.

I sing along with the songs I've heard on the radio a million times and jump around with my friends, but I just can't quite totally get on board with tonight. Maybe I just need more alcohol.

"Where to next?" Shannon asks once we've left the arena and the ringing in our ears has begun to fade.

"Your choice," James says, looking down at her with utter devotion shining in his eyes. It wasn't a great surprise when Shannon sent a photo of her giant engagement ring to our group chat a couple of months ago. We all knew it was coming—Danni especially, seeing as it turned out that she helped choose the ring.

Shannon directs us all to a cocktail bar a few streets over and I make quick work of manoeuvring my way through the crowd to get to the bar, my need for a drink beginning to get the better of me. The others disappear off somewhere in the hope of finding a table

"Can we have two jugs of..." I quickly glance at the menu. "Margaritas please."

"Coming right up, sweetheart." The barman winks at me before his eyes drop to my chest. Hooking up on a night out isn't really my thing, but hell if it doesn't make me feel a little better about myself. He's cute too, and just the kind of guy who would give both my parents a heart attack if I were to bring him home. Both his forearms are covered in tattoos, he's got gauges in both his ears, and a lip ring. A smile tugs at the corner of my mouth as I imagine the looks on their faces.

My gran's words suddenly hit me.

Just breathe.

My hand lifts and my fingers run over the healing skin just below my bra. My smile widens.

I watch the barman prepare our cocktails, my eyes focused on the ink on his arms. I've always been obsessed by art, any kind of art, and that most definitely includes on skin.

I'm lost in my own head, so when he places the jugs in front of me, I startle, feeling ridiculous.

"T-Thank you," I mutter, but when I lift my eyes, I find him staring intently at me.

"You're welcome. I'm Christian, by the way."

"Oh, hi." A sly smile creeps onto my lips. "I'm Biff."

"Biff?" His brows draw together in a way I'm all too used to when I say my name.

"It's short for Tabitha."

"That's pretty. So... uh... how do you feel about—"

"Christian, a little help?" one of the other barmen shouts, pulling Christian's attention from me.

"Sorry, I'll hopefully see you again later?"

I nod at him, not wanting to give him any false hope. Like I said, he's cute, but after my last string of bad dates and even worse short-term boyfriends, I'm happy flying solo right now. I've got a top of the range vibrating friend in my bedside table; I don't need a man.

Picking up the tray in front of me, I turn and go in search of my friends. It takes forever, but eventually I find them tucked around a tiny table in the back corner of the bar.

"What the hell took so long? We thought you'd pulled and abandoned us."

"Yes and no," I say, ensuring every head turns my way.

"Tell us more," Danni, my best friend, demands.

"It was nothing. The barman was about to ask me out, but it got busy."

"Why the hell did you come back? Get over there. We all know you could do with a little... loosening up," James says with a wink.

"I'm good. He wasn't my type."

"Oh, of course. You only date posh boys."

"That is not true."

"Is it not?" Danni asks, chipping in once she's filled all the glasses.

"No..." I think back over the previous few guys they met. "Wayne wasn't posh," I argue when I realise they're kind of right.

"No, he was just a wanker."

Blowing out a long breath, I try to come up with an argument, but quite honestly, it's true. My shoulders slump as I realise that I've been subconsciously dating guys my parents would approve of. It's like my need to follow their orders is so well ingrained by now that I don't even realise I'm doing it. Shame that their ideas about my life, what I should do, and whom I should date don't exactly line up with mine.

Glancing over my shoulder at the bar, I catch a glimpse of Christian's head. Maybe I should take him up on his almost offer. What's the worst that could happen?

Deciding some liquid courage is in order, I grab my margherita and swallow half down in one go.

I'm so fed up of attempting to live my parents' idea of a perfect life. I promised Gran I'd do things my way. I need to start living up to my promise.

BY THE TIME I'm tipsy enough to walk back to the bar and chat up Christian, he's nowhere to be seen. I'm kind of disappointed seeing as the others had convinced me to throw caution to the wind (something that I'm really bad at doing), but I think I'm mostly relieved to be able go home and lock myself inside my flat alone and not have to worry about anyone else.

With my arm linked through Danni's, we make our way out to the street, ready to make our journeys home, and Shannon jumps into an idling Uber while Danni waits for another to go in the opposite direction.

"You sure you don't want to be dropped off? I don't mind."

"No, I'm sure. I could do with the fresh air." It's not a lie—the alcohol from one too many cocktails is making my head a little fuzzy. I hate going to sleep with the room spinning. I'd much rather that feeling fade before lying down.

"Okay. Promise me you'll text me when you're home."

"I promise." I wrap my arms around my best friend and then wave her off in her own Uber.

Turning on my heels, I start the short walk home.

I've been a London girl all my life, and while some might be afraid to walk home after dark, I love it. I love seeing a different side to this city, the quiet side when most people are hiding in their flats, not flooding the streets on their daily commutes.

My mind is flicking back and forth between my promise to Gran and my missed opportunity tonight when a shop front that I walk past on almost a daily basis makes me stop.

It's a tattoo studio I've been inside of once in my life. I never really pay it much attention, but the new sign in the window catches my eye and I stop to look.

Admin help wanted. Enquire within.

Something stirs in my belly, and it's not just my need to do something to piss my parents off—although getting a job in a place like this is sure to do that. I'm pretty sure it's excitement.

Tattoos fascinate me, or more so, the artists.

I'm surprised to see the open sign still illuminated, so before I can change my mind, I push the door open. A little bell rings above it, and after a few seconds of standing in reception alone, a head pops out from around the door.

"Evening. What can I do you for?" The guy's smile is soft and kind despite his otherwise slightly harsh features and ink.

"Oh um..." I hesitate under his intense dark stare. I glance over my shoulder, the back of the piece of paper catching my eye and reminding me why I walked in here. "I just saw the job ad in the window. Is the position still open?"

His eyes drop from mine and take in what I'm wearing. Seeing as tonight's outing involved a rock concert, I'm dressed much like him in all black and looking a little edgy with my skinny black jeans, ripped AC/DC t-shirt and heavy black makeup. I must admit it's not a look I usually go for, but it was fitting for tonight.

He nods, apparently happy with what he sees.

"Experience?" he asks, making my stomach drop.

"Not really, but I'm studying for a Masters so I'm not an idiot. I know my way around a computer, Excel, and I'm super organised."

"Right..." he trails off, like he's thinking about the best way to get rid of me.

"I'm a really quick learner. I'm punctual, methodical and really easy to get along with."

"It's okay, you had me sold at organised. I'm Dawson, although everyone around here calls me D."

"Nice to meet you." I stick my hand out for him to shake, and an amused smile plays at his lips. Stretching out an inked arm, he takes my hand and gives it a very firm shake that my dad would be impressed by—if he could look past the tattoos, that is. "I'm Tabitha, but everyone calls me Biff."

"Biff, I like it. When can you start?"

"Don't you want to interview me?"

"You sound like you could be perfect. When can you start?"

"Err... tomorrow?" I ask, totally taken aback. He doesn't know me from Adam.

"Yes!" He practically snaps my hand off. "Can you be here for two o'clock? I can show you around before clients start turning up. I'll apologise now for dropping you in the deep end, we've not had anyone for a few weeks and things are starting to get a little crazy."

"I can cope with crazy."

"Good to know. This place can be nuts." I smile at him, more grateful than he could know to have a distraction and a focus.

My Masters should be enough to keep my mind busy, but since Gran went, I can't seem to lose myself in it like I could previously. Hopefully, sorting this place's admin out might be exactly what I need.

"Two o'clock tomorrow then," I say, turning to leave. "I'll bring ID. Do you need a reference? I've done some voluntary work recently, I'm sure they'll write something for me."

"Just turn up on time and do your job and you're golden."

I walk out with more of a spring in my step than I have in a long time. I'm determined to find something that's going to make me happy, not just my parents. I've lived in their shadow for long enough.

I LOOK myself over before leaving my flat for my first shift at the tattoo studio. I'm dressed a little more like myself today in a pair of dark skinny jeans, a white blouse and a black blazer. It's simple and smart. I'm not sure if there's a dress code—D never specified what I should wear. With my hair straightened and hanging down my back and my makeup light, I feel like I can take on whatever crazy he throws at me.

With a final spritz of perfume, I grab my bag from the unit in the hall and pull open my door. My home is a top floor flat in an old London warehouse. They were converted a few years ago by my father's company, and I managed to get myself first dibs. They might drive me insane on the best of days, but at least I get this place rent-free. It almost makes up for their controlling and stuck-up ways... almost.

Ignoring the lift like I always do, I head for the stairs. My heels click against the polished concrete until I'm at the bottom and out to the busy city. I love London. I love that no matter what the time, there's always something going on or someone who's awake.

The spring afternoon is still a little fresh, making me regret not grabbing my coat, or even a scarf, before I left. I pull my blazer tighter around myself and make the short journey to the shop.

The door's locked when I get there, and the bright neon sign that clearly showed it was open last night is currently saying closed.

Unsure of what to do, I lift my hand to knock. Only a second later, the shop front is illuminated, and the sound of movement inside filters down to me, but when the door opens it's not the guy from last night.

"Oh... uh... hi. Is... uh... D here?"

The guy folds his arms over his chest and looks me up and down. He chuckles, although I've no idea what he finds so amusing.

"D," he shouts over his shoulder, "there's some posh bird here to see you."

My teeth grind that he's stereotyped me quite so quickly, but I refuse to allow him to see that his assumptions about me affect me in any way.

"Ah, good. I was worried you might change your mind."

"Not at all," I say, stepping past the judgemental arsehole and into the studio reception-cum-waiting room.

"That's Spike. Feel free to ignore him. He's not got laid in about a million years, it makes him a little cranky." I fight to contain a laugh, especially when I turn toward Spike to find his lips pursed and his eyes narrowed in frustration. All it does is confirm that D's words are correct.

"Is that fucking necessary? Posh doesn't need to know how inactive my cock is, especially not when she's only just walked through the fucking door. Unless..." He stalks towards me and I automatically back up. I can't deny that he's a good looking guy, but there's no way I'm going there.

"I don't think so."

"You sure? You look like you could do with a bit of rough." He winks, and I want the ground to swallow me up.

"Down, Spike. This is Tabitha, or Biff. She's our new admin, so I suggest you be nice to her if you want to stop organising your own appointments and shit. I don't need a sexual harassment case on my hands before she's even fucking started."

I can't help but laugh at the look on Spike's face. "Don't worry. I'm sure you'll find some desperate old spinster soon."

He looks me up and down again, something in his eyes changed. "Appearances aside, I think you're going to get on well here."

I smile at him. "Mine's a coffee. Milk, no sugar. I'm already sweet enough." His chin drops.

"I thought you were our new assistant. Why am I still making the coffee?"

"Know your place, Spike. Now do as the lady says. You know my order."

"Yeah, it comes with a side of fuck off!" He flips D off before disappearing through a door that I can only assume goes to a kitchen.

"I probably should have warned you that you've agreed to work around a bunch of arseholes."

"I know how to handle myself around horny men, don't worry."

After finishing my A levels, before I grew any kind of backbone where my parents were concerned, I agreed to work for my dad. I was his little office bitch and spent an horrendous year of my life being bossed around by men who thought that just because they had a cock hanging between their legs it made them better than me. I might have fucking hated that year, but it taught me a few things, not just about business but also how to deal with men who think they're something fucking special just because they're a tiny bit successful and make more money than me. I've no doubt that my time at Anderson Development Group gave me all the skills I'm going to need to handle these artists.

"So I see. So, this is your desk. When you're on shift you'll be the first person people see when they're inside, so it's important that you look good. But from what I've seen, I don't think we'll have an issue. I've sorted you out logins for the computer and the software we use. Most of it is pretty self-explanatory. I'm pretty IT illiterate and I've figured most of it out, put it that way."

D's showing me how they book clients in when someone else joins us. This time it's someone I recognise from my previous visit, although it's immediately obvious that he doesn't remember me like I do him. But then I guess he was the one delivering the pain, not receiving it.

"Biff, this is Titch. Titch, this is Biff, our new admin. Be nice."

"Nice? I'm always nice. Nice to meet you, Biff. You have any issues with this one, you come and see me. He might look tough, but I know all his secrets." Titch winks, a smile curling at his lips that shows he's a little more interested than he's making out, and quickly disappears towards his room.

It's not long until the first clients of the afternoon arrive, and I'm left alone to try to get to grips with everything.

Between clients, D pops his head out of his room to check I'm okay, and every hour I make a round of coffee for everyone. That sure seems to get me in their good books.

"I think I could get used to having you around," Spike says when I deliver probably his fourth coffee of the day. "Only thing that would make it better is if it were whisky."

"Not sure the person at the end of your needle would agree." He chuckles and turns back to the design he was working on when I interrupted.

My first day flies by. D tells me to head home not long after nine o'clock. They've all got hours of tattooing to go yet, seeing as Saturday night is their busiest night of the week, but he insists I get a decent night's sleep.

ONE-CLICK now to continue reading.